ANN M. MARTIN

THE BABY-SITTERS CLUB

KRISTY'S BIG DAY

A GRAPHIC NOVEL BY
GALE GALLIGAN
WITH COLOR BY BRADEN LAMB

graphix

An Imprint of

SCHOLASTIC

All rights reserved. Published by Graphix, an imprint of
Scholastic Inc., *Publishers since 1920*. SCHOLASTIC, GRAPHIX,
THE BABY-SITTERS CLUB, and associated logos are trademarks
and/or registered trademarks of Scholastic Inc.

Library of Congress Control Number: 2017955790

ISBN 978-1-338-06768-2 (hardcover)
ISBN 978-1-338-06761-3 (paperback)

10 9 8 7 6 5 4 3 2 1   18 19 20 21 22

Printed in China   62
First edition, September 2018

Edited by Cassandra Pelham Fulton and David Levithan
Book design by Phil Falco
Creative Director: David Saylor

For Max, William, Durinn, Nate, and Lily.

And for Patrick, who is much older than these
cool babies, but still manages to have a good time.

G. G.

KRISTY THOMAS
PRESIDENT

CLAUDIA KISHI
VICE PRESIDENT

MARY ANNE SPIER
SECRETARY

STACEY MCGILL
TREASURER

DAWN SCHAFER
ALTERNATE OFFICER

MALLORY PIKE
JUNIOR OFFICER

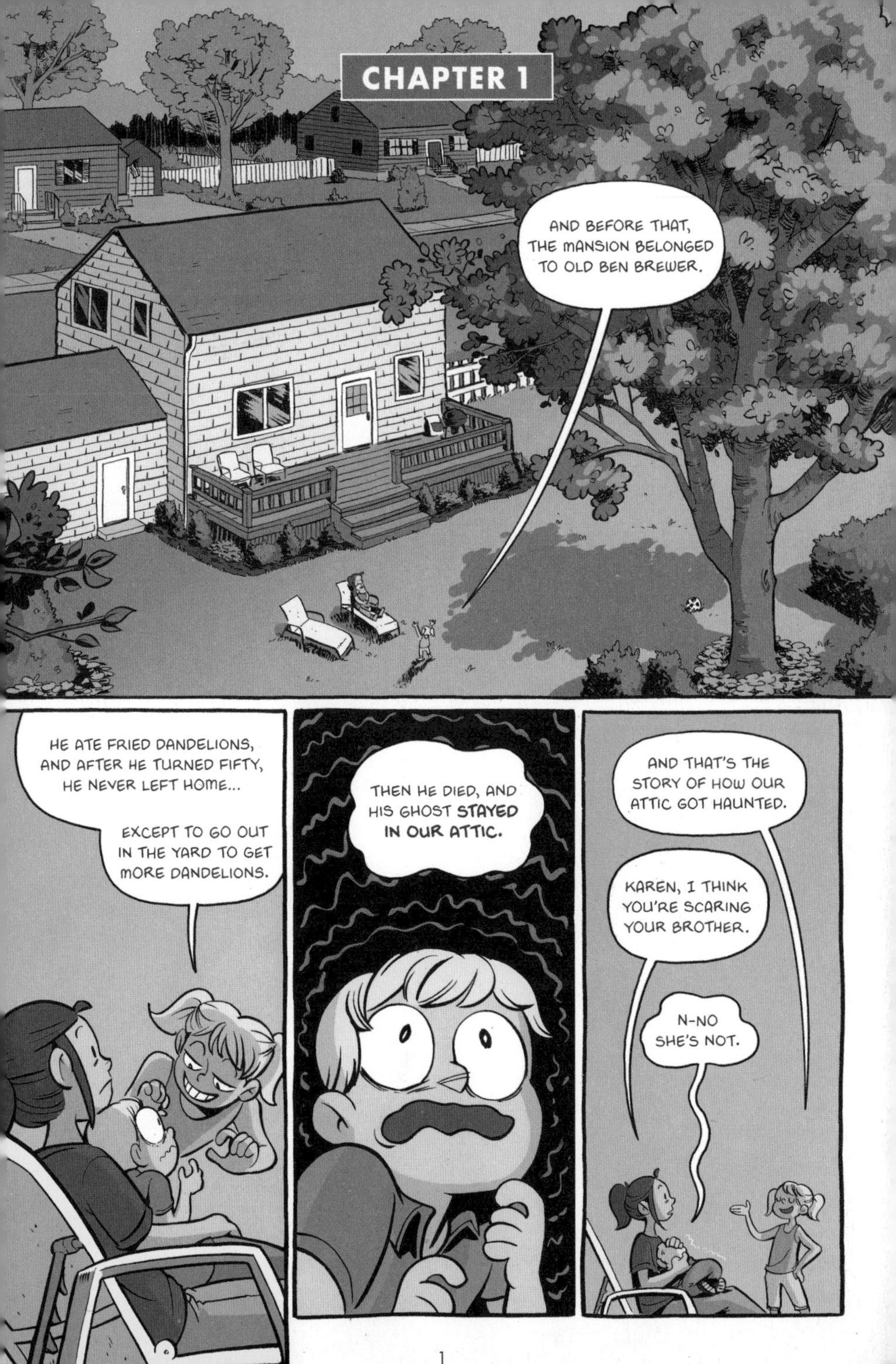
CHAPTER 1
AND BEFORE THAT, THE MANSION BELONGED TO OLD BEN BREWER.
HE ATE FRIED DANDELIONS, AND AFTER HE TURNED FIFTY, HE NEVER LEFT HOME...
EXCEPT TO GO OUT IN THE YARD TO GET MORE DANDELIONS.
THEN HE DIED, AND HIS GHOST **STAYED IN OUR ATTIC.**
AND THAT'S THE STORY OF HOW OUR ATTIC GOT HAUNTED.
KAREN, I THINK YOU'RE SCARING YOUR BROTHER.
N-NO SHE'S NOT.

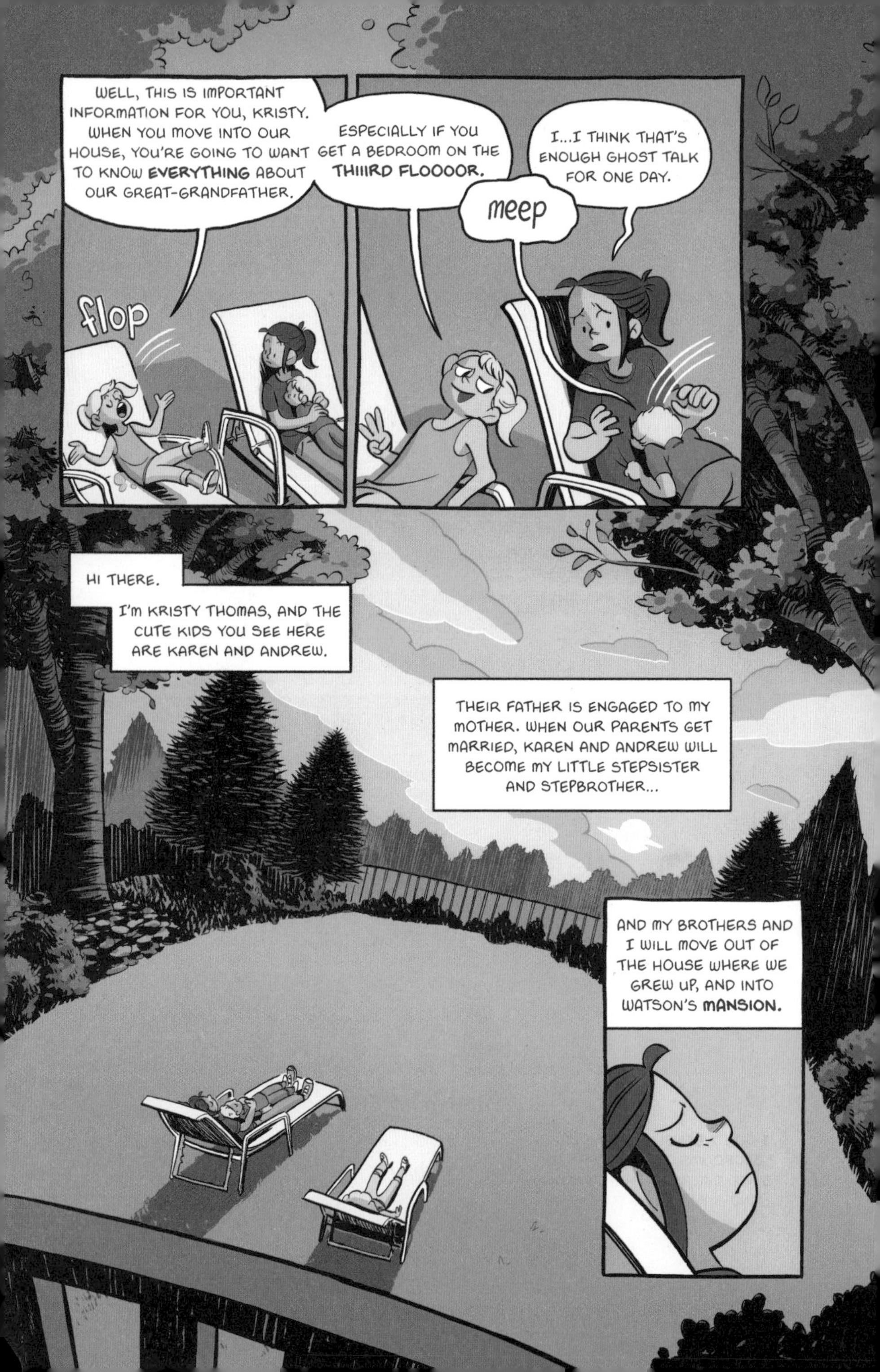
WELL, THIS IS IMPORTANT INFORMATION FOR YOU, KRISTY. WHEN YOU MOVE INTO OUR HOUSE, YOU'RE GOING TO WANT TO KNOW EVERYTHING ABOUT OUR GREAT-GRANDFATHER.
flop
ESPECIALLY IF YOU GET A BEDROOM ON THE THIIIRD FLOOOOR.
meep
I...I THINK THAT'S ENOUGH GHOST TALK FOR ONE DAY.
HI THERE.
I'M KRISTY THOMAS, AND THE CUTE KIDS YOU SEE HERE ARE KAREN AND ANDREW.
THEIR FATHER IS ENGAGED TO MY MOTHER. WHEN OUR PARENTS GET MARRIED, KAREN AND ANDREW WILL BECOME MY LITTLE STEPSISTER AND STEPBROTHER...
AND MY BROTHERS AND I WILL MOVE OUT OF THE HOUSE WHERE WE GREW UP, AND INTO WATSON'S MANSION.

THERE ARE PROS AND CONS. THE PROS: I WASN'T KIDDING ABOUT THE MANSION -- WATSON'S RICH. LIKE, **MILLIONAIRE-RICH.**

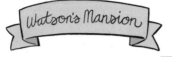

Watson's Mansion

CHARLIE AND SAM, MY OLDER BROTHERS, WILL FINALLY GET THEIR OWN ROOMS.

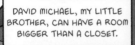

DAVID MICHAEL, MY LITTLE BROTHER, CAN HAVE A ROOM BIGGER THAN A CLOSET.

oooo

XMAS

I DON'T BENEFIT AT ALL WHERE BEDROOMS ARE CONCERNED, SINCE I ALREADY HAVE MY OWN AND I THINK IT'S JUST FINE.

WHAT'S THE **CON,** YOU ASK?

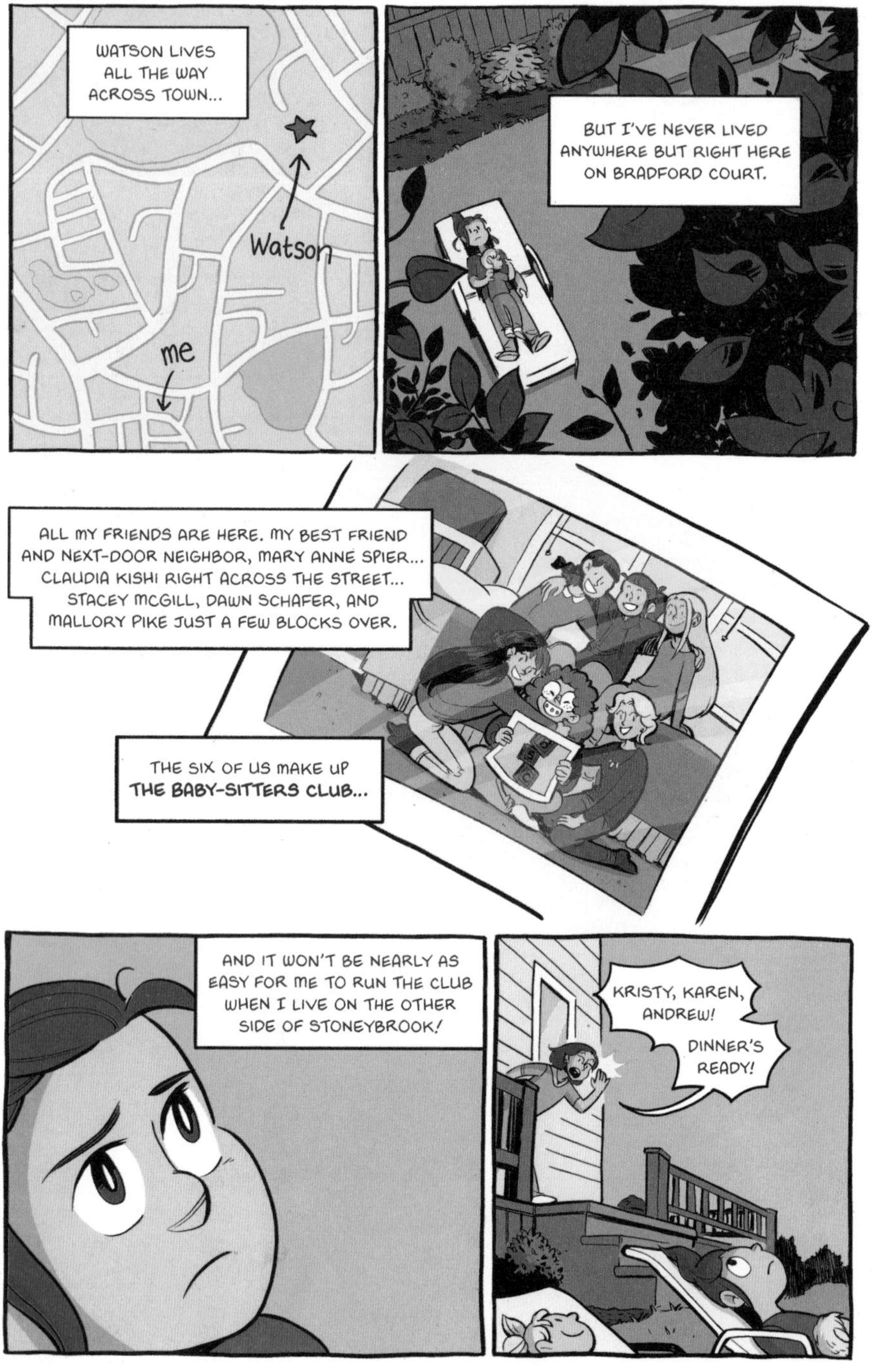
WATSON LIVES ALL THE WAY ACROSS TOWN...
Watson
me
BUT I'VE NEVER LIVED ANYWHERE BUT RIGHT HERE ON BRADFORD COURT.
ALL MY FRIENDS ARE HERE. MY BEST FRIEND AND NEXT-DOOR NEIGHBOR, MARY ANNE SPIER... CLAUDIA KISHI RIGHT ACROSS THE STREET... STACEY MCGILL, DAWN SCHAFER, AND MALLORY PIKE JUST A FEW BLOCKS OVER.
THE SIX OF US MAKE UP **THE BABY-SITTERS CLUB...**
AND IT WON'T BE NEARLY AS EASY FOR ME TO RUN THE CLUB WHEN I LIVE ON THE OTHER SIDE OF STONEYBROOK!
KRISTY, KAREN, ANDREW!
DINNER'S READY!

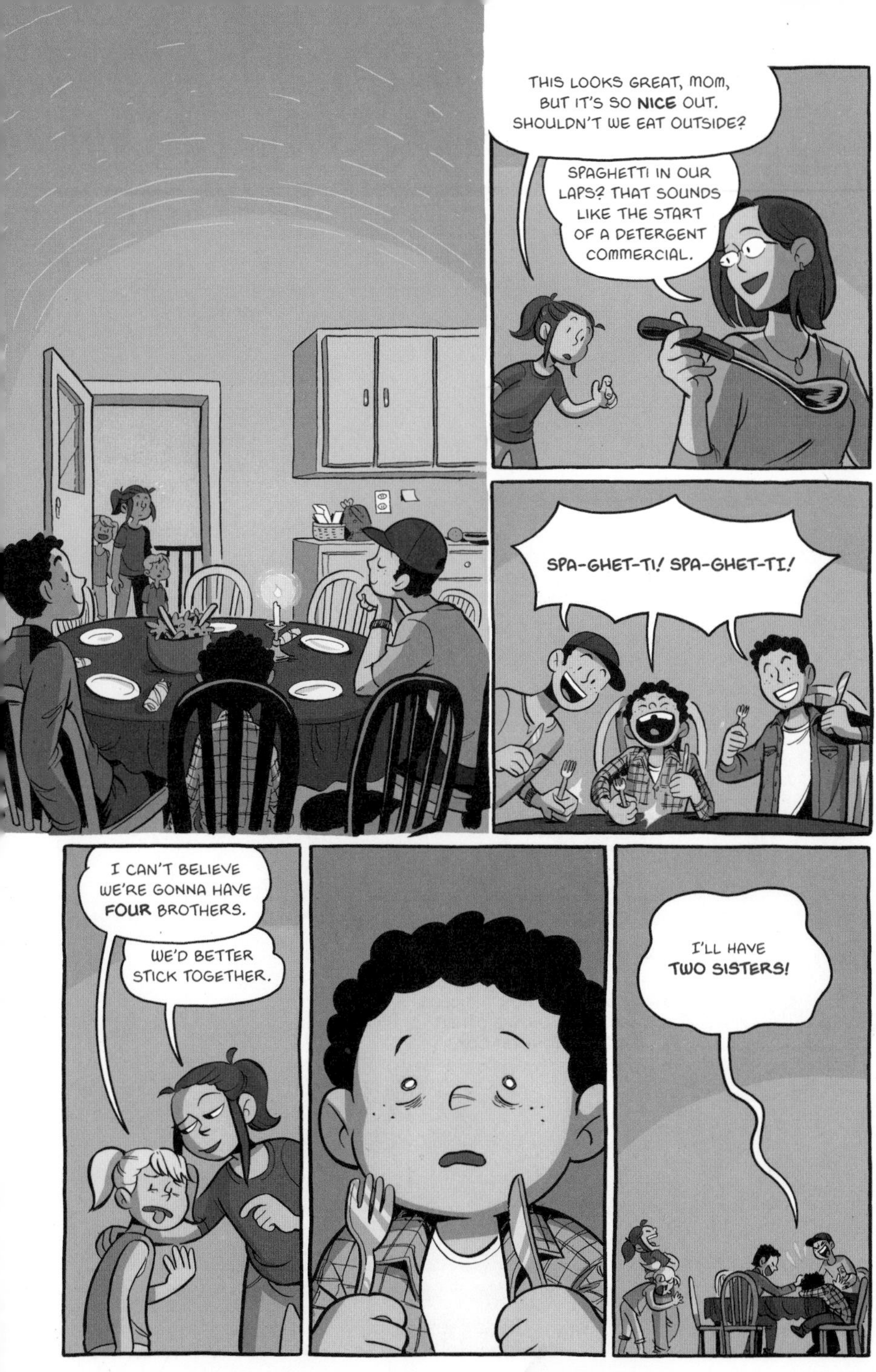
THIS LOOKS GREAT, MOM, BUT IT'S SO NICE OUT. SHOULDN'T WE EAT OUTSIDE?
SPAGHETTI IN OUR LAPS? THAT SOUNDS LIKE THE START OF A DETERGENT COMMERCIAL.
SPA-GHET-TI! SPA-GHET-TI!
I CAN'T BELIEVE WE'RE GONNA HAVE FOUR BROTHERS.
WE'D BETTER STICK TOGETHER.
I'LL HAVE TWO SISTERS!

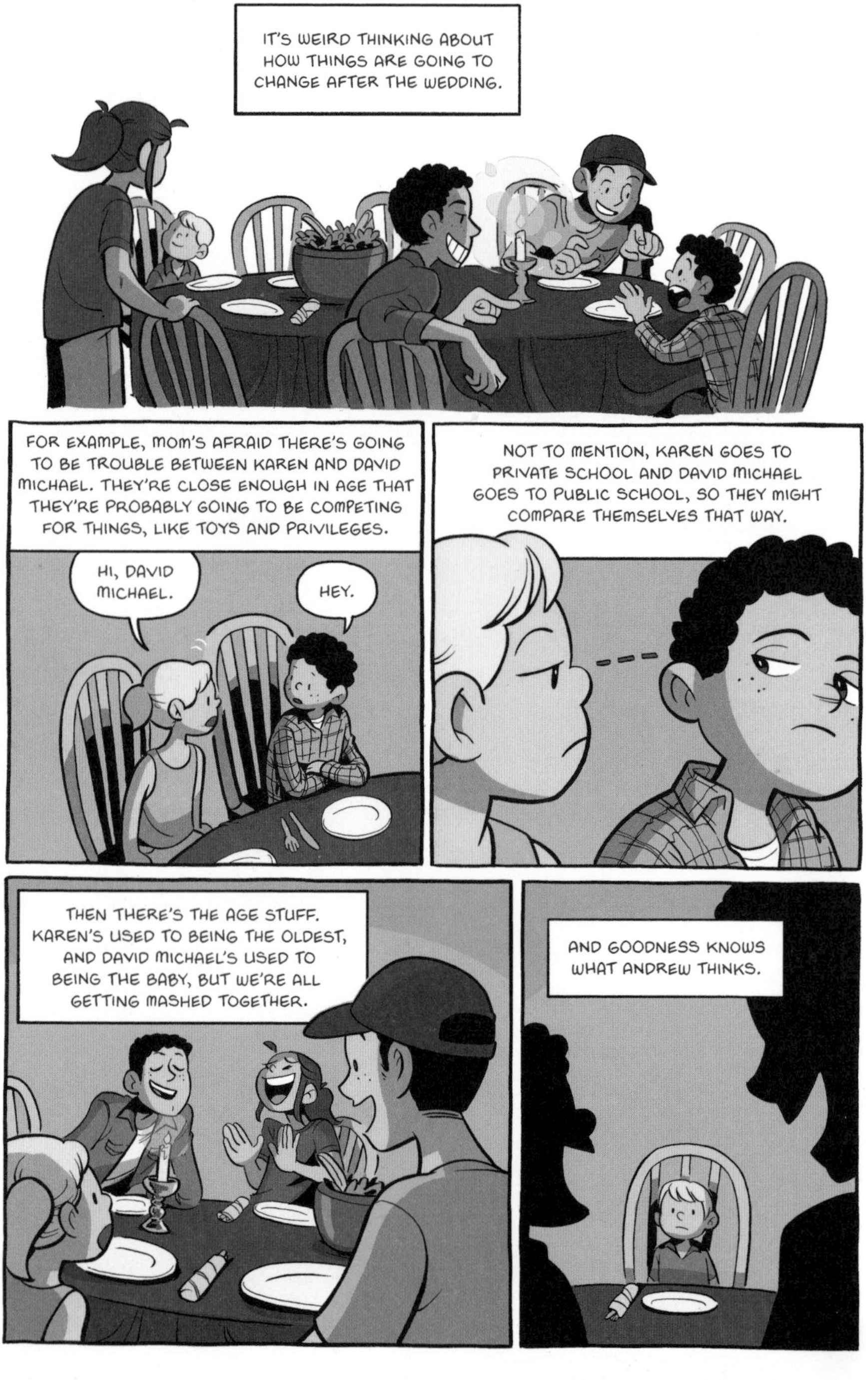
IT'S WEIRD THINKING ABOUT HOW THINGS ARE GOING TO CHANGE AFTER THE WEDDING.
FOR EXAMPLE, MOM'S AFRAID THERE'S GOING TO BE TROUBLE BETWEEN KAREN AND DAVID MICHAEL. THEY'RE CLOSE ENOUGH IN AGE THAT THEY'RE PROBABLY GOING TO BE COMPETING FOR THINGS, LIKE TOYS AND PRIVILEGES.
HI, DAVID MICHAEL.
HEY.
NOT TO MENTION, KAREN GOES TO PRIVATE SCHOOL AND DAVID MICHAEL GOES TO PUBLIC SCHOOL, SO THEY MIGHT COMPARE THEMSELVES THAT WAY.
THEN THERE'S THE AGE STUFF. KAREN'S USED TO BEING THE OLDEST, AND DAVID MICHAEL'S USED TO BEING THE BABY, BUT WE'RE ALL GETTING MASHED TOGETHER.
AND GOODNESS KNOWS WHAT ANDREW THINKS.

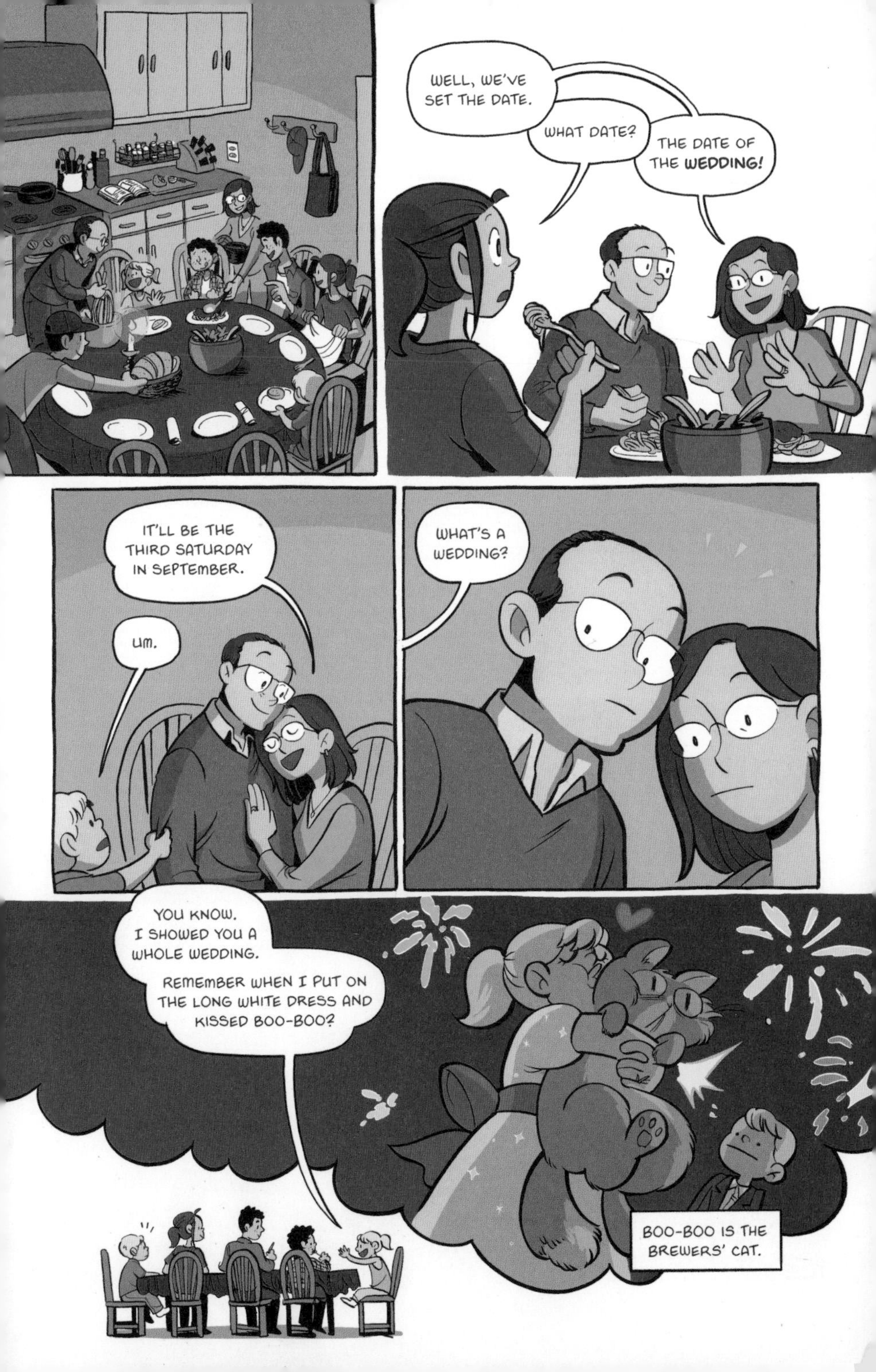
WELL, WE'VE SET THE DATE.
WHAT DATE?
THE DATE OF THE **WEDDING!**
IT'LL BE THE THIRD SATURDAY IN SEPTEMBER.
UM.
WHAT'S A WEDDING?
YOU KNOW. I SHOWED YOU A WHOLE WEDDING.
REMEMBER WHEN I PUT ON THE LONG WHITE DRESS AND KISSED BOO-BOO?
BOO-BOO IS THE BREWERS' CAT.

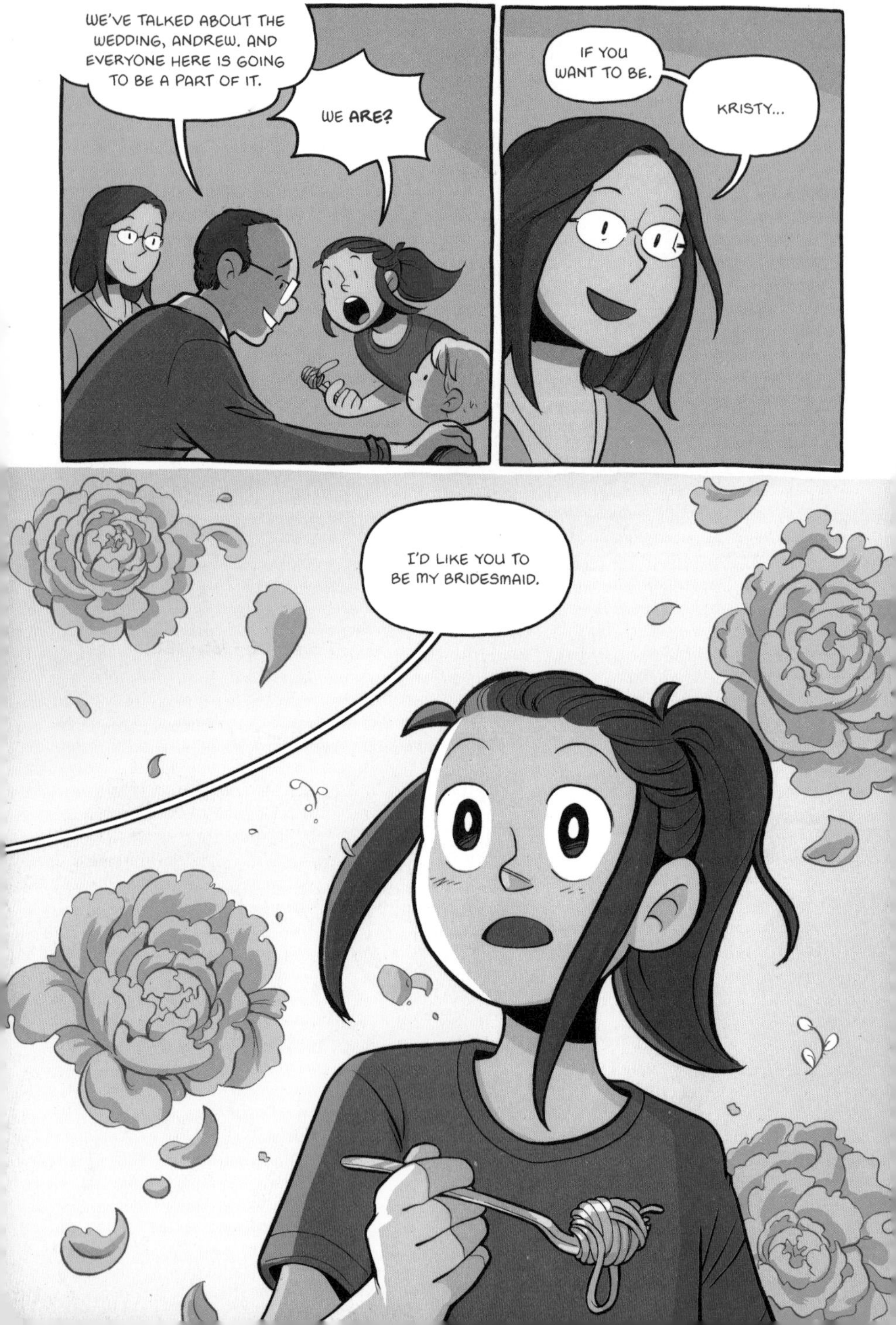
WE'VE TALKED ABOUT THE WEDDING, ANDREW. AND EVERYONE HERE IS GOING TO BE A PART OF IT.
WE **ARE?**
IF YOU WANT TO BE.
KRISTY...
I'D LIKE YOU TO BE MY BRIDESMAID.

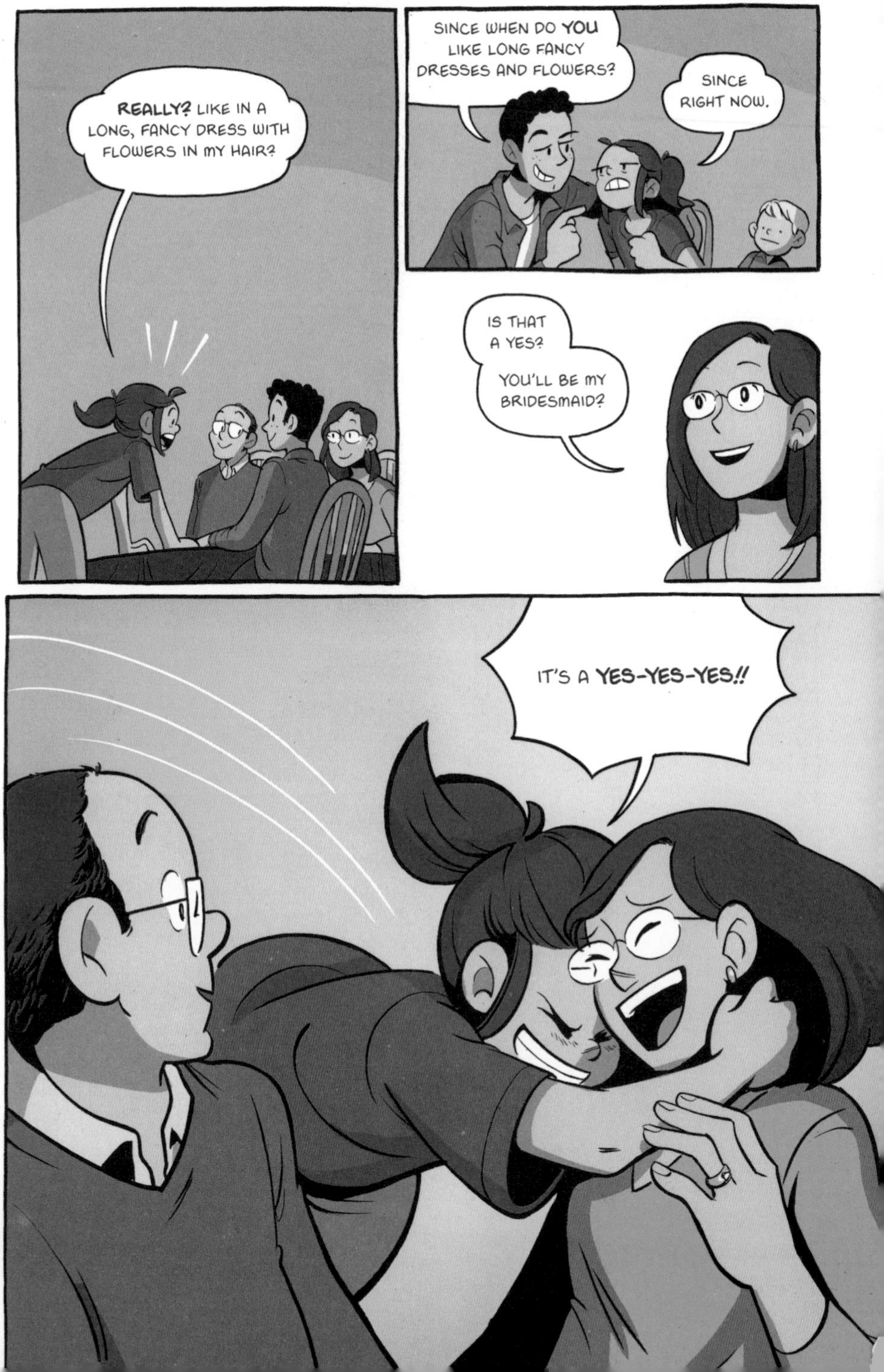
REALLY? LIKE IN A LONG, FANCY DRESS WITH FLOWERS IN MY HAIR?
SINCE WHEN DO YOU LIKE LONG FANCY DRESSES AND FLOWERS?
SINCE RIGHT NOW.
IS THAT A YES?
YOU'LL BE MY BRIDESMAID?
IT'S A YES-YES-YES!!

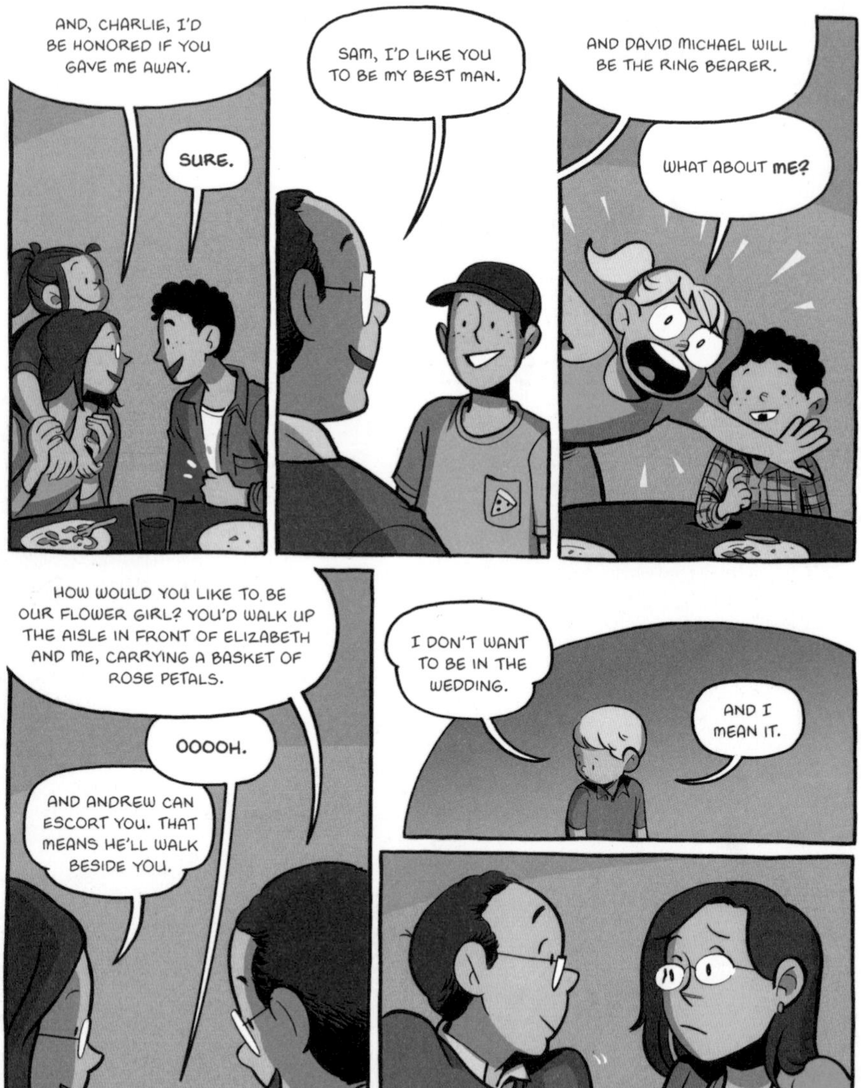
AND, CHARLIE, I'D BE HONORED IF YOU GAVE ME AWAY.
SURE.
SAM, I'D LIKE YOU TO BE MY BEST MAN.
AND DAVID MICHAEL WILL BE THE RING BEARER.
WHAT ABOUT ME?
HOW WOULD YOU LIKE TO BE OUR FLOWER GIRL? YOU'D WALK UP THE AISLE IN FRONT OF ELIZABETH AND ME, CARRYING A BASKET OF ROSE PETALS.
OOOOH.
AND ANDREW CAN ESCORT YOU. THAT MEANS HE'LL WALK BESIDE YOU.
I DON'T WANT TO BE IN THE WEDDING.
AND I MEAN IT.
WELL, THINK IT OVER. WE'D LIKE YOU TO BE IN THE WEDDING, BUT IT'S UP TO YOU, OKAY?
OKAY.

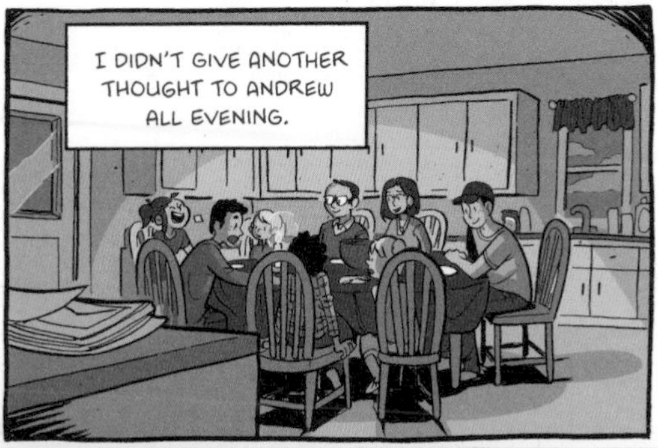
I DIDN'T GIVE ANOTHER THOUGHT TO ANDREW ALL EVENING.

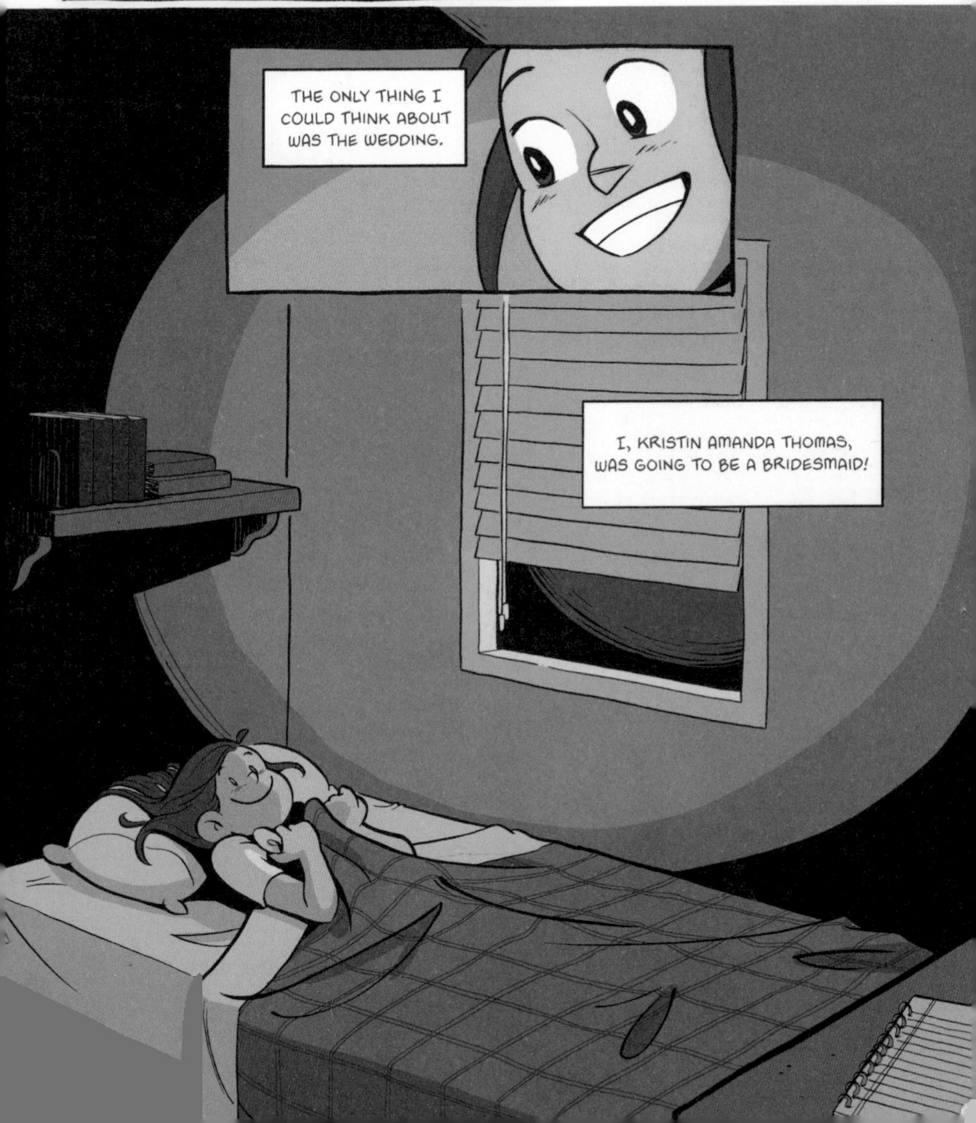
THE ONLY THING I COULD THINK ABOUT WAS THE WEDDING.
I, KRISTIN AMANDA THOMAS, WAS GOING TO BE A BRIDESMAID!

CHAPTER 2

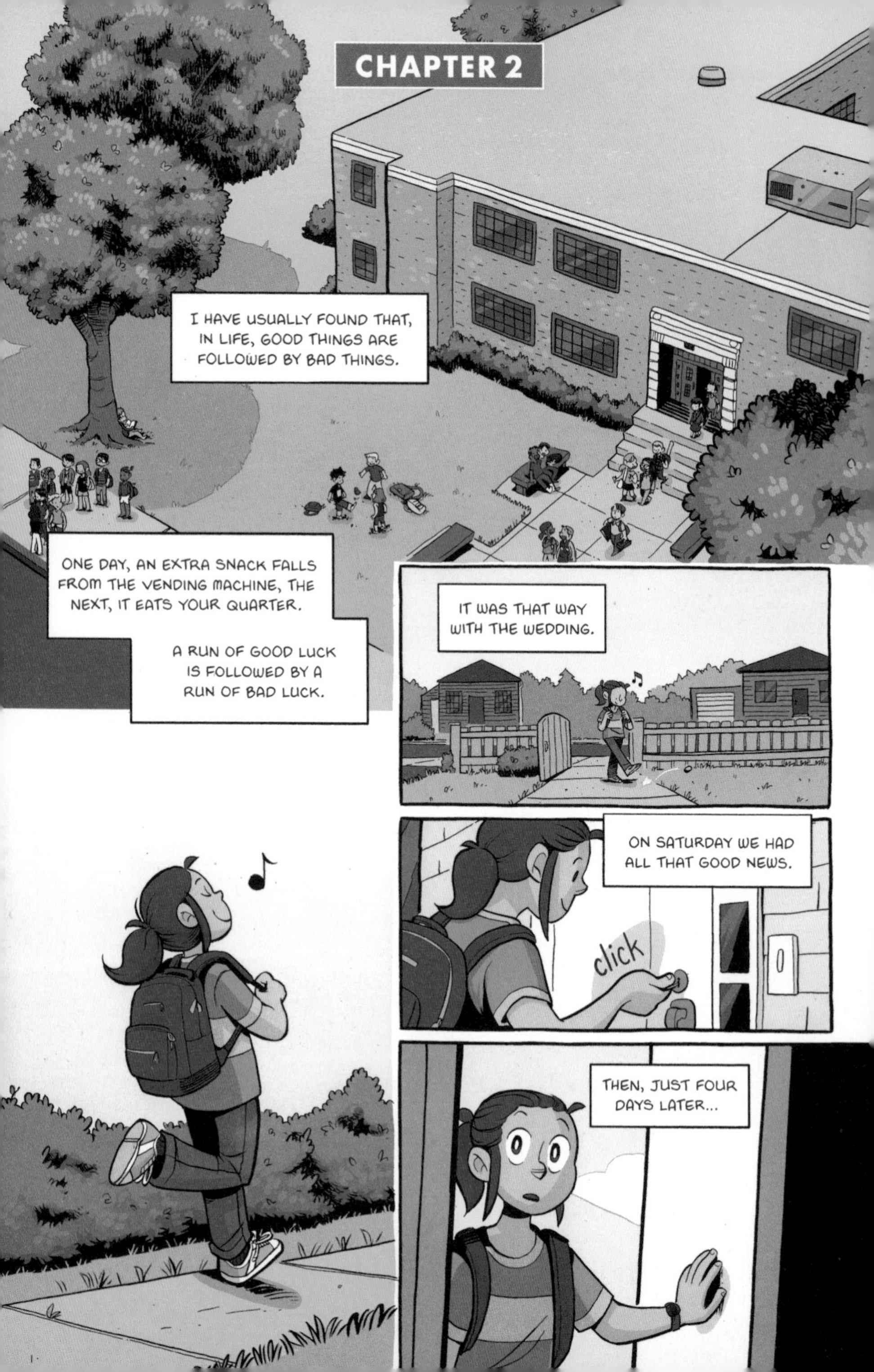
I HAVE USUALLY FOUND THAT, IN LIFE, GOOD THINGS ARE FOLLOWED BY BAD THINGS.
ONE DAY, AN EXTRA SNACK FALLS FROM THE VENDING MACHINE, THE NEXT, IT EATS YOUR QUARTER.
A RUN OF GOOD LUCK IS FOLLOWED BY A RUN OF BAD LUCK.
IT WAS THAT WAY WITH THE WEDDING.
ON SATURDAY WE HAD ALL THAT GOOD NEWS.
click
THEN, JUST FOUR DAYS LATER...

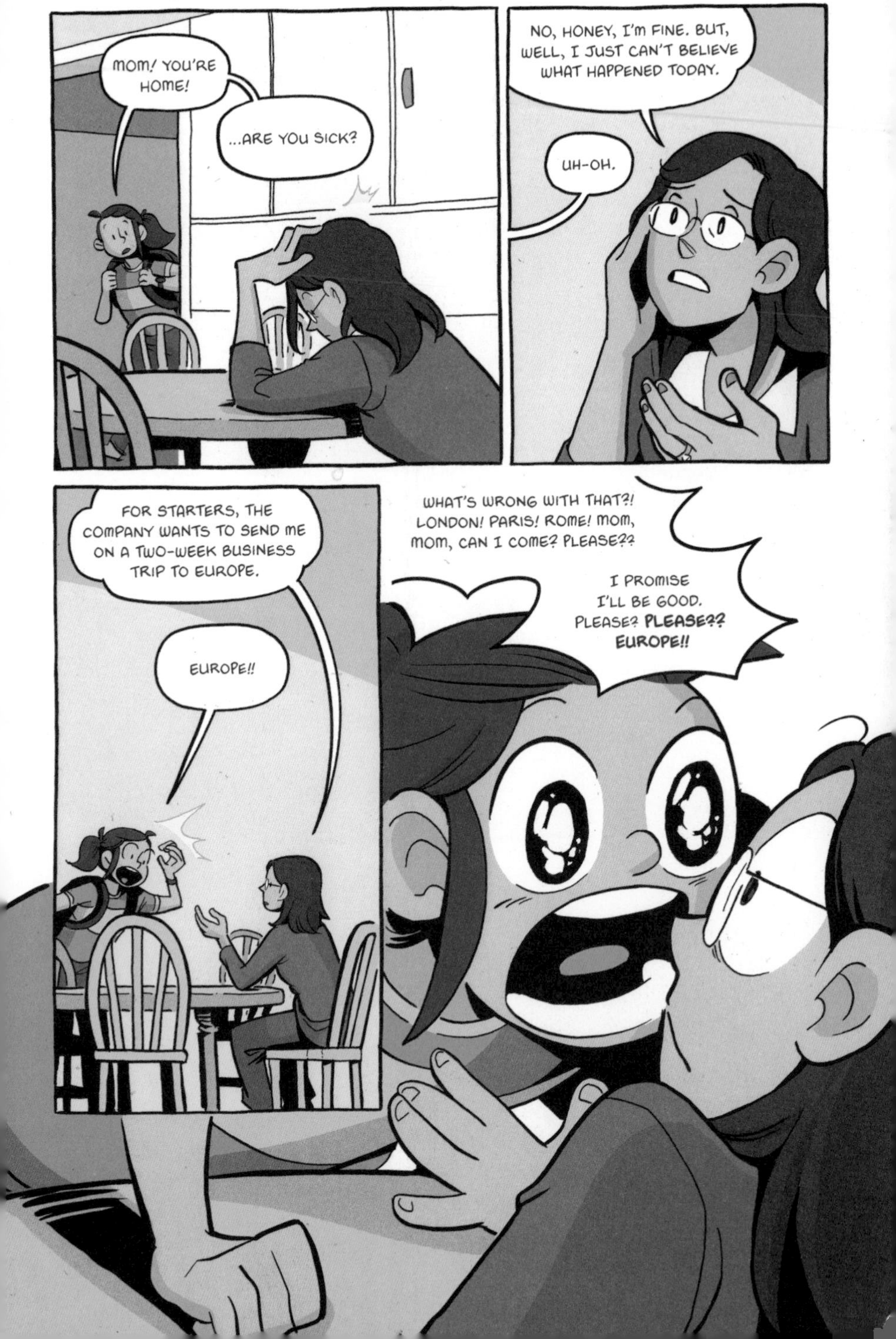
MOM! YOU'RE HOME!
...ARE YOU SICK?
NO, HONEY, I'M FINE. BUT, WELL, I JUST CAN'T BELIEVE WHAT HAPPENED TODAY.
UH-OH.
FOR STARTERS, THE COMPANY WANTS TO SEND ME ON A TWO-WEEK BUSINESS TRIP TO EUROPE.
EUROPE!!
WHAT'S WRONG WITH THAT?! LONDON! PARIS! ROME! MOM, MOM, CAN I COME? PLEASE??
I PROMISE I'LL BE GOOD. PLEASE? **PLEASE??** **EUROPE!!**

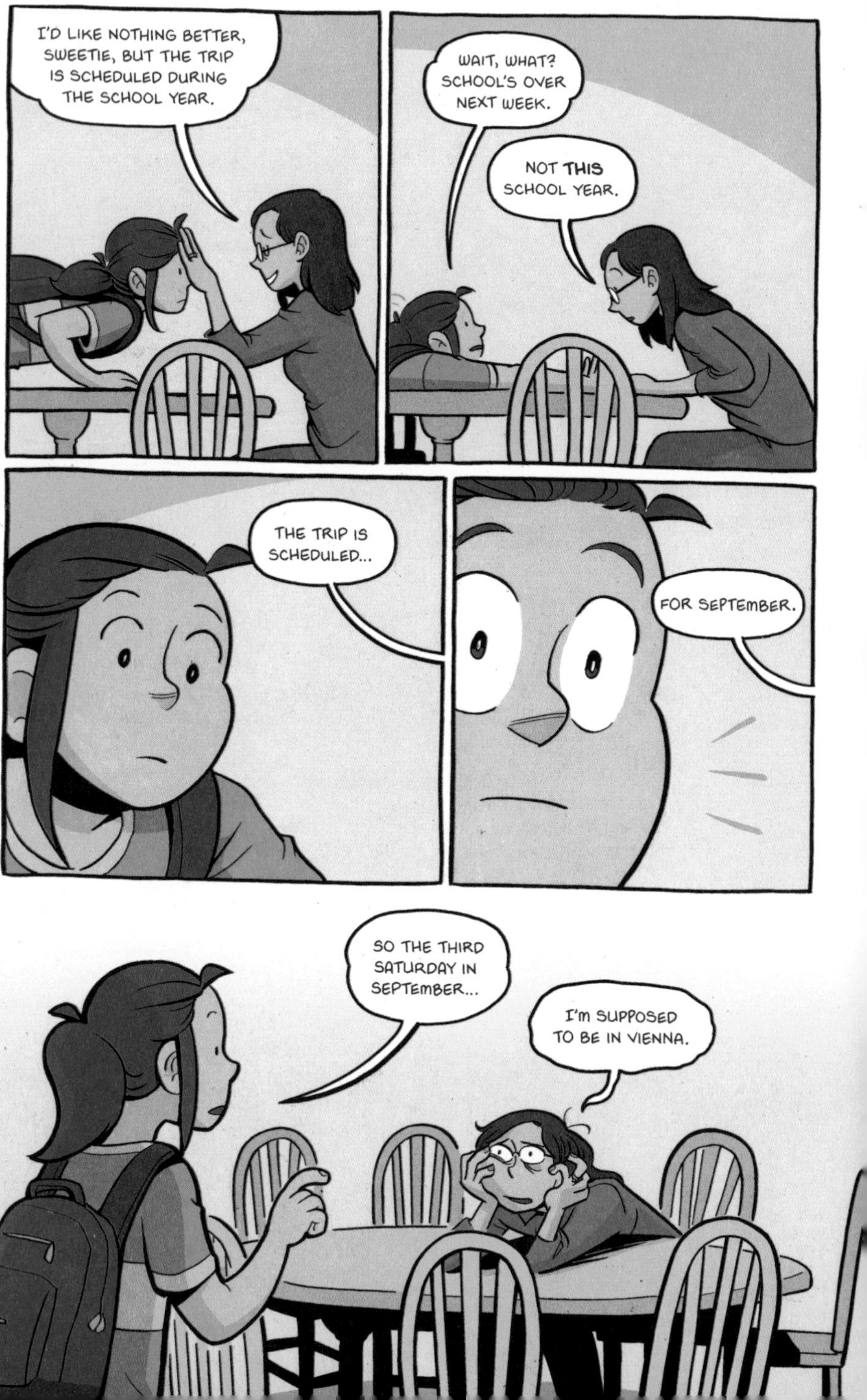
I'D LIKE NOTHING BETTER, SWEETIE, BUT THE TRIP IS SCHEDULED DURING THE SCHOOL YEAR.
WAIT, WHAT? SCHOOL'S OVER NEXT WEEK.
NOT **THIS** SCHOOL YEAR.
THE TRIP IS SCHEDULED...
FOR SEPTEMBER.
SO THE THIRD SATURDAY IN SEPTEMBER...
I'M SUPPOSED TO BE IN VIENNA.

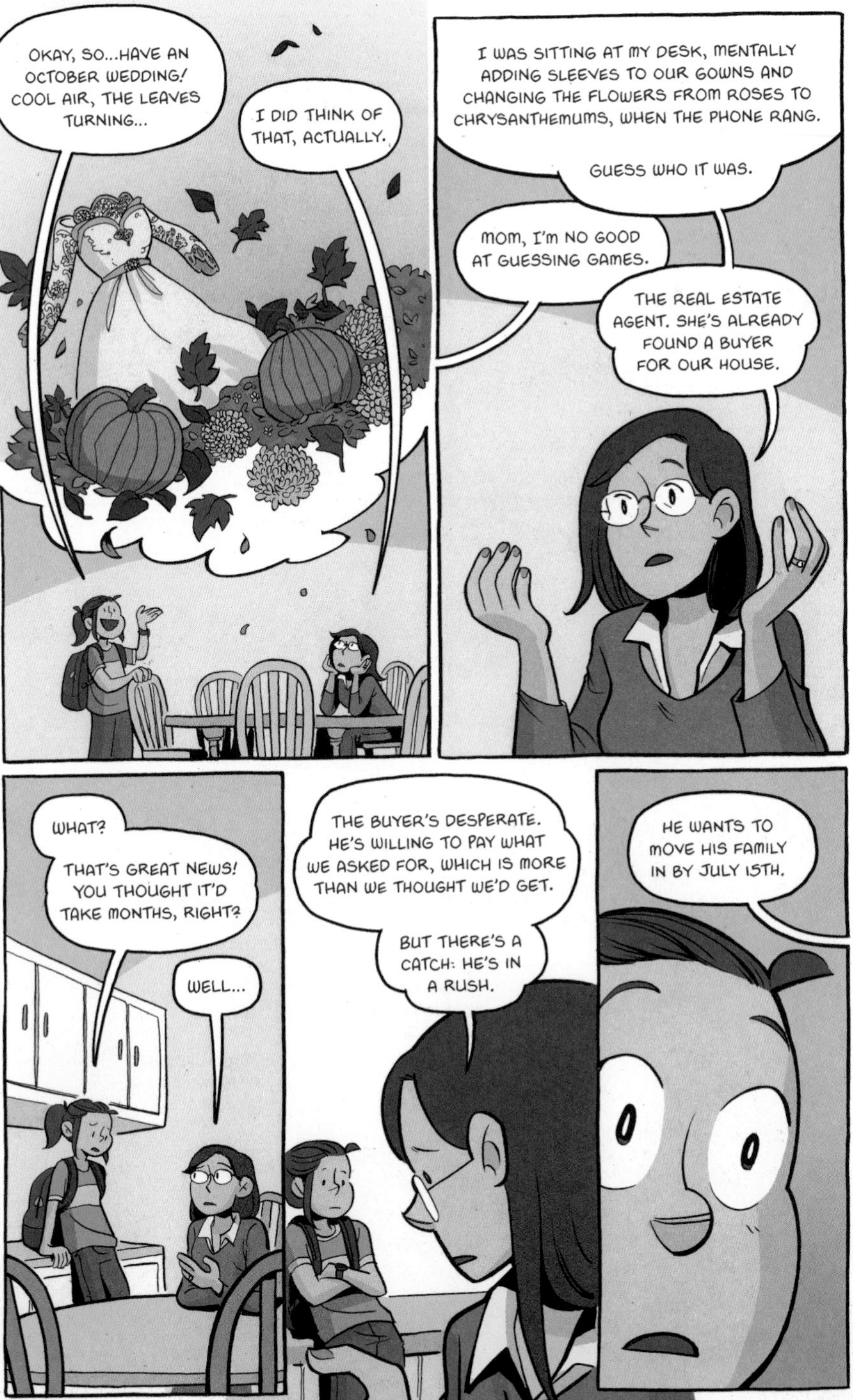
OKAY, SO...HAVE AN OCTOBER WEDDING! COOL AIR, THE LEAVES TURNING...
I DID THINK OF THAT, ACTUALLY.
I WAS SITTING AT MY DESK, MENTALLY ADDING SLEEVES TO OUR GOWNS AND CHANGING THE FLOWERS FROM ROSES TO CHRYSANTHEMUMS, WHEN THE PHONE RANG.
GUESS WHO IT WAS.
MOM, I'M NO GOOD AT GUESSING GAMES.
THE REAL ESTATE AGENT. SHE'S ALREADY FOUND A BUYER FOR OUR HOUSE.
WHAT?
THAT'S GREAT NEWS! YOU THOUGHT IT'D TAKE MONTHS, RIGHT?
WELL...
THE BUYER'S DESPERATE. HE'S WILLING TO PAY WHAT WE ASKED FOR, WHICH IS MORE THAN WE THOUGHT WE'D GET.
BUT THERE'S A CATCH: HE'S IN A RUSH.
HE WANTS TO MOVE HIS FAMILY IN BY JULY 15TH.

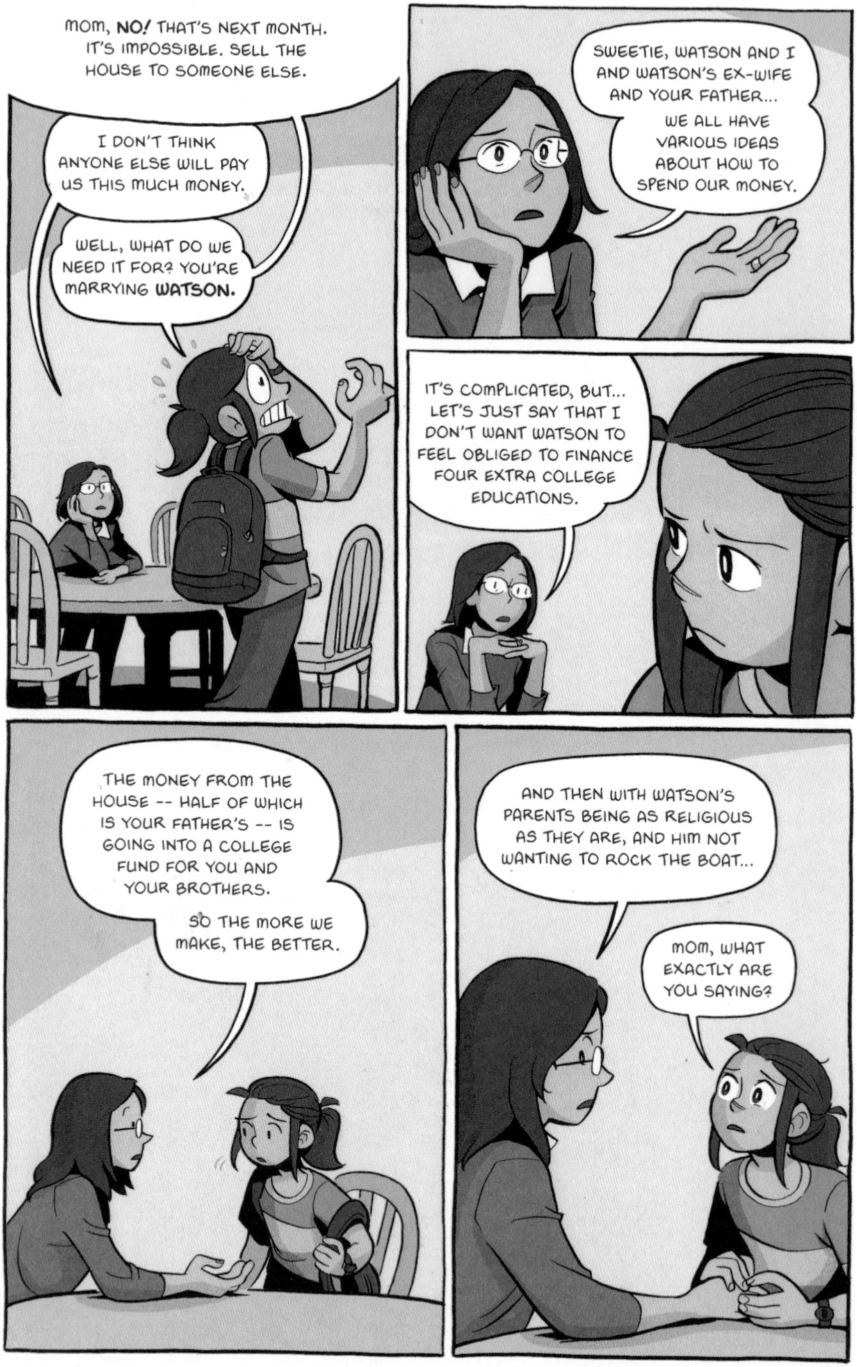
MOM, NO! THAT'S NEXT MONTH. IT'S IMPOSSIBLE. SELL THE HOUSE TO SOMEONE ELSE.
I DON'T THINK ANYONE ELSE WILL PAY US THIS MUCH MONEY.
WELL, WHAT DO WE NEED IT FOR? YOU'RE MARRYING WATSON.
SWEETIE, WATSON AND I AND WATSON'S EX-WIFE AND YOUR FATHER...
WE ALL HAVE VARIOUS IDEAS ABOUT HOW TO SPEND OUR MONEY.
IT'S COMPLICATED, BUT... LET'S JUST SAY THAT I DON'T WANT WATSON TO FEEL OBLIGED TO FINANCE FOUR EXTRA COLLEGE EDUCATIONS.
THE MONEY FROM THE HOUSE -- HALF OF WHICH IS YOUR FATHER'S -- IS GOING INTO A COLLEGE FUND FOR YOU AND YOUR BROTHERS.
SO THE MORE WE MAKE, THE BETTER.
AND THEN WITH WATSON'S PARENTS BEING AS RELIGIOUS AS THEY ARE, AND HIM NOT WANTING TO ROCK THE BOAT...
MOM, WHAT EXACTLY ARE YOU SAYING?

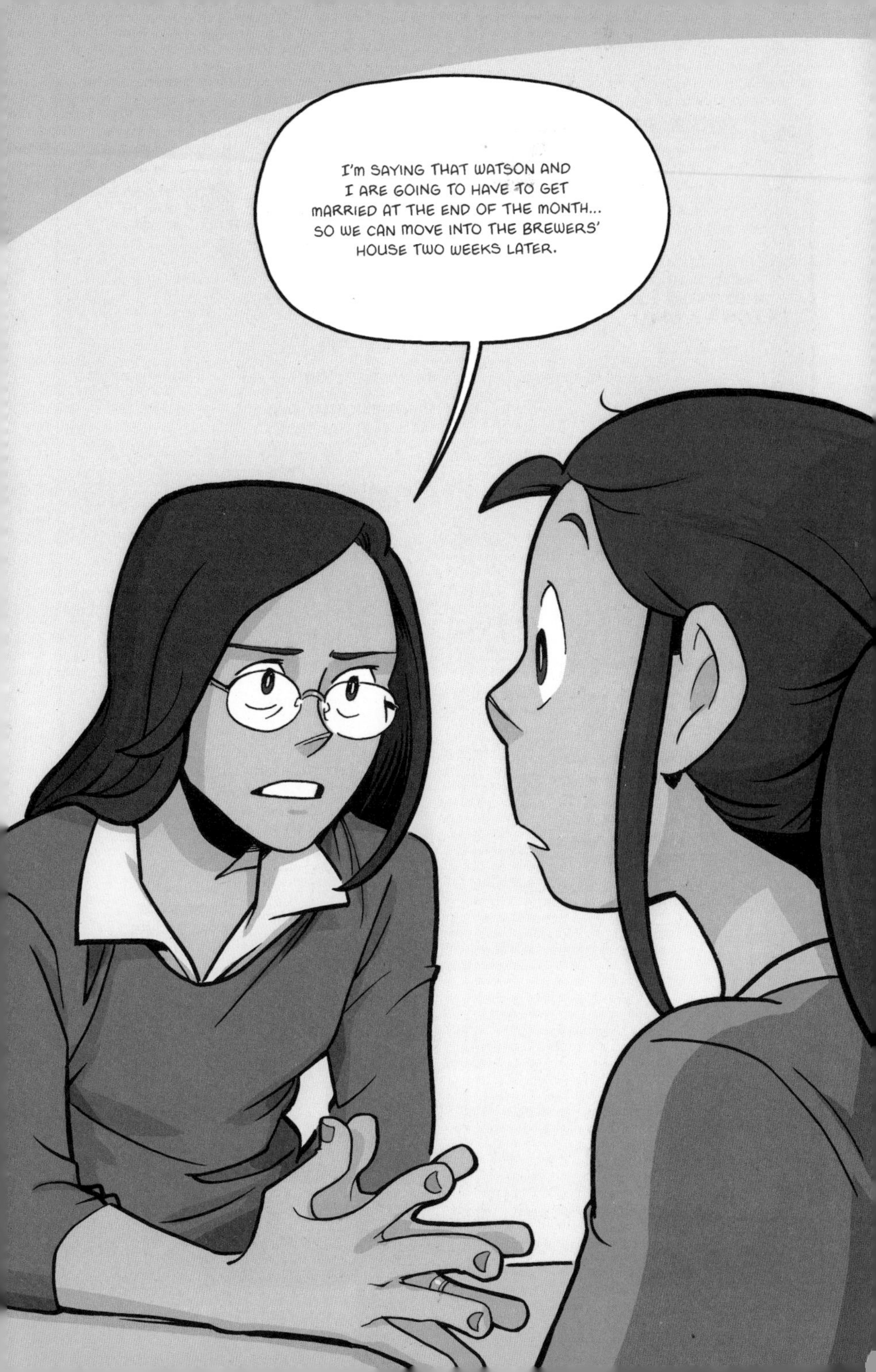
I'M SAYING THAT WATSON AND I ARE GOING TO HAVE TO GET MARRIED AT THE END OF THE MONTH... SO WE CAN MOVE INTO THE BREWERS' HOUSE TWO WEEKS LATER.

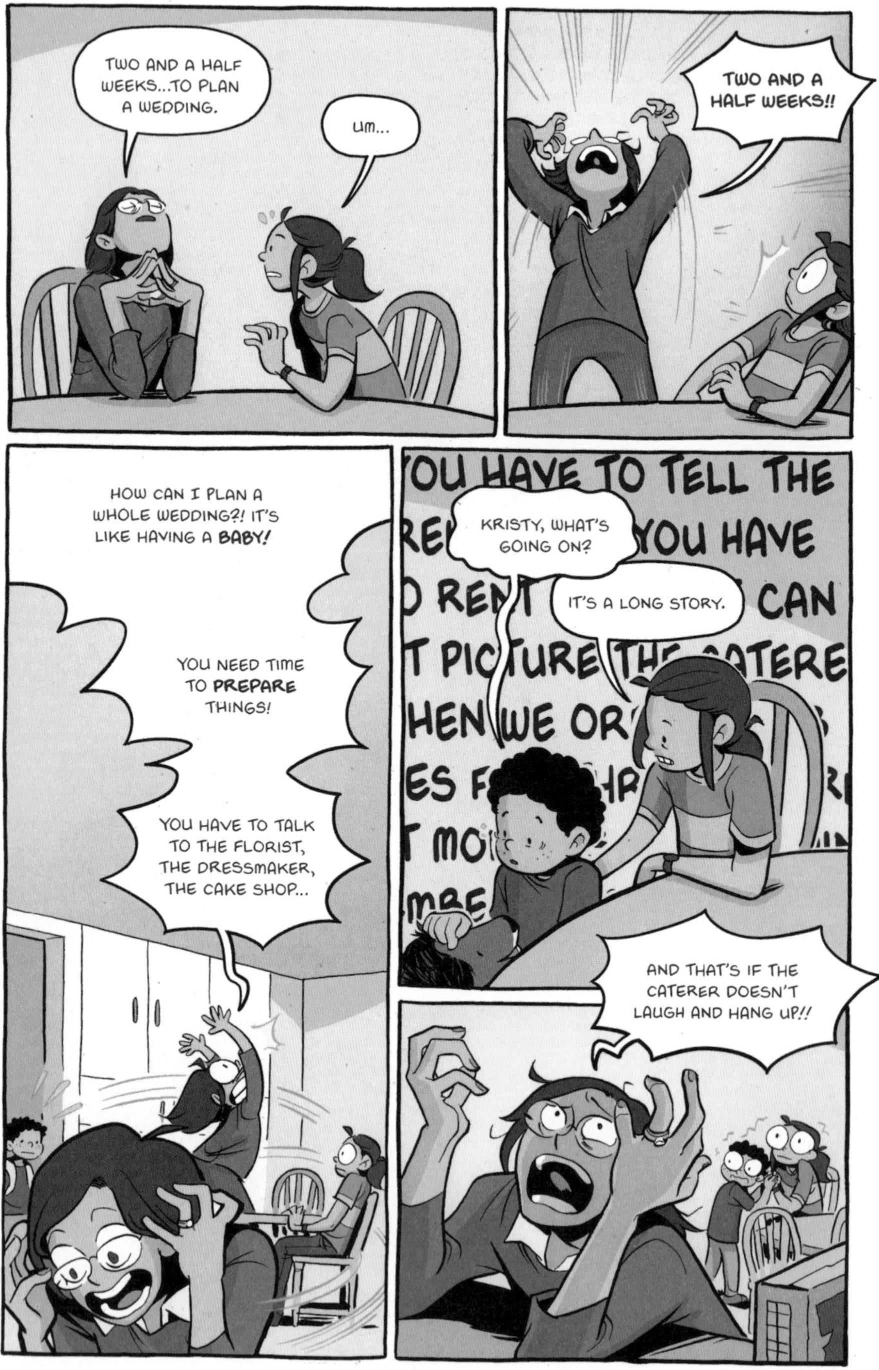
TWO AND A HALF WEEKS...TO PLAN A WEDDING.
UM...
TWO AND A HALF WEEKS!!
HOW CAN I PLAN A WHOLE WEDDING?! IT'S LIKE HAVING A BABY!
YOU NEED TIME TO PREPARE THINGS!
YOU HAVE TO TALK TO THE FLORIST, THE DRESSMAKER, THE CAKE SHOP...
KRISTY, WHAT'S GOING ON?
IT'S A LONG STORY.
AND THAT'S IF THE CATERER DOESN'T LAUGH AND HANG UP!!

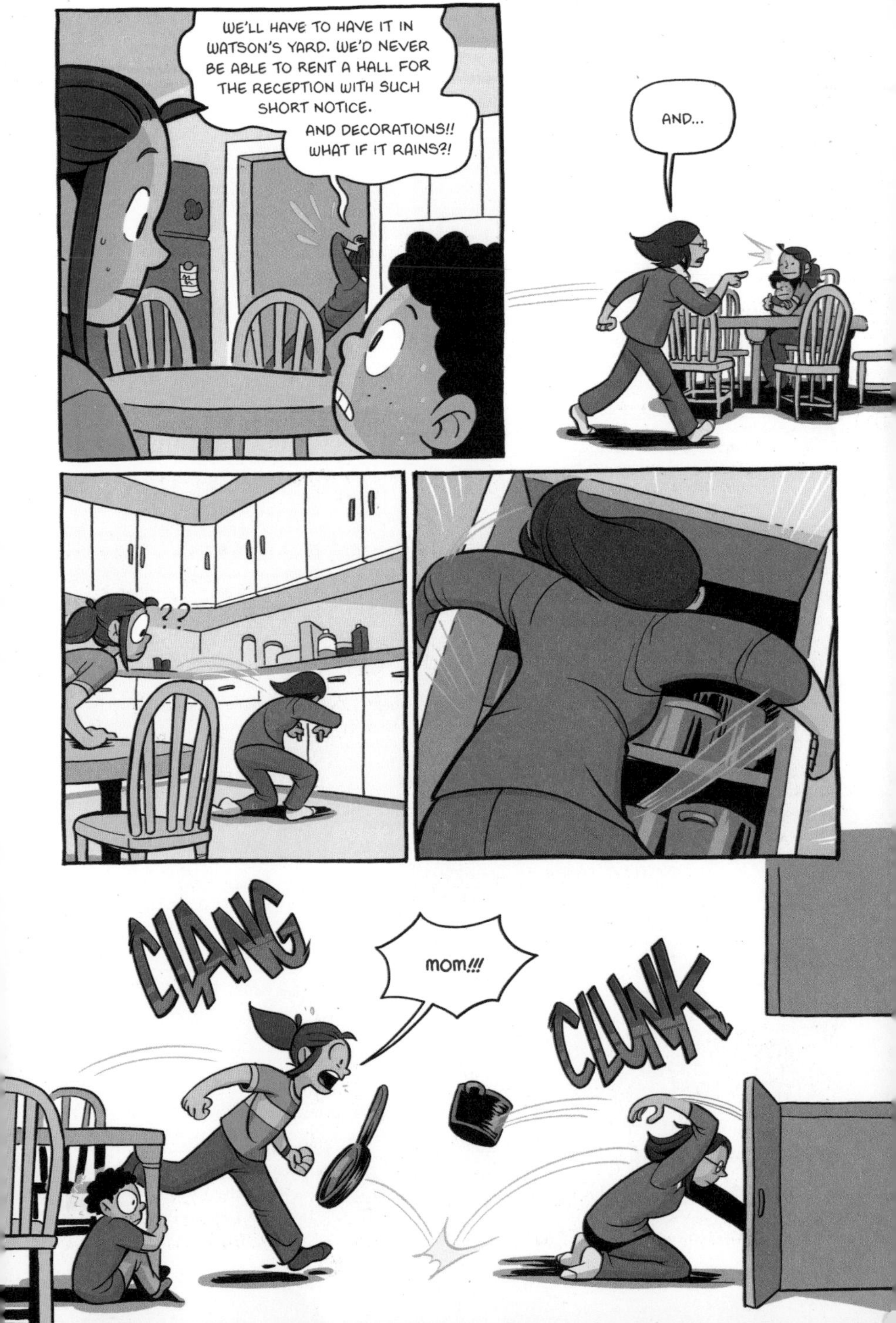
WE'LL HAVE TO HAVE IT IN WATSON'S YARD. WE'D NEVER BE ABLE TO RENT A HALL FOR THE RECEPTION WITH SUCH SHORT NOTICE.
AND DECORATIONS!! WHAT IF IT RAINS?!
AND...
??
CLANG
MOM!!!
CLUNK

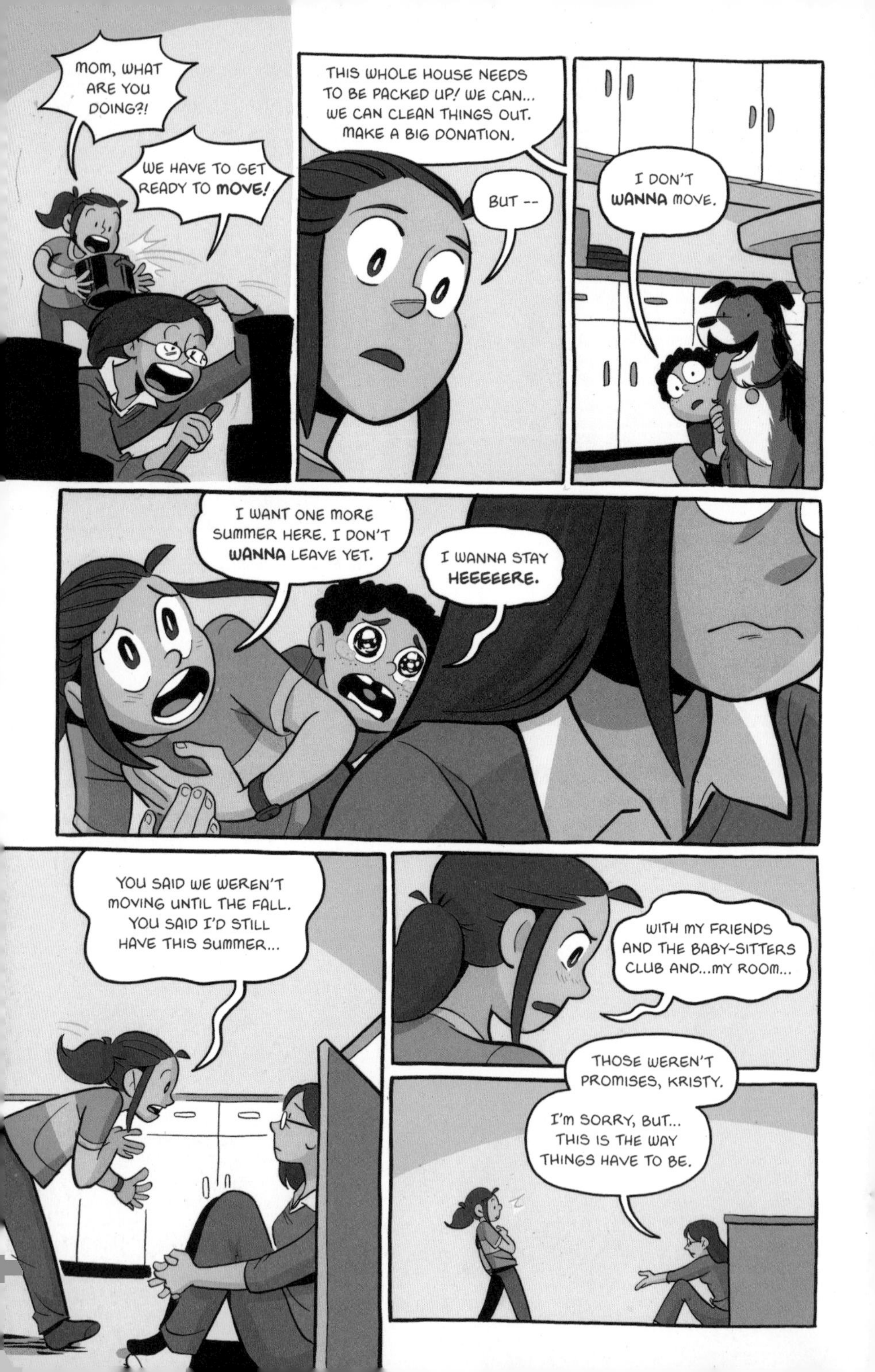

MOM, WHAT ARE YOU DOING?!
WE HAVE TO GET READY TO **MOVE!**
THIS WHOLE HOUSE NEEDS TO BE PACKED UP! WE CAN... WE CAN CLEAN THINGS OUT. MAKE A BIG DONATION.
BUT --
I DON'T **WANNA** MOVE.
I WANT ONE MORE SUMMER HERE. I DON'T **WANNA** LEAVE YET.
I WANNA STAY **HEEEEERE.**
YOU SAID WE WEREN'T MOVING UNTIL THE FALL. YOU SAID I'D STILL HAVE THIS SUMMER...
WITH MY FRIENDS AND THE BABY-SITTERS CLUB AND...MY ROOM...
THOSE WEREN'T PROMISES, KRISTY.
I'M SORRY, BUT... THIS IS THE WAY THINGS HAVE TO BE.

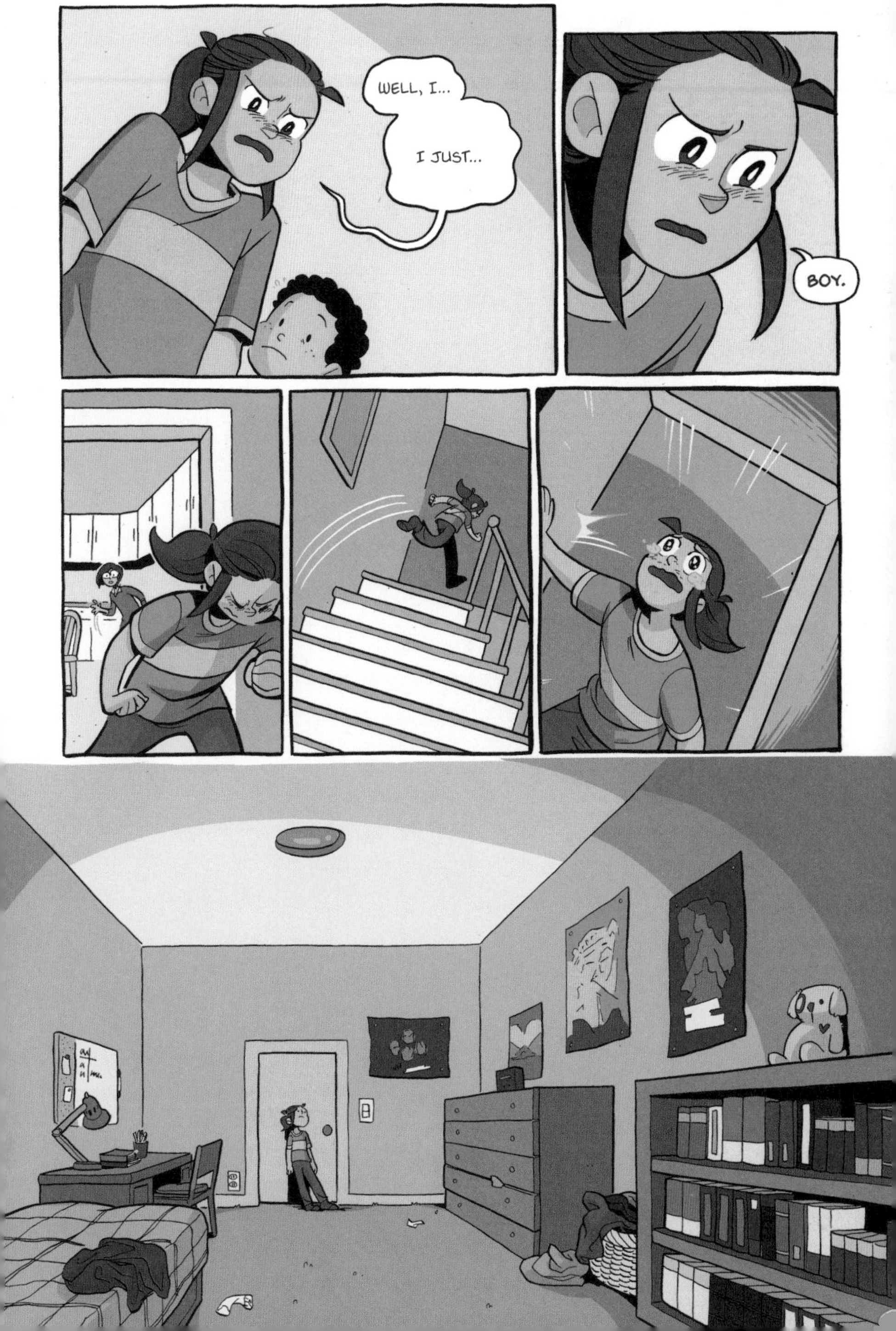
WELL, I...
I JUST...
BOY.

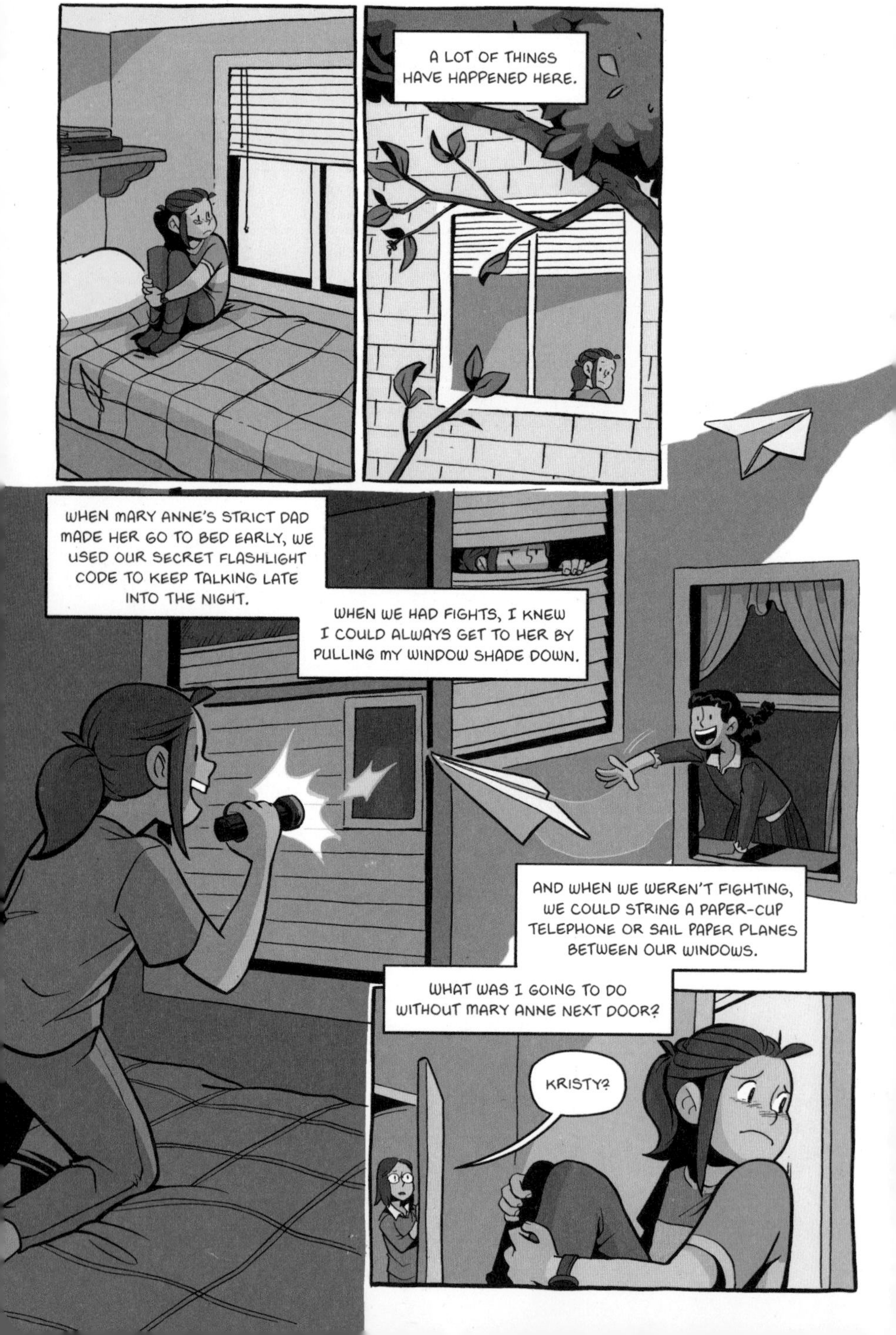
A LOT OF THINGS HAVE HAPPENED HERE.
WHEN MARY ANNE'S STRICT DAD MADE HER GO TO BED EARLY, WE USED OUR SECRET FLASHLIGHT CODE TO KEEP TALKING LATE INTO THE NIGHT.
WHEN WE HAD FIGHTS, I KNEW I COULD ALWAYS GET TO HER BY PULLING MY WINDOW SHADE DOWN.
AND WHEN WE WEREN'T FIGHTING, WE COULD STRING A PAPER-CUP TELEPHONE OR SAIL PAPER PLANES BETWEEN OUR WINDOWS.
WHAT WAS I GOING TO DO WITHOUT MARY ANNE NEXT DOOR?
KRISTY?

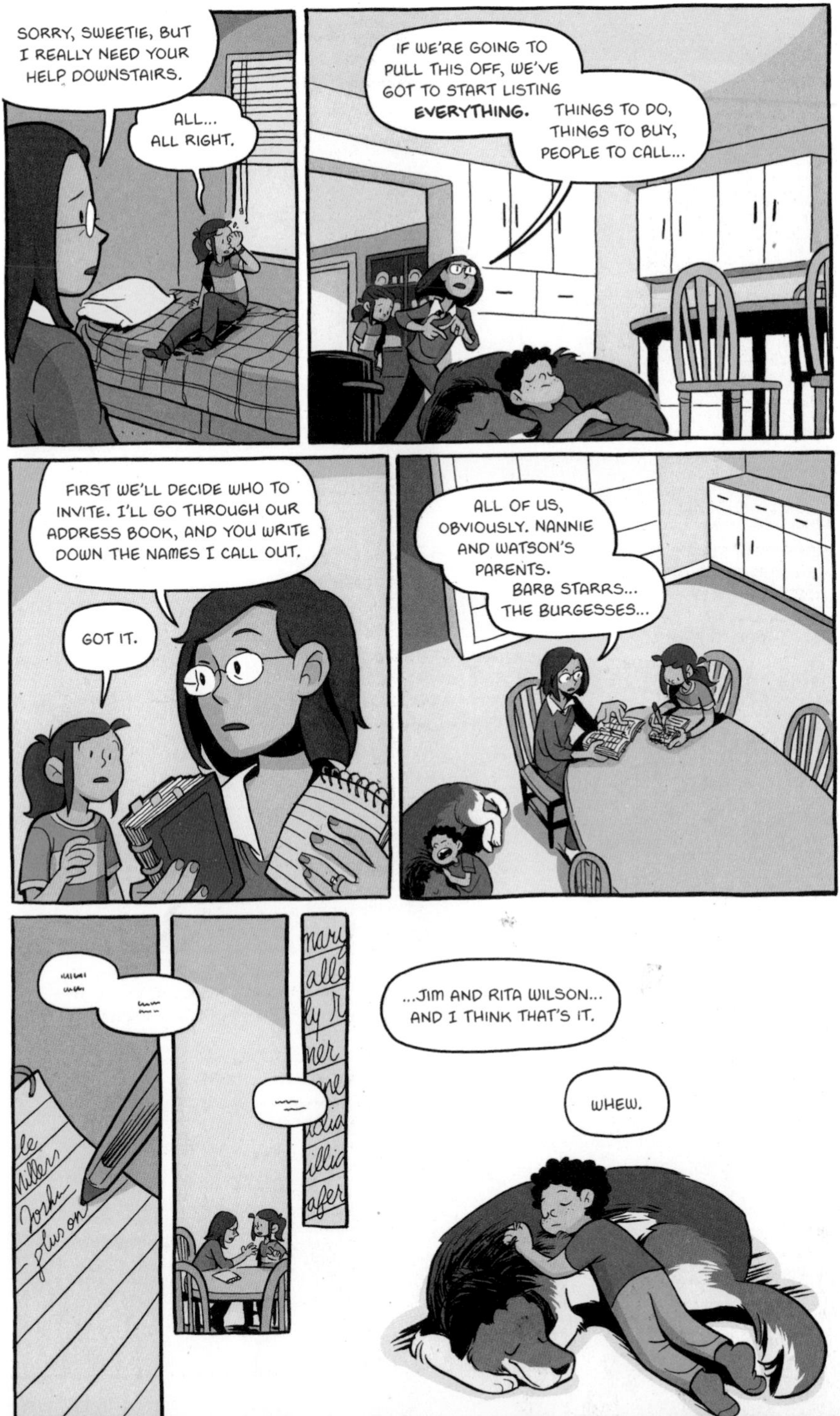
SORRY, SWEETIE, BUT I REALLY NEED YOUR HELP DOWNSTAIRS.
ALL... ALL RIGHT.
IF WE'RE GOING TO PULL THIS OFF, WE'VE GOT TO START LISTING **EVERYTHING.** THINGS TO DO, THINGS TO BUY, PEOPLE TO CALL...
FIRST WE'LL DECIDE WHO TO INVITE. I'LL GO THROUGH OUR ADDRESS BOOK, AND YOU WRITE DOWN THE NAMES I CALL OUT.
GOT IT.
ALL OF US, OBVIOUSLY. NANNIE AND WATSON'S PARENTS.
BARB STARRS... THE BURGESSES...
...JIM AND RITA WILSON... AND I THINK THAT'S IT.
WHEW.

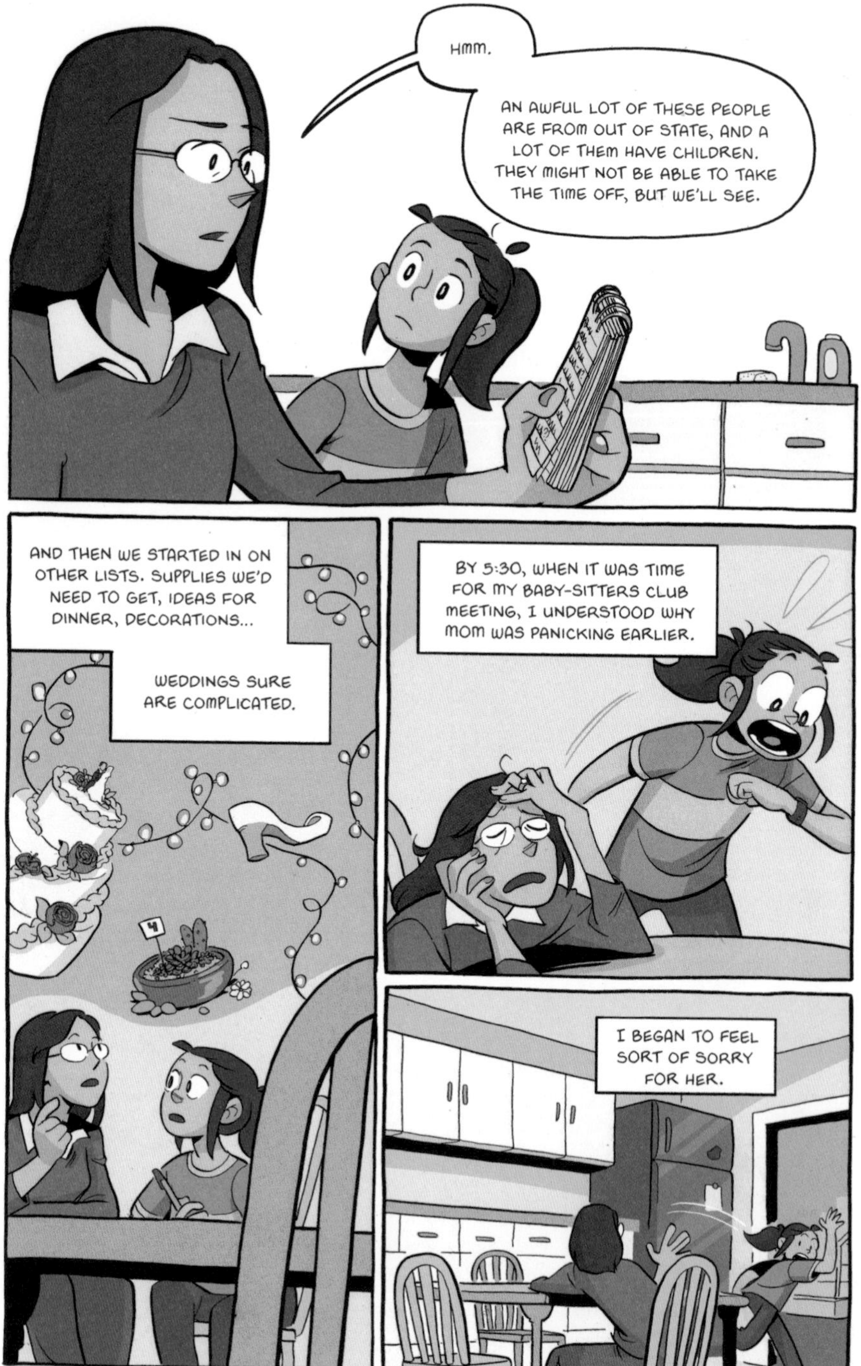
HMM.
AN AWFUL LOT OF THESE PEOPLE ARE FROM OUT OF STATE, AND A LOT OF THEM HAVE CHILDREN. THEY MIGHT NOT BE ABLE TO TAKE THE TIME OFF, BUT WE'LL SEE.
AND THEN WE STARTED IN ON OTHER LISTS. SUPPLIES WE'D NEED TO GET, IDEAS FOR DINNER, DECORATIONS...
WEDDINGS SURE ARE COMPLICATED.
BY 5:30, WHEN IT WAS TIME FOR MY BABY-SITTERS CLUB MEETING, I UNDERSTOOD WHY MOM WAS PANICKING EARLIER.
I BEGAN TO FEEL SORT OF SORRY FOR HER.

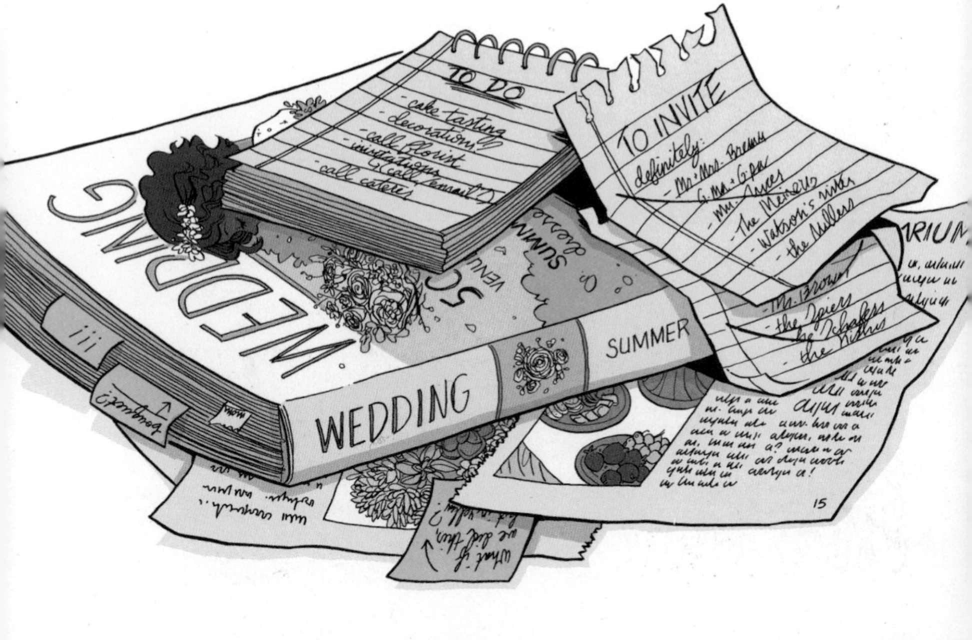
TO DO
- cake tasting
- decorations
- call florist
- invitations
(call, email?)
- call caterers
TO INVITE
definitely:
- the Millers
WEDDING
SUMMER
WEDDING
15

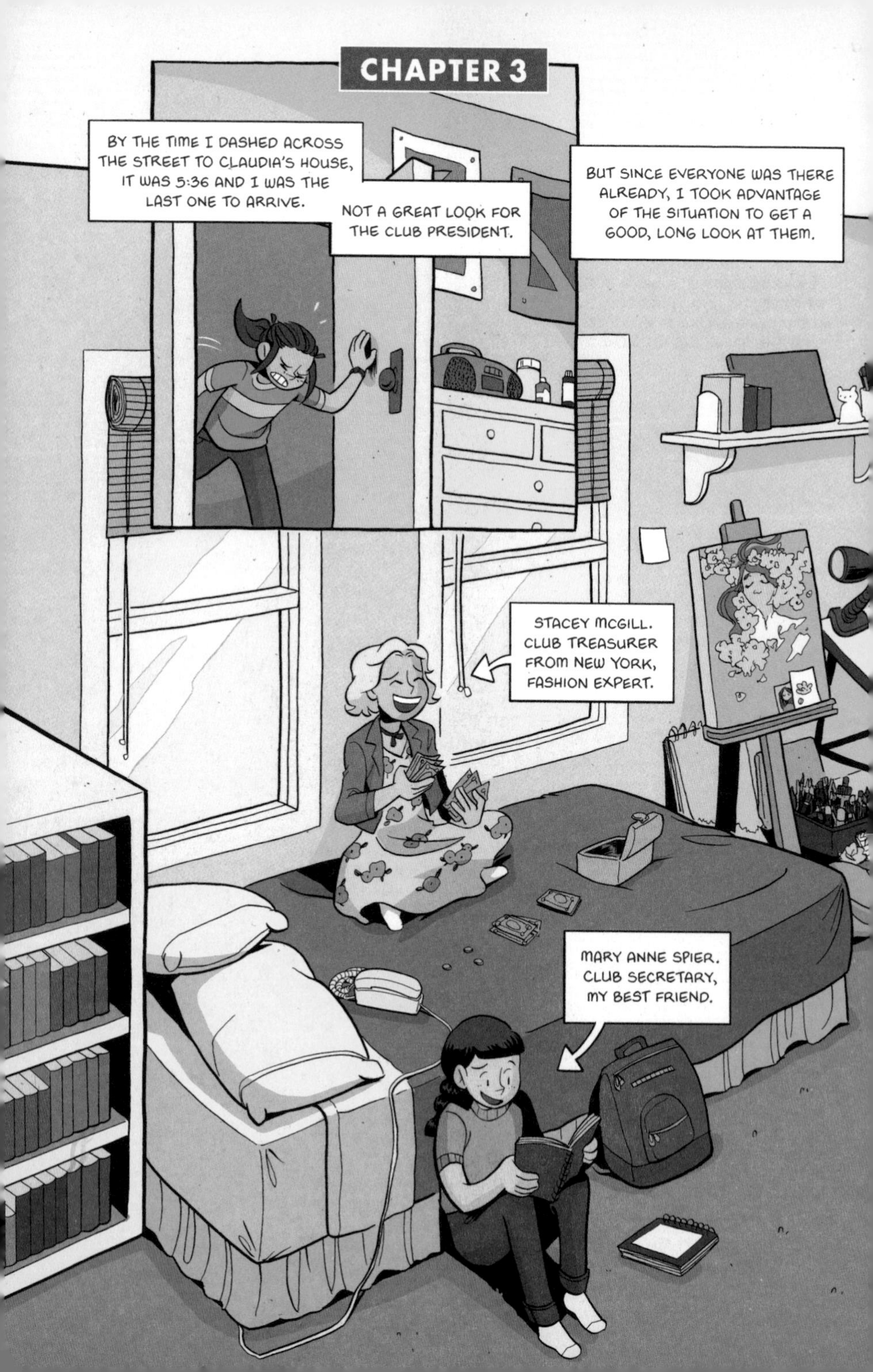

CHAPTER 3
BY THE TIME I DASHED ACROSS THE STREET TO CLAUDIA'S HOUSE, IT WAS 5:36 AND I WAS THE LAST ONE TO ARRIVE.
NOT A GREAT LOOK FOR THE CLUB PRESIDENT.
BUT SINCE EVERYONE WAS THERE ALREADY, I TOOK ADVANTAGE OF THE SITUATION TO GET A GOOD, LONG LOOK AT THEM.
STACEY MCGILL. CLUB TREASURER FROM NEW YORK, FASHION EXPERT.
MARY ANNE SPIER. CLUB SECRETARY, MY BEST FRIEND.

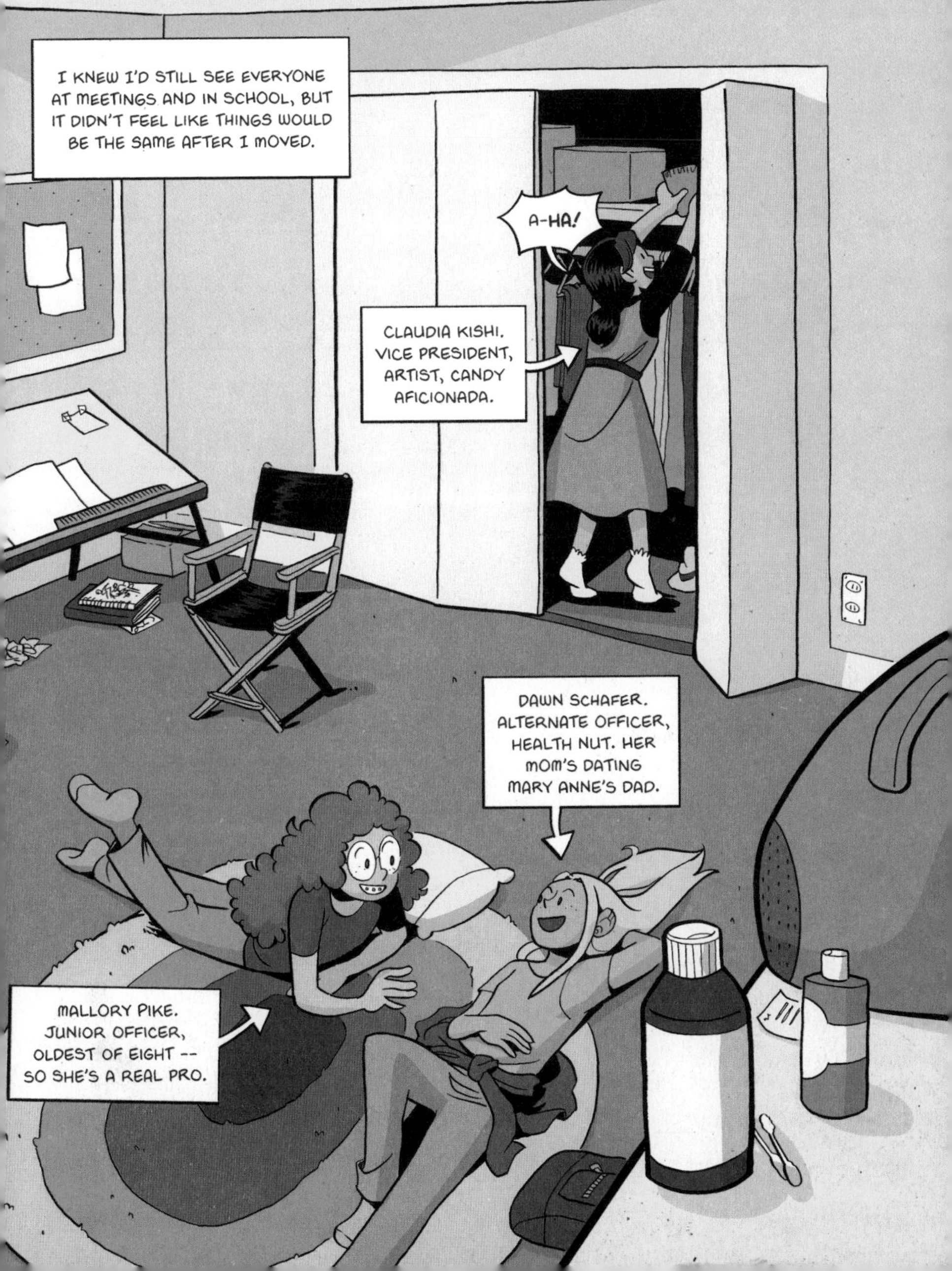
I KNEW I'D STILL SEE EVERYONE AT MEETINGS AND IN SCHOOL, BUT IT DIDN'T FEEL LIKE THINGS WOULD BE THE SAME AFTER I MOVED.
A-HA!
CLAUDIA KISHI. VICE PRESIDENT, ARTIST, CANDY AFICIONADA.
DAWN SCHAFER. ALTERNATE OFFICER, HEALTH NUT. HER MOM'S DATING MARY ANNE'S DAD.
MALLORY PIKE. JUNIOR OFFICER, OLDEST OF EIGHT -- SO SHE'S A REAL PRO.

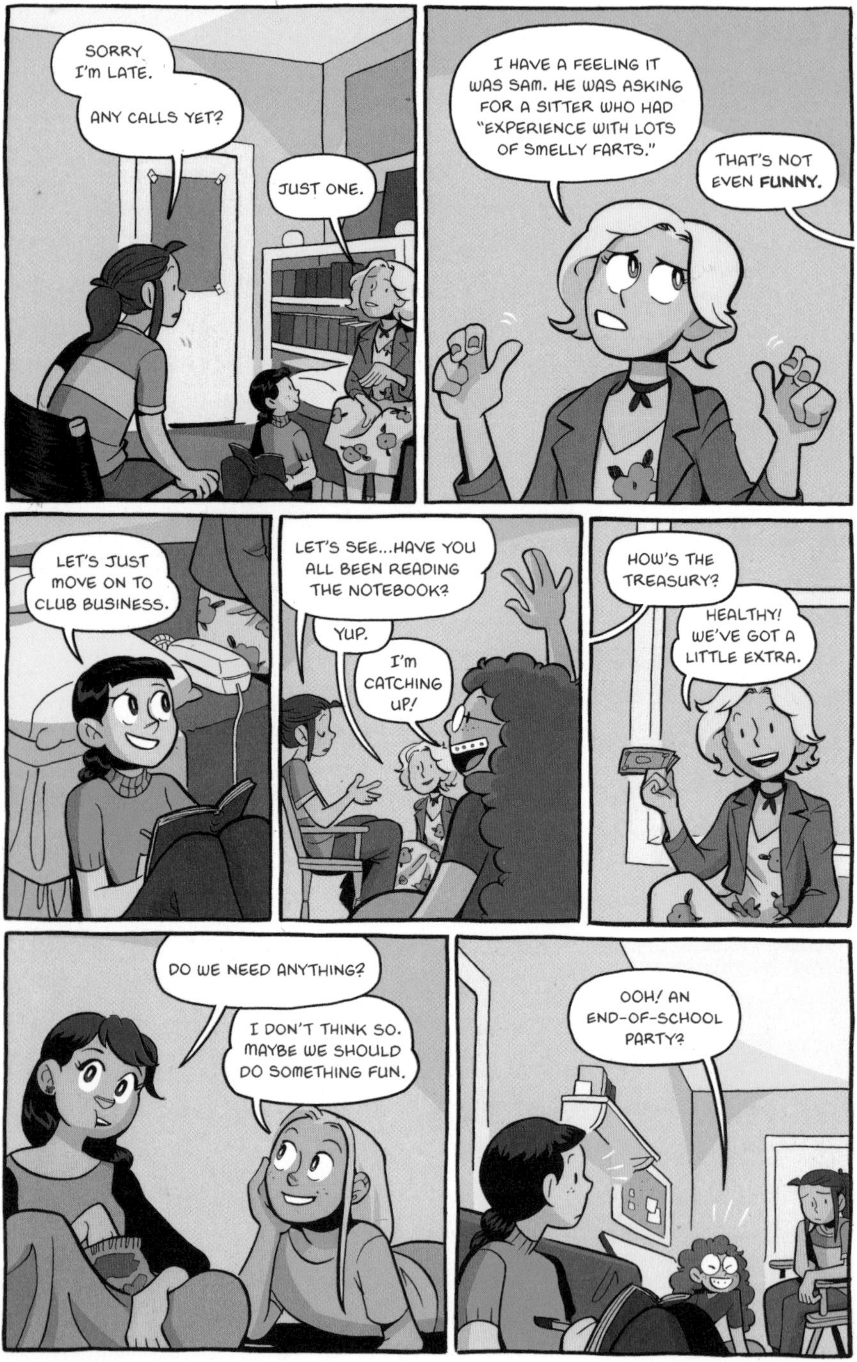
SORRY I'M LATE.
ANY CALLS YET?
JUST ONE.
I HAVE A FEELING IT WAS SAM. HE WAS ASKING FOR A SITTER WHO HAD "EXPERIENCE WITH LOTS OF SMELLY FARTS."
THAT'S NOT EVEN **FUNNY.**
LET'S JUST MOVE ON TO CLUB BUSINESS.
LET'S SEE...HAVE YOU ALL BEEN READING THE NOTEBOOK?
YUP.
I'M CATCHING UP!
HOW'S THE TREASURY?
HEALTHY! WE'VE GOT A LITTLE EXTRA.
DO WE NEED ANYTHING?
I DON'T THINK SO. MAYBE WE SHOULD DO SOMETHING FUN.
OOH! AN END-OF-SCHOOL PARTY?

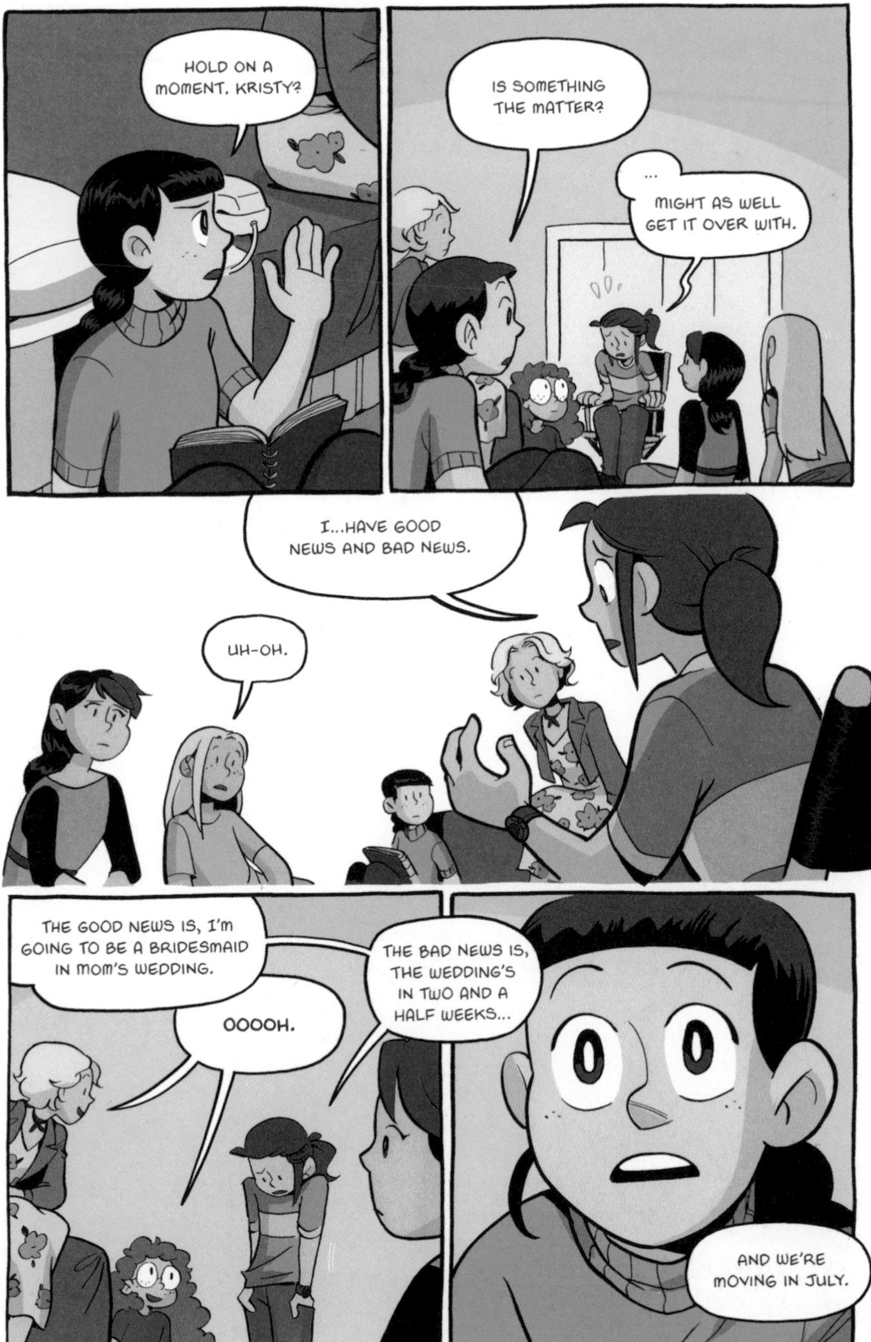
HOLD ON A MOMENT. KRISTY?
IS SOMETHING THE MATTER?
...
MIGHT AS WELL GET IT OVER WITH.
I...HAVE GOOD NEWS AND BAD NEWS.
UH-OH.
THE GOOD NEWS IS, I'M GOING TO BE A BRIDESMAID IN MOM'S WEDDING.
OOOOH.
THE BAD NEWS IS, THE WEDDING'S IN TWO AND A HALF WEEKS...
AND WE'RE MOVING IN JULY.

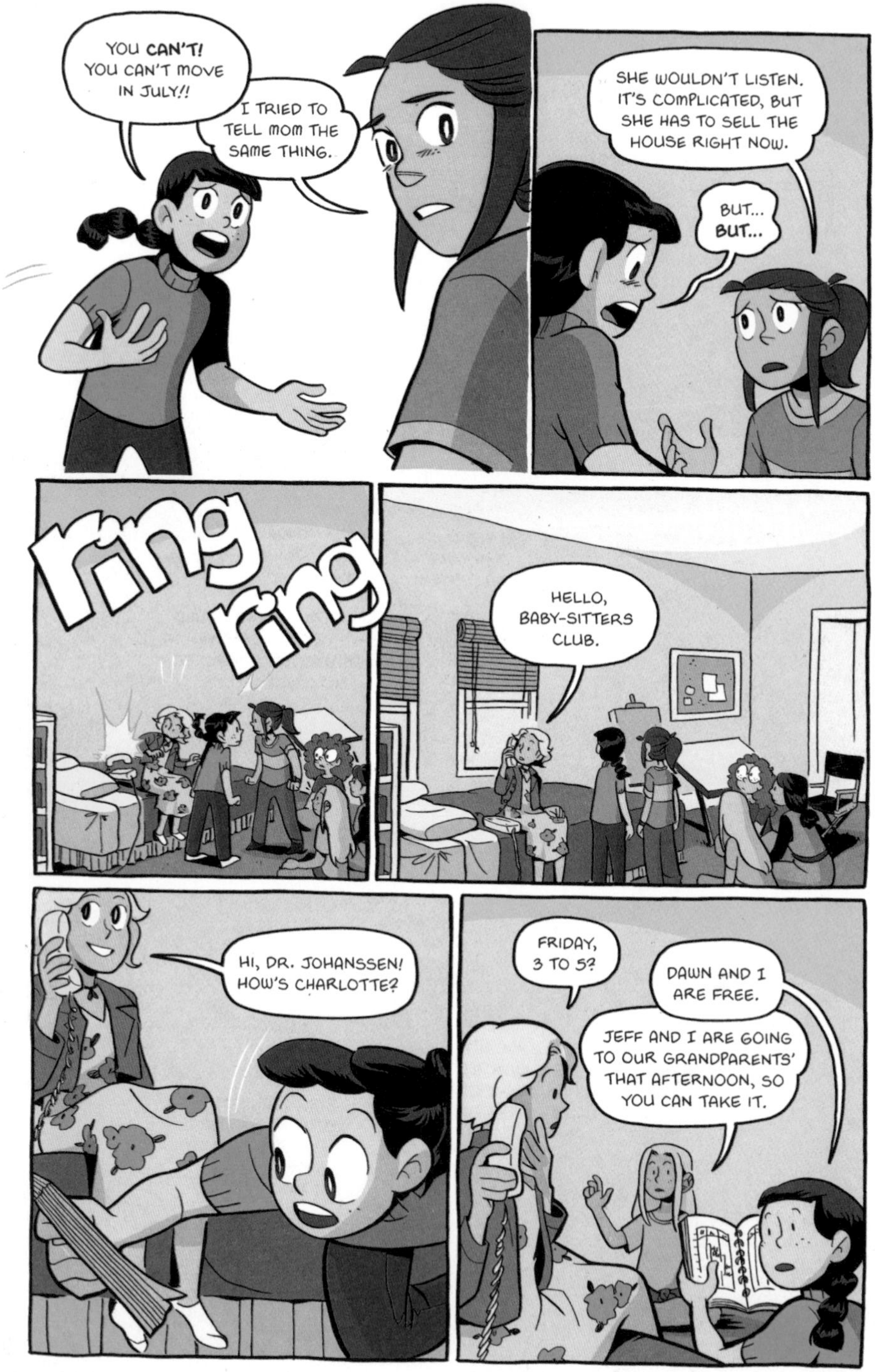
YOU **CAN'T!** YOU CAN'T MOVE IN JULY!!
I TRIED TO TELL MOM THE SAME THING.
SHE WOULDN'T LISTEN. IT'S COMPLICATED, BUT SHE HAS TO SELL THE HOUSE RIGHT NOW.
BUT... **BUT...**
RING RING
HELLO, BABY-SITTERS CLUB.
HI, DR. JOHANSSEN! HOW'S CHARLOTTE?
FRIDAY, 3 TO 5?
DAWN AND I ARE FREE.
JEFF AND I ARE GOING TO OUR GRANDPARENTS' THAT AFTERNOON, SO YOU CAN TAKE IT.

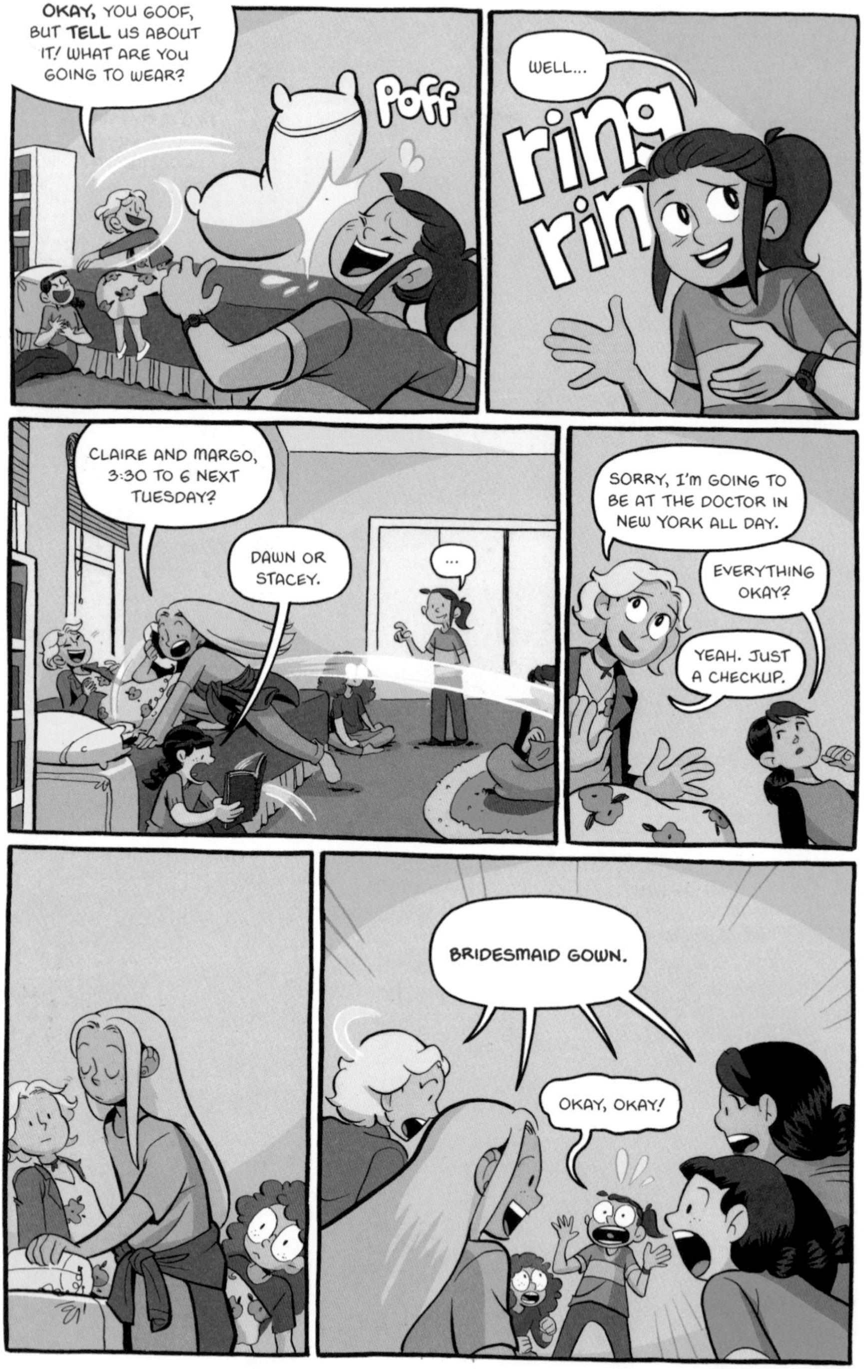
OKAY, YOU GOOF, BUT TELL US ABOUT IT! WHAT ARE YOU GOING TO WEAR?
Poff
WELL...
ring ring
CLAIRE AND MARGO, 3:30 TO 6 NEXT TUESDAY?
DAWN OR STACEY.
...
SORRY, I'M GOING TO BE AT THE DOCTOR IN NEW YORK ALL DAY.
EVERYTHING OKAY?
YEAH. JUST A CHECKUP.
BRIDESMAID GOWN.
OKAY, OKAY!

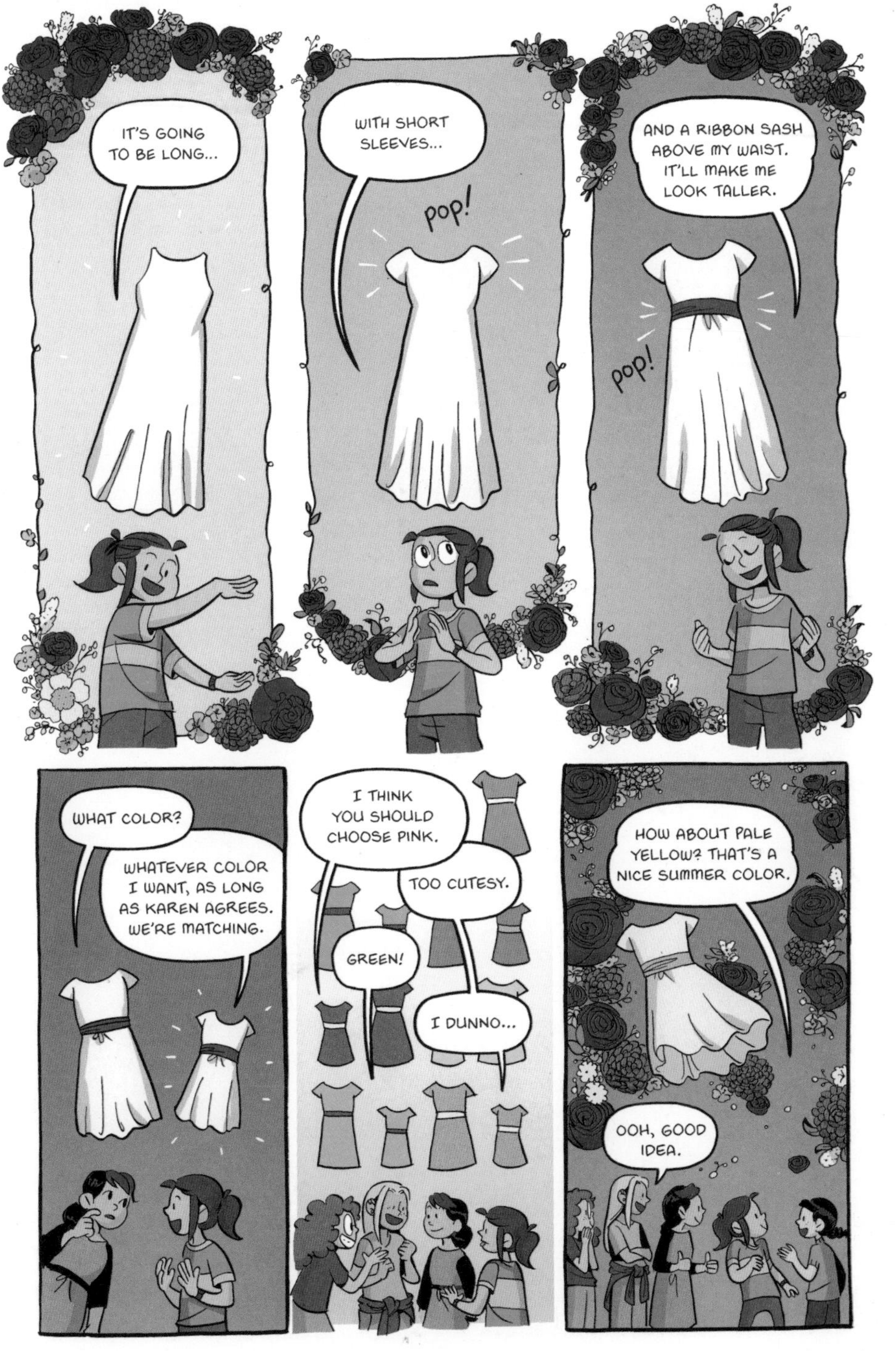
IT'S GOING TO BE LONG...
WITH SHORT SLEEVES...
POP!
AND A RIBBON SASH ABOVE MY WAIST. IT'LL MAKE ME LOOK TALLER.
POP!
WHAT COLOR?
WHATEVER COLOR I WANT, AS LONG AS KAREN AGREES. WE'RE MATCHING.
I THINK YOU SHOULD CHOOSE PINK.
TOO CUTESY.
GREEN!
I DUNNO...
HOW ABOUT PALE YELLOW? THAT'S A NICE SUMMER COLOR.
OOH, GOOD IDEA.

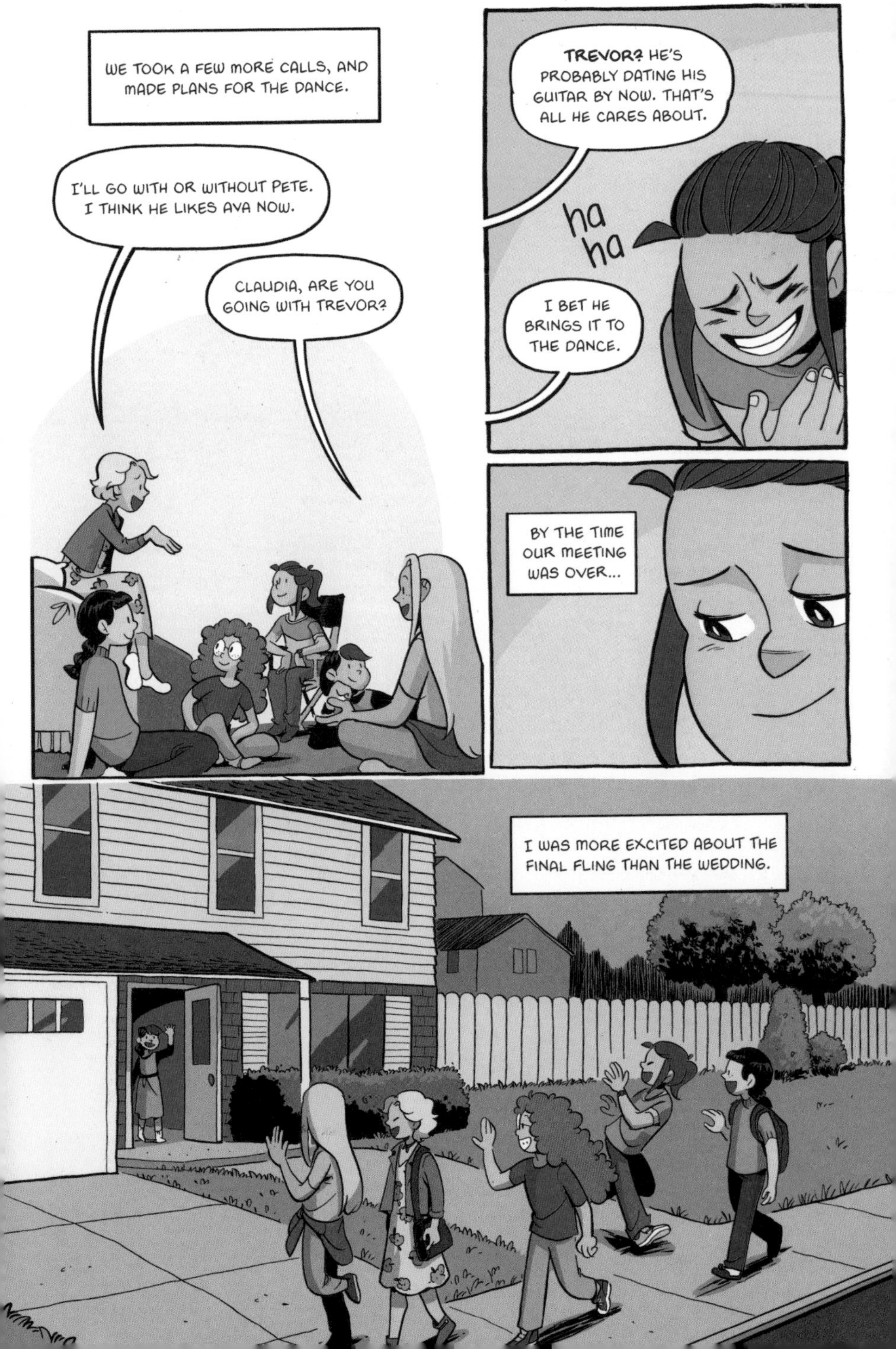
WE TOOK A FEW MORE CALLS, AND MADE PLANS FOR THE DANCE.
I'LL GO WITH OR WITHOUT PETE. I THINK HE LIKES AVA NOW.
CLAUDIA, ARE YOU GOING WITH TREVOR?
TREVOR? HE'S PROBABLY DATING HIS GUITAR BY NOW. THAT'S ALL HE CARES ABOUT.
ha ha
I BET HE BRINGS IT TO THE DANCE.
BY THE TIME OUR MEETING WAS OVER...
I WAS MORE EXCITED ABOUT THE FINAL FLING THAN THE WEDDING.

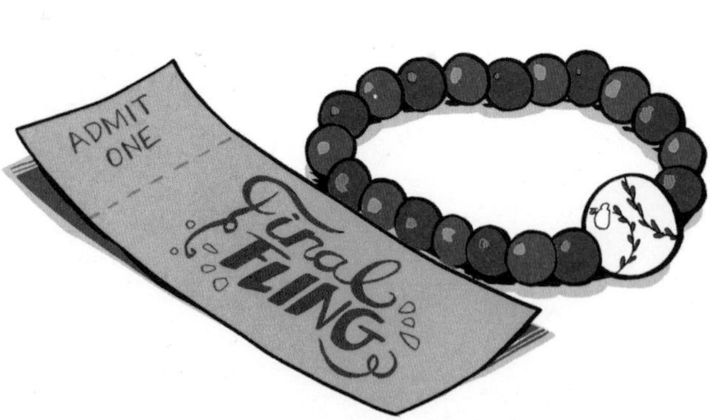
ADMIT ONE
Final FLING

CHAPTER 4

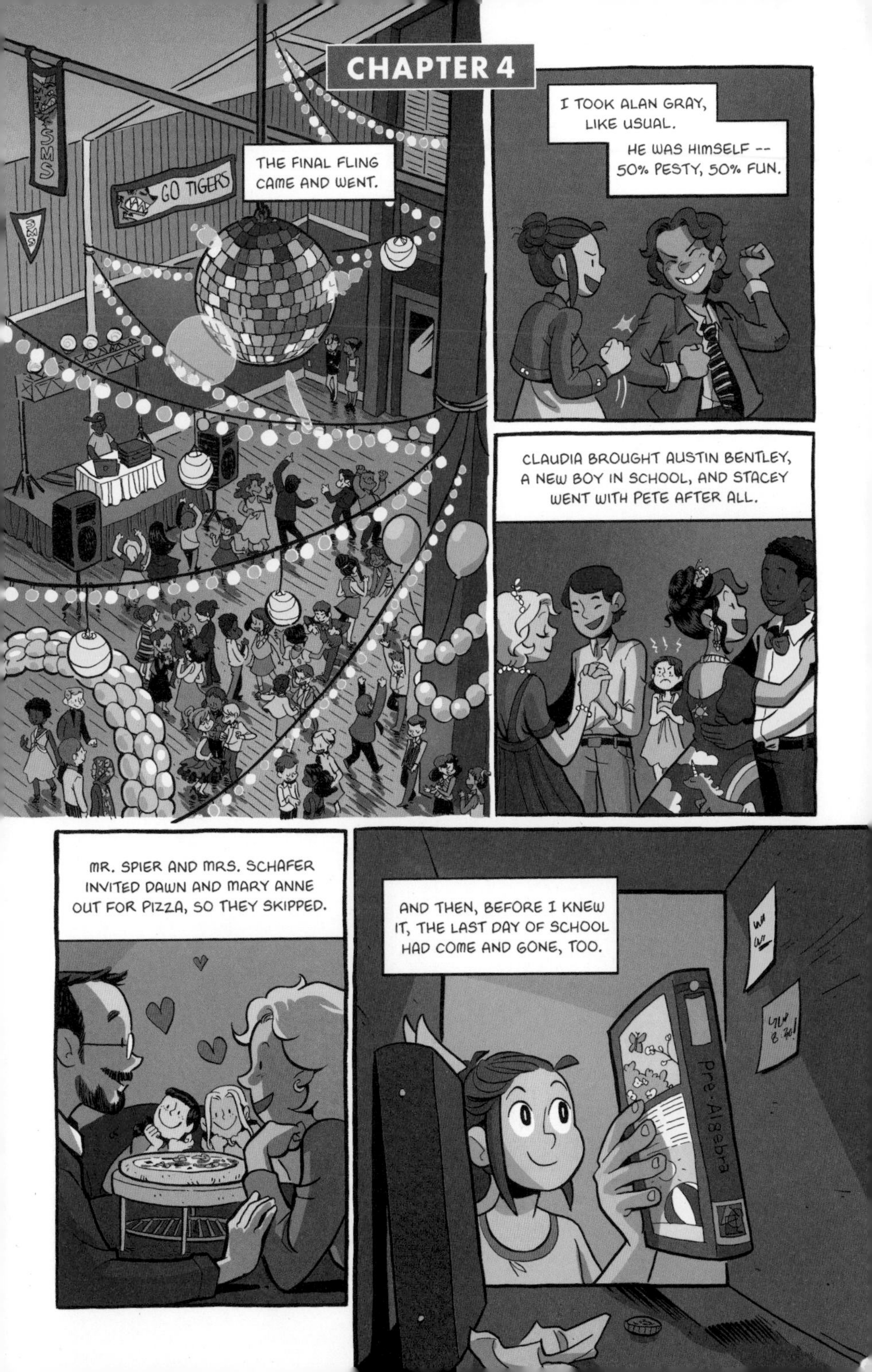

SMS
GO TIGERS
SMS
THE FINAL FLING CAME AND WENT.
I TOOK ALAN GRAY, LIKE USUAL.
HE WAS HIMSELF -- 50% PESTY, 50% FUN.
CLAUDIA BROUGHT AUSTIN BENTLEY, A NEW BOY IN SCHOOL, AND STACEY WENT WITH PETE AFTER ALL.
MR. SPIER AND MRS. SCHAFER INVITED DAWN AND MARY ANNE OUT FOR PIZZA, SO THEY SKIPPED.
AND THEN, BEFORE I KNEW IT, THE LAST DAY OF SCHOOL HAD COME AND GONE, TOO.
Pre-Algebra

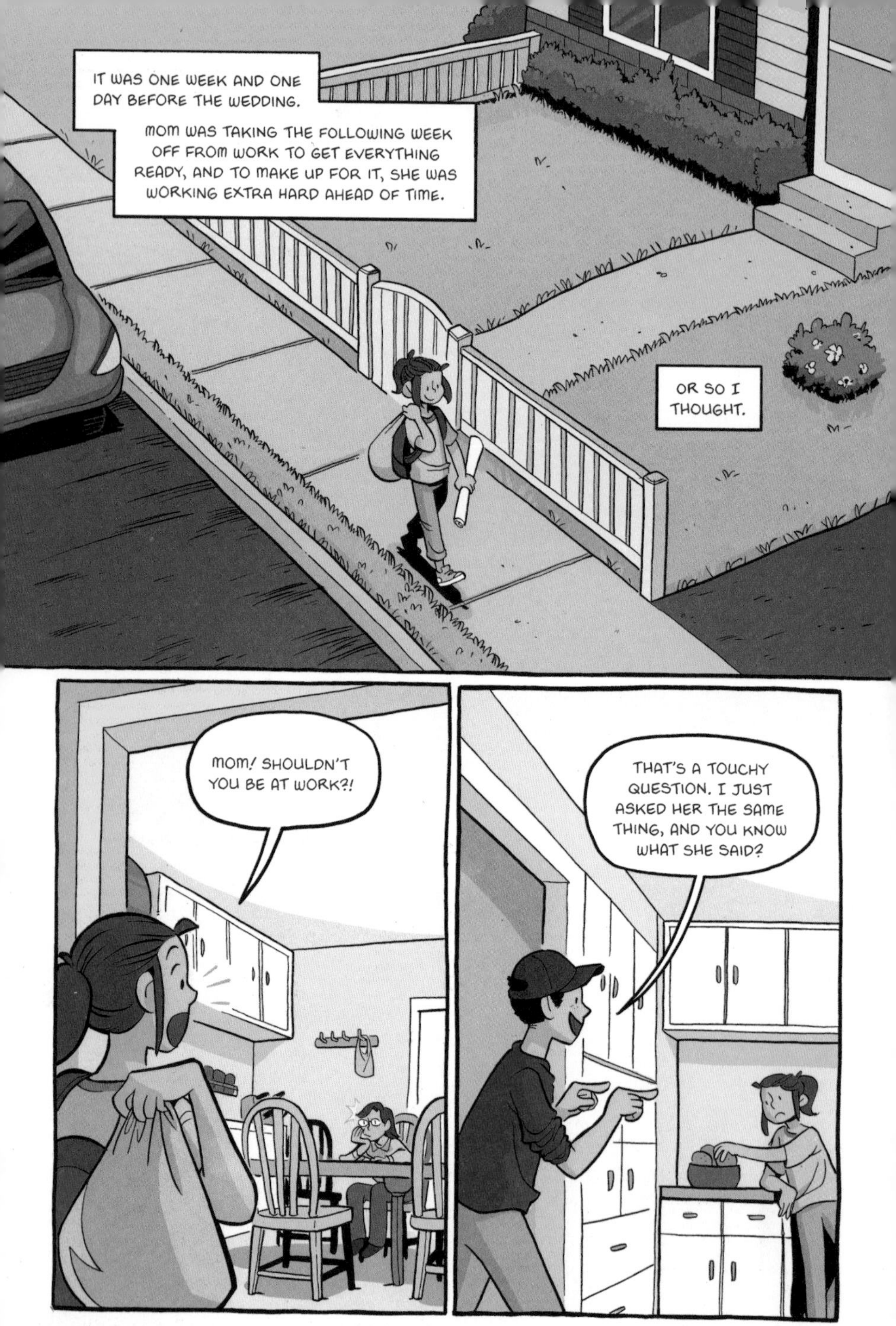
IT WAS ONE WEEK AND ONE DAY BEFORE THE WEDDING.
MOM WAS TAKING THE FOLLOWING WEEK OFF FROM WORK TO GET EVERYTHING READY, AND TO MAKE UP FOR IT, SHE WAS WORKING EXTRA HARD AHEAD OF TIME.
OR SO I THOUGHT.
MOM! SHOULDN'T YOU BE AT WORK?!
THAT'S A TOUCHY QUESTION. I JUST ASKED HER THE SAME THING, AND YOU KNOW WHAT SHE SAID?

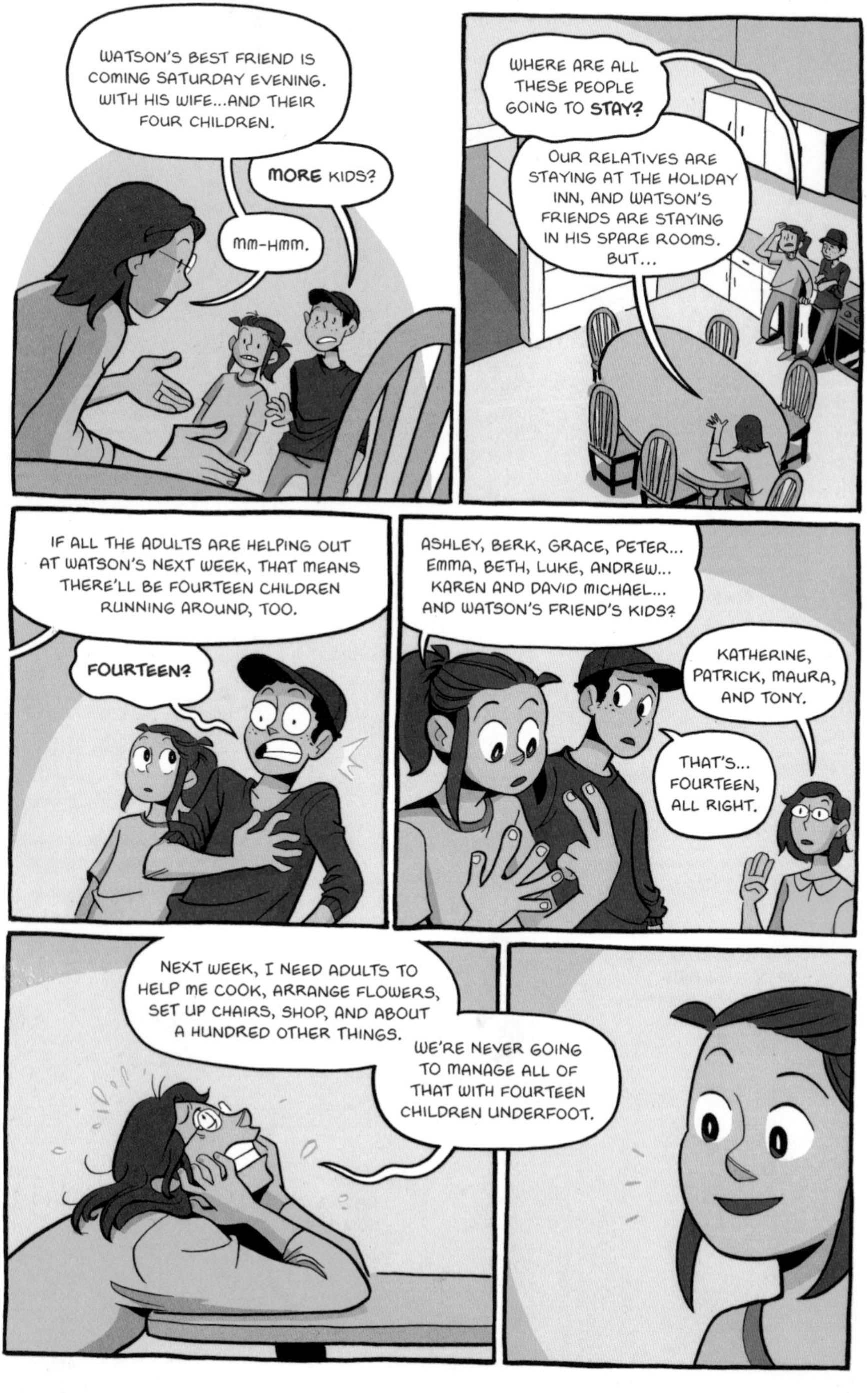
WATSON'S BEST FRIEND IS COMING SATURDAY EVENING. WITH HIS WIFE...AND THEIR FOUR CHILDREN.
MORE KIDS?
MM-HMM.
WHERE ARE ALL THESE PEOPLE GOING TO STAY?
OUR RELATIVES ARE STAYING AT THE HOLIDAY INN, AND WATSON'S FRIENDS ARE STAYING IN HIS SPARE ROOMS. BUT...
IF ALL THE ADULTS ARE HELPING OUT AT WATSON'S NEXT WEEK, THAT MEANS THERE'LL BE FOURTEEN CHILDREN RUNNING AROUND, TOO.
FOURTEEN?
ASHLEY, BERK, GRACE, PETER... EMMA, BETH, LUKE, ANDREW... KAREN AND DAVID MICHAEL... AND WATSON'S FRIEND'S KIDS?
KATHERINE, PATRICK, MAURA, AND TONY.
THAT'S... FOURTEEN, ALL RIGHT.
NEXT WEEK, I NEED ADULTS TO HELP ME COOK, ARRANGE FLOWERS, SET UP CHAIRS, SHOP, AND ABOUT A HUNDRED OTHER THINGS.
WE'RE NEVER GOING TO MANAGE ALL OF THAT WITH FOURTEEN CHILDREN UNDERFOOT.

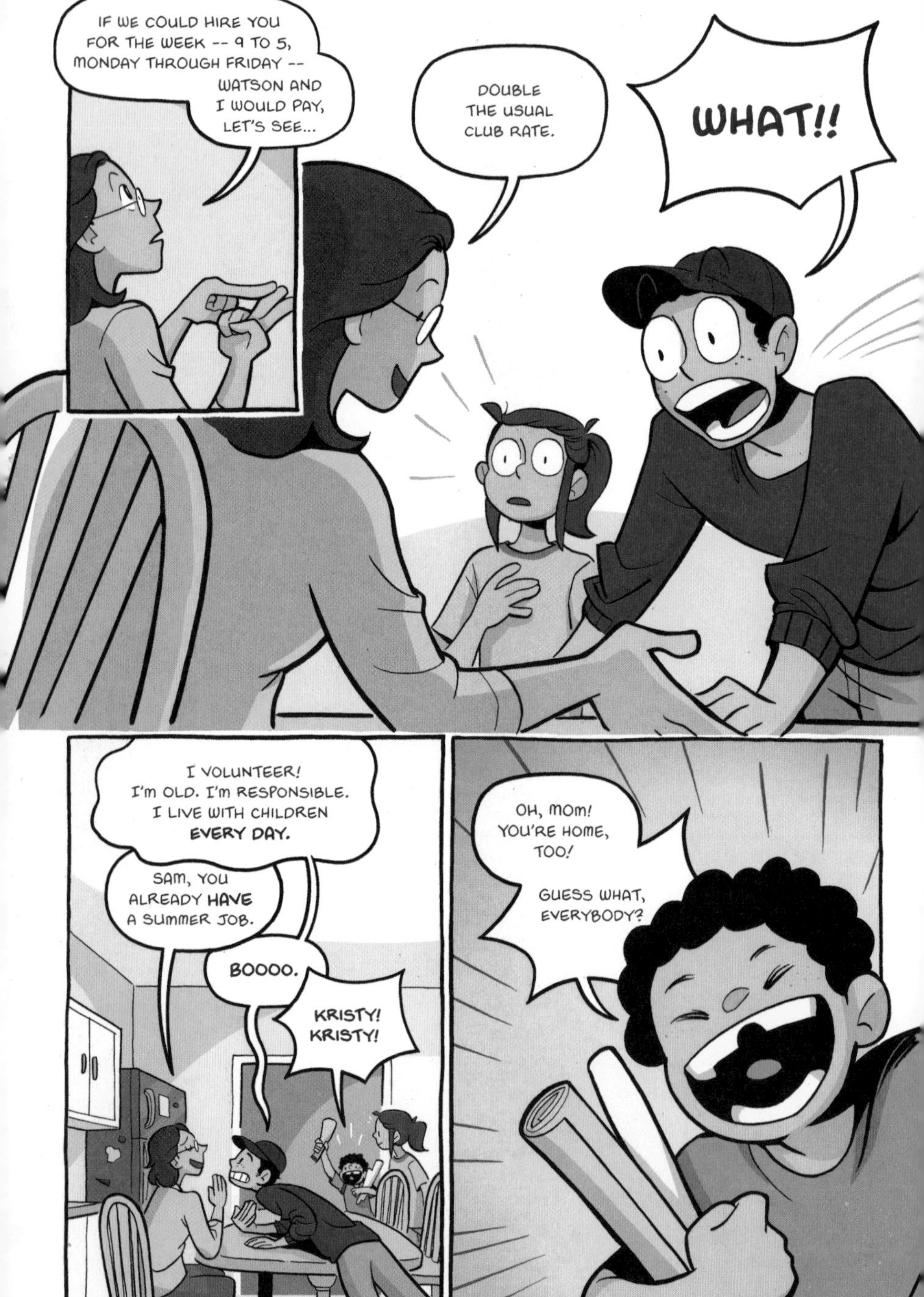
IF WE COULD HIRE YOU FOR THE WEEK -- 9 TO 5, MONDAY THROUGH FRIDAY -- WATSON AND I WOULD PAY, LET'S SEE...
DOUBLE THE USUAL CLUB RATE.
WHAT!!
I VOLUNTEER! I'M OLD. I'M RESPONSIBLE. I LIVE WITH CHILDREN EVERY DAY.
SAM, YOU ALREADY HAVE A SUMMER JOB.
BOOOO.
KRISTY! KRISTY!
OH, MOM! YOU'RE HOME, TOO!
GUESS WHAT, EVERYBODY?

"CITIZENSHIP AWARD."
Citizenship Awar
"THIS CERTIFIES THAT DAVID MICHAEL THOMAS HAS BEEN CHOSEN BEST CITIZEN OF THE YEAR IN MR. BOWMAN'S ROOM, BY HIS PEERS."
that
Thomas
his peers.
Principal
Vice Principal
THAT MEANS THE OTHER KIDS. THEY **VOTED** FOR ME.
DUH.
HONEY, CONGRATULATIONS! WE'LL HAVE TO FRAME THIS.
CAN WE PUT IT ON THE AWARDS WALL?
OF **COURSE.**

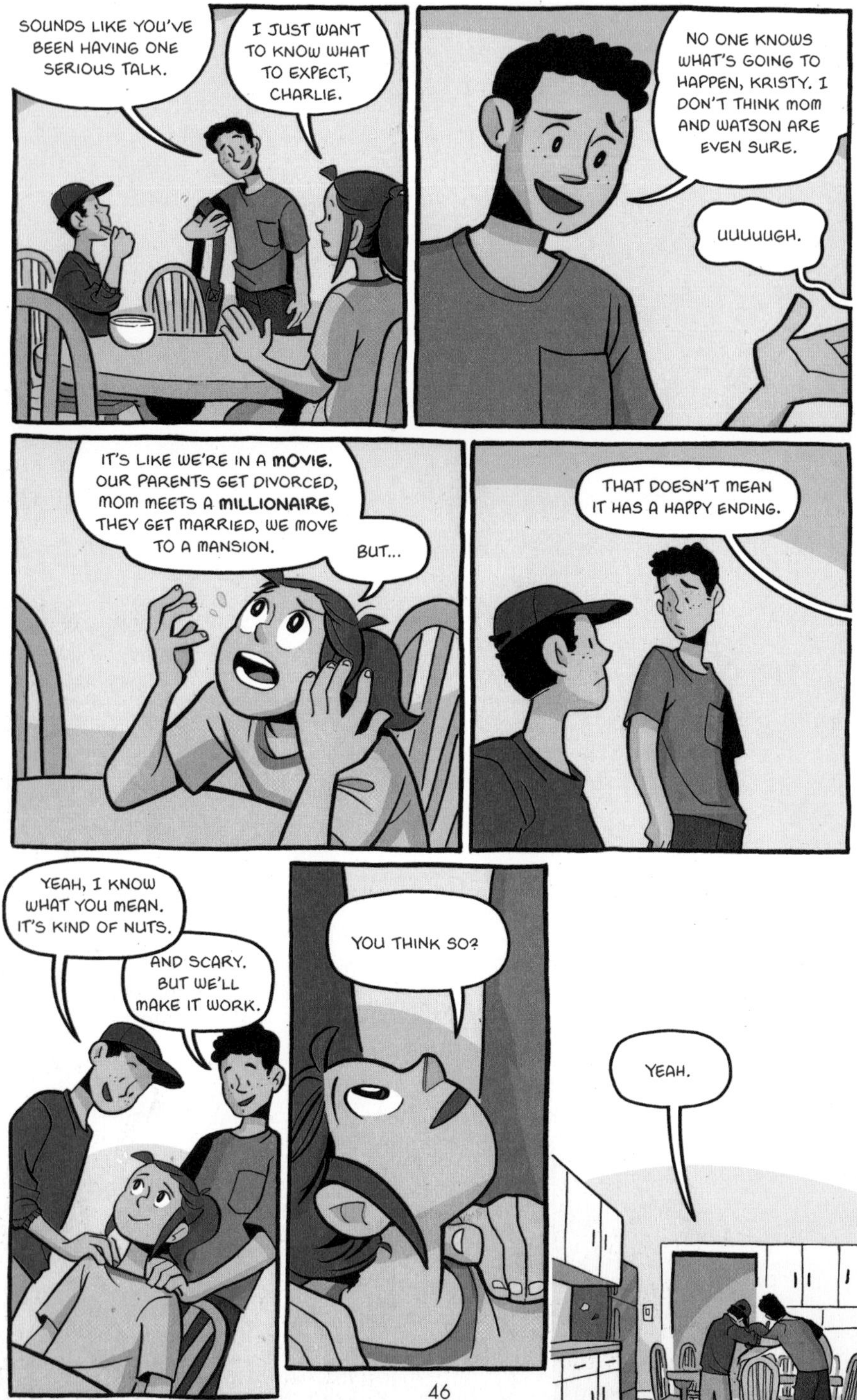
SOUNDS LIKE YOU'VE BEEN HAVING ONE SERIOUS TALK.
I JUST WANT TO KNOW WHAT TO EXPECT, CHARLIE.
NO ONE KNOWS WHAT'S GOING TO HAPPEN, KRISTY. I DON'T THINK MOM AND WATSON ARE EVEN SURE.
UUUUUGH.
IT'S LIKE WE'RE IN A **MOVIE**. OUR PARENTS GET DIVORCED, MOM MEETS A **MILLIONAIRE**, THEY GET MARRIED, WE MOVE TO A MANSION.
BUT...
THAT DOESN'T MEAN IT HAS A HAPPY ENDING.
YEAH, I KNOW WHAT YOU MEAN. IT'S KIND OF NUTS.
AND SCARY. BUT WE'LL MAKE IT WORK.
YOU THINK SO?
YEAH.

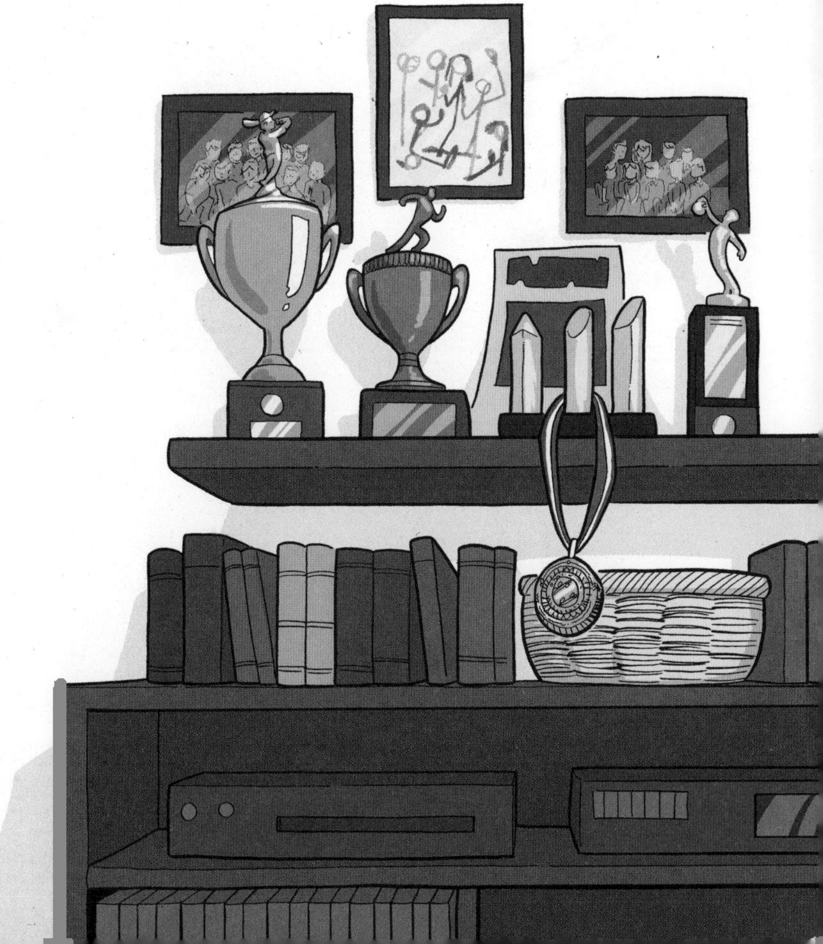

CHAPTER 5

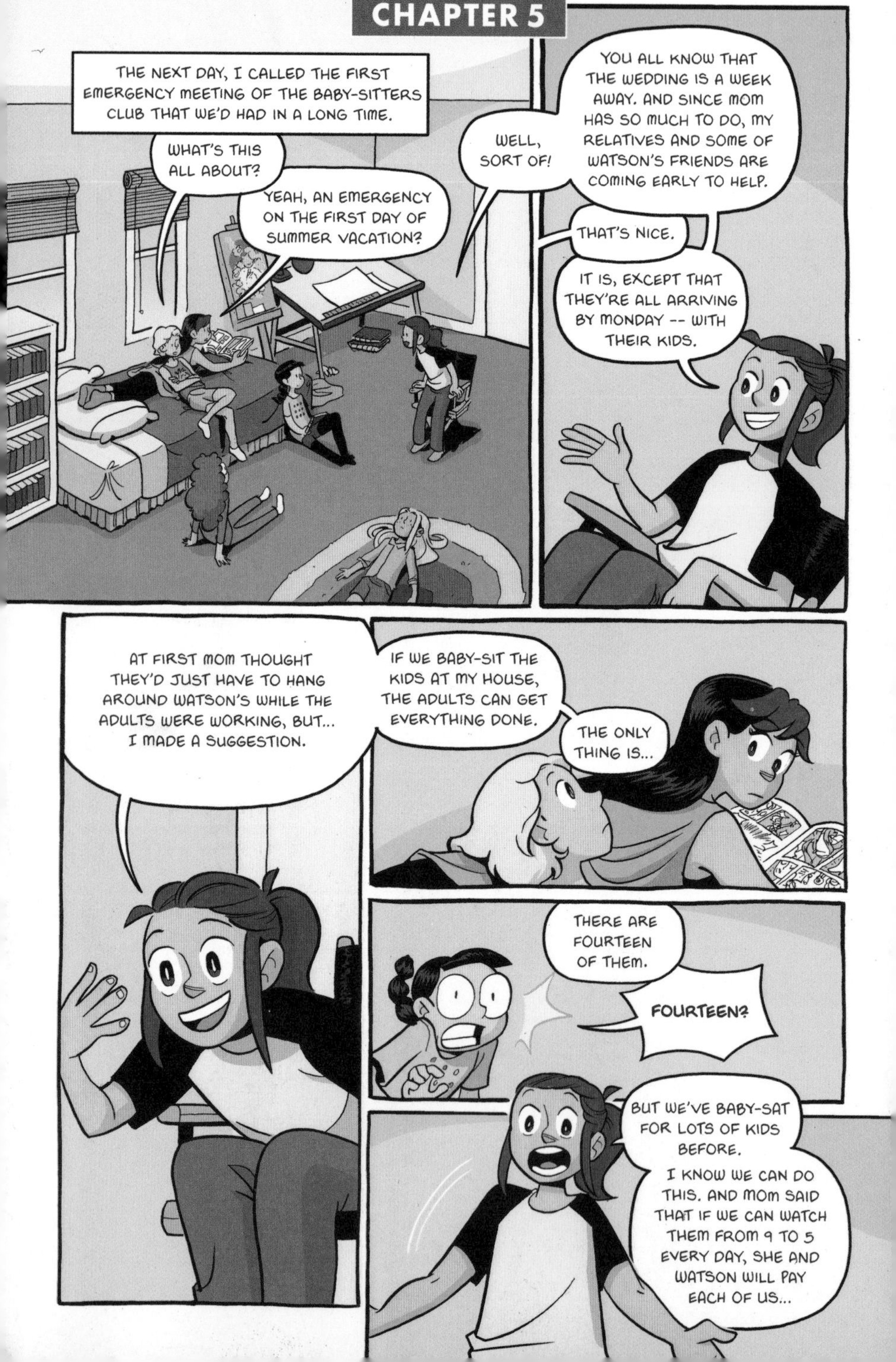
THE NEXT DAY, I CALLED THE FIRST EMERGENCY MEETING OF THE BABY-SITTERS CLUB THAT WE'D HAD IN A LONG TIME.
WHAT'S THIS ALL ABOUT?
YEAH, AN EMERGENCY ON THE FIRST DAY OF SUMMER VACATION?
WELL, SORT OF!
YOU ALL KNOW THAT THE WEDDING IS A WEEK AWAY. AND SINCE MOM HAS SO MUCH TO DO, MY RELATIVES AND SOME OF WATSON'S FRIENDS ARE COMING EARLY TO HELP.
THAT'S NICE.
IT IS, EXCEPT THAT THEY'RE ALL ARRIVING BY MONDAY -- WITH THEIR KIDS.
AT FIRST MOM THOUGHT THEY'D JUST HAVE TO HANG AROUND WATSON'S WHILE THE ADULTS WERE WORKING, BUT... I MADE A SUGGESTION.
IF WE BABY-SIT THE KIDS AT MY HOUSE, THE ADULTS CAN GET EVERYTHING DONE.
THE ONLY THING IS...
THERE ARE FOURTEEN OF THEM.
FOURTEEN?
BUT WE'VE BABY-SAT FOR LOTS OF KIDS BEFORE.
I KNOW WE CAN DO THIS. AND MOM SAID THAT IF WE CAN WATCH THEM FROM 9 TO 5 EVERY DAY, SHE AND WATSON WILL PAY EACH OF US...

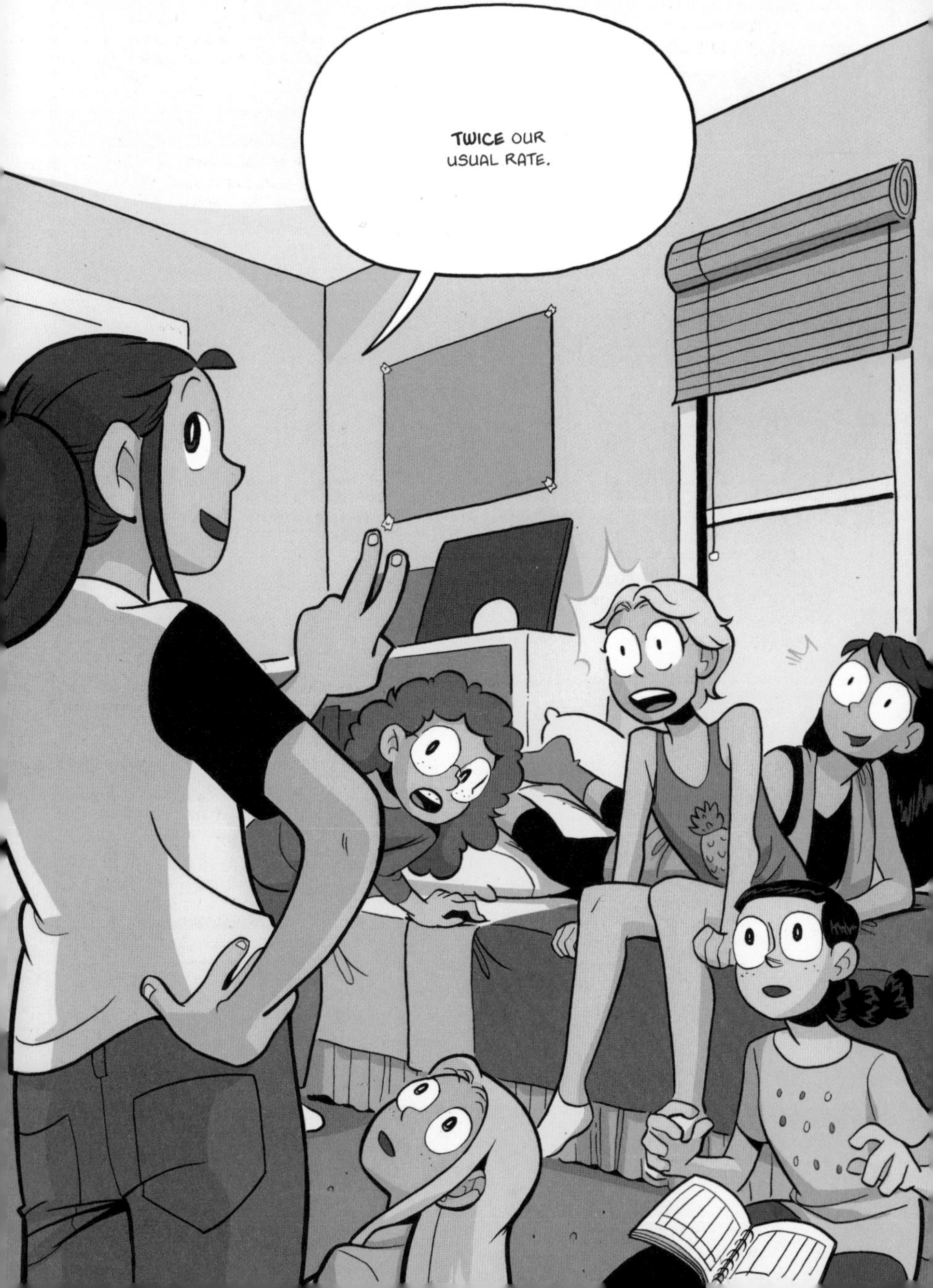
TWICE OUR USUAL RATE.

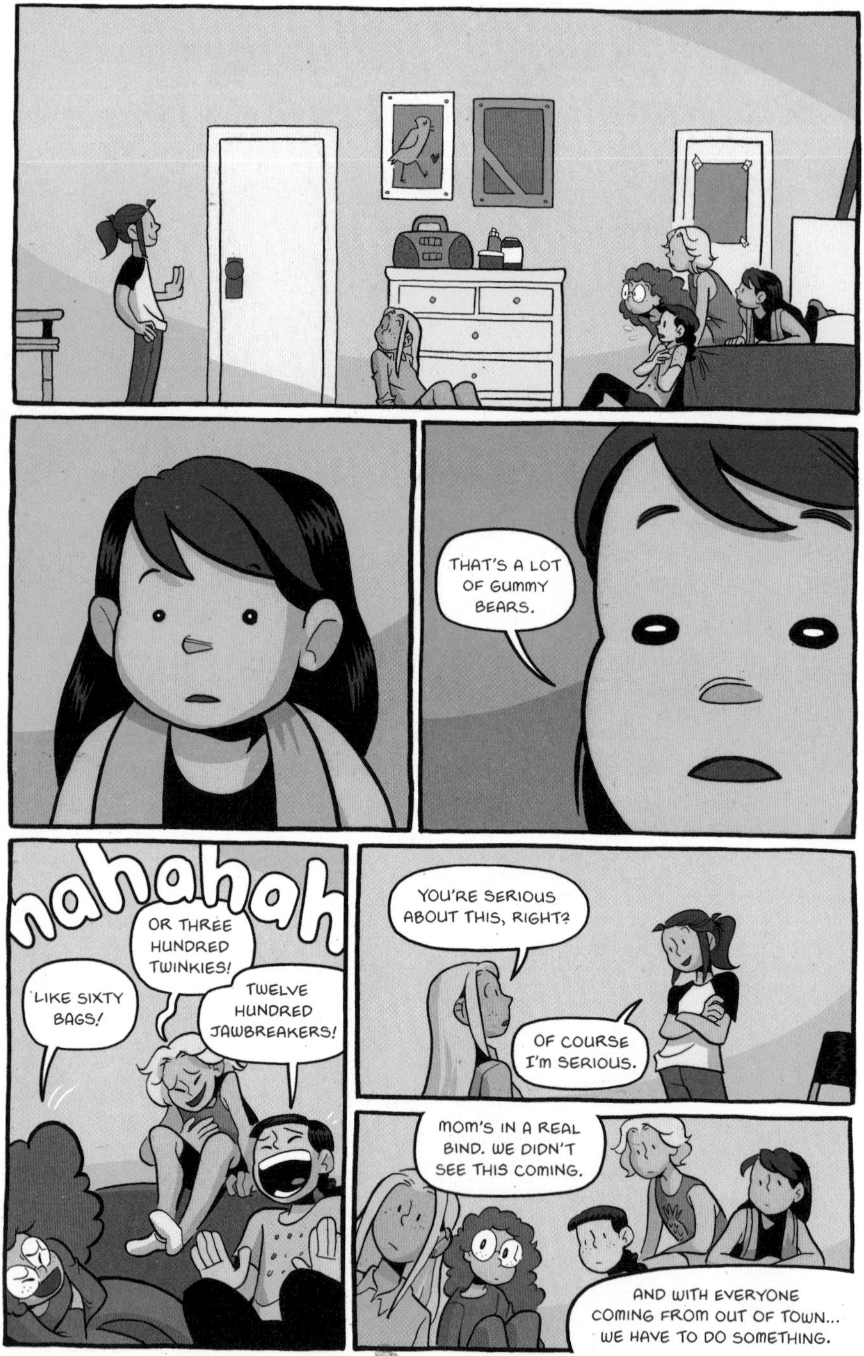
THAT'S A LOT OF GUMMY BEARS.
HAHAHAH
LIKE SIXTY BAGS!
OR THREE HUNDRED TWINKIES!
TWELVE HUNDRED JAWBREAKERS!
YOU'RE SERIOUS ABOUT THIS, RIGHT?
OF COURSE I'M SERIOUS.
MOM'S IN A REAL BIND. WE DIDN'T SEE THIS COMING.
AND WITH EVERYONE COMING FROM OUT OF TOWN... WE HAVE TO DO SOMETHING.

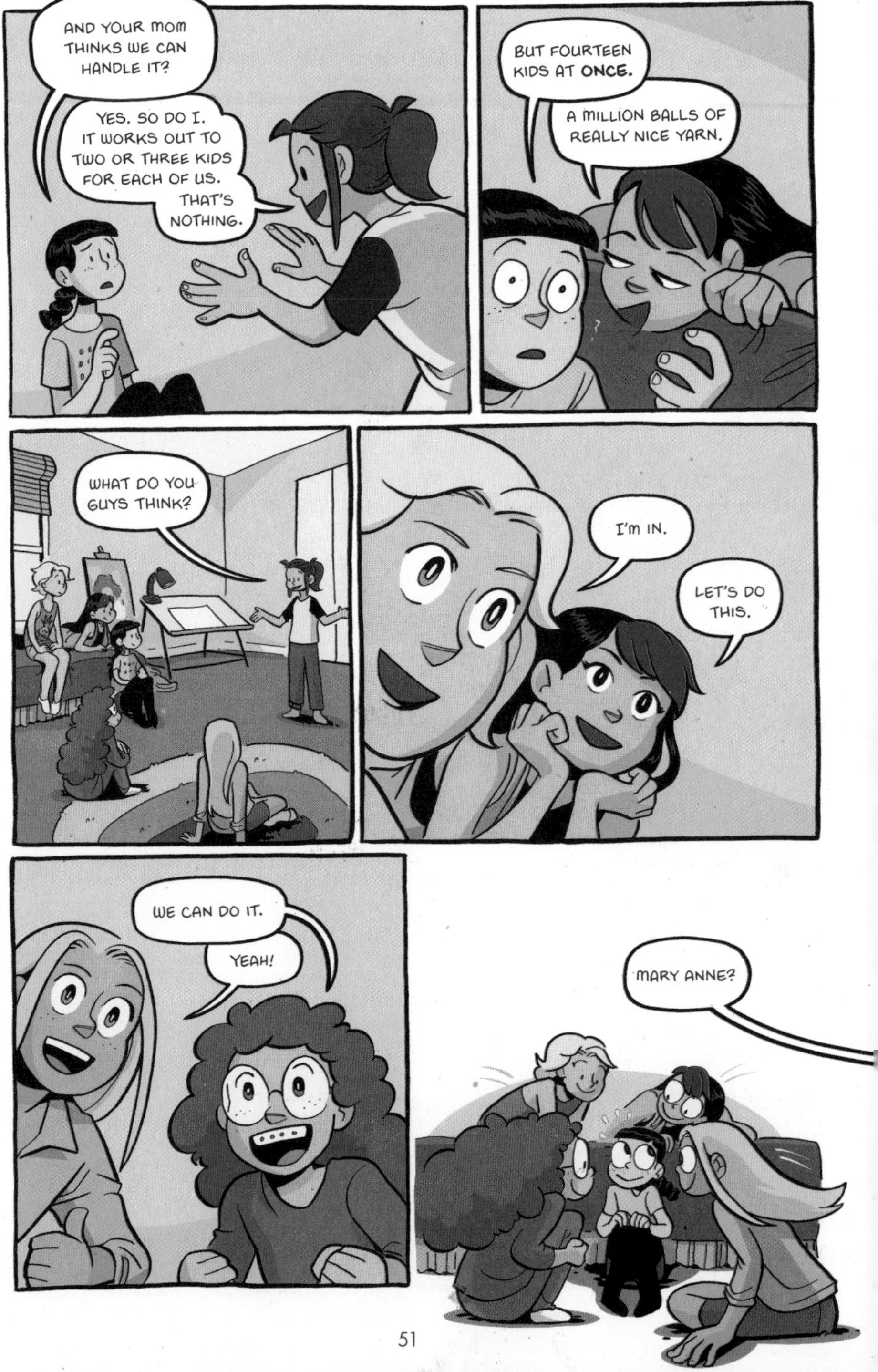
AND YOUR MOM THINKS WE CAN HANDLE IT?
YES. SO DO I. IT WORKS OUT TO TWO OR THREE KIDS FOR EACH OF US.
THAT'S NOTHING.
BUT FOURTEEN KIDS AT **ONCE.**
A MILLION BALLS OF REALLY NICE YARN.
WHAT DO YOU GUYS THINK?
I'M IN.
LET'S DO THIS.
WE CAN DO IT.
YEAH!
MARY ANNE?

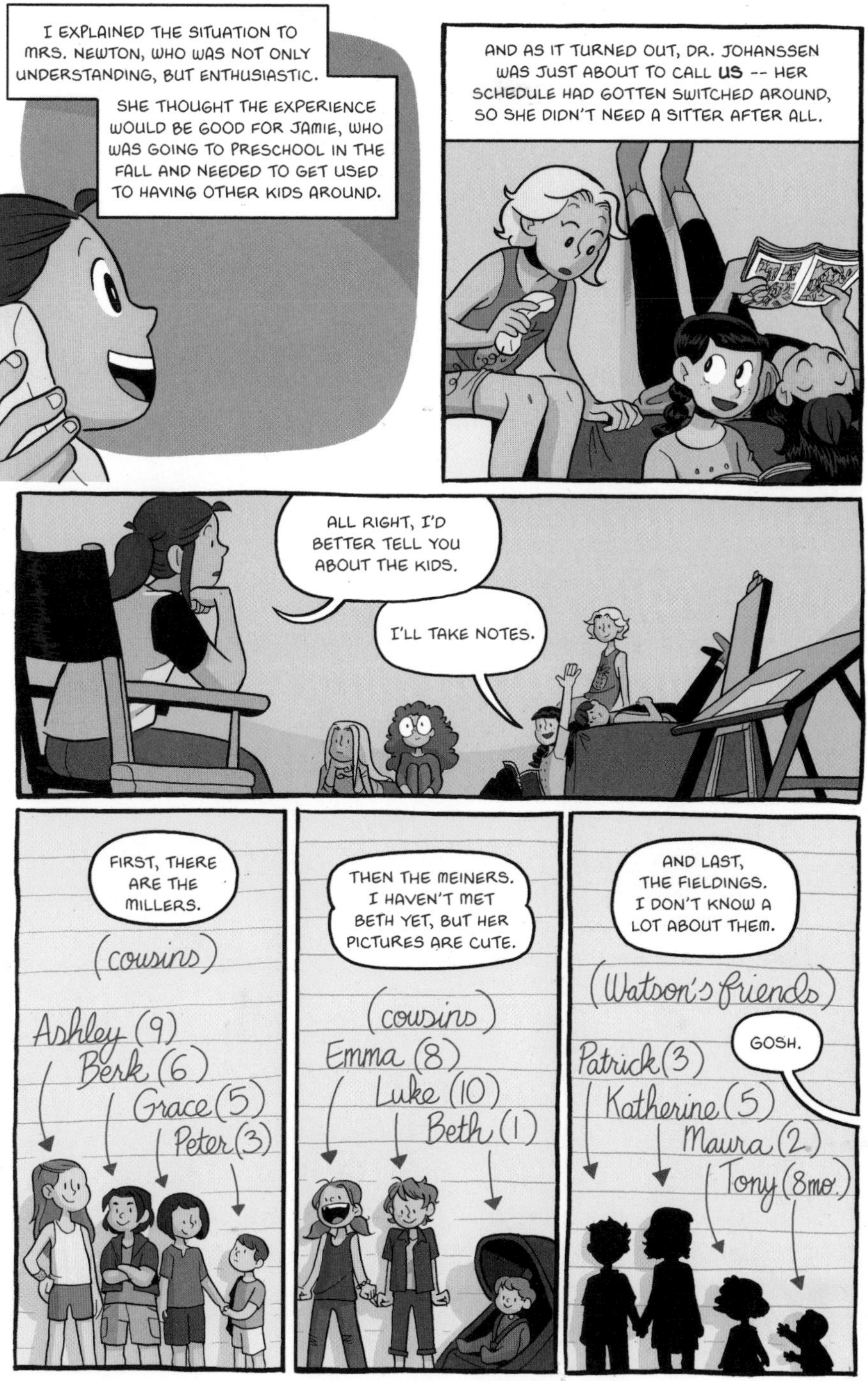
I EXPLAINED THE SITUATION TO MRS. NEWTON, WHO WAS NOT ONLY UNDERSTANDING, BUT ENTHUSIASTIC.
SHE THOUGHT THE EXPERIENCE WOULD BE GOOD FOR JAMIE, WHO WAS GOING TO PRESCHOOL IN THE FALL AND NEEDED TO GET USED TO HAVING OTHER KIDS AROUND.
AND AS IT TURNED OUT, DR. JOHANSSEN WAS JUST ABOUT TO CALL US -- HER SCHEDULE HAD GOTTEN SWITCHED AROUND, SO SHE DIDN'T NEED A SITTER AFTER ALL.
ALL RIGHT, I'D BETTER TELL YOU ABOUT THE KIDS.
I'LL TAKE NOTES.
FIRST, THERE ARE THE MILLERS.
(cousins)
Ashley (9)
Berk (6)
Grace (5)
Peter (3)
THEN THE MEINERS. I HAVEN'T MET BETH YET, BUT HER PICTURES ARE CUTE.
(cousins)
Emma (8)
Luke (10)
Beth (1)
AND LAST, THE FIELDINGS. I DON'T KNOW A LOT ABOUT THEM.
(Watson's friends)
GOSH.
Patrick (3)
Katherine (5)
Maura (2)
Tony (8mo.)

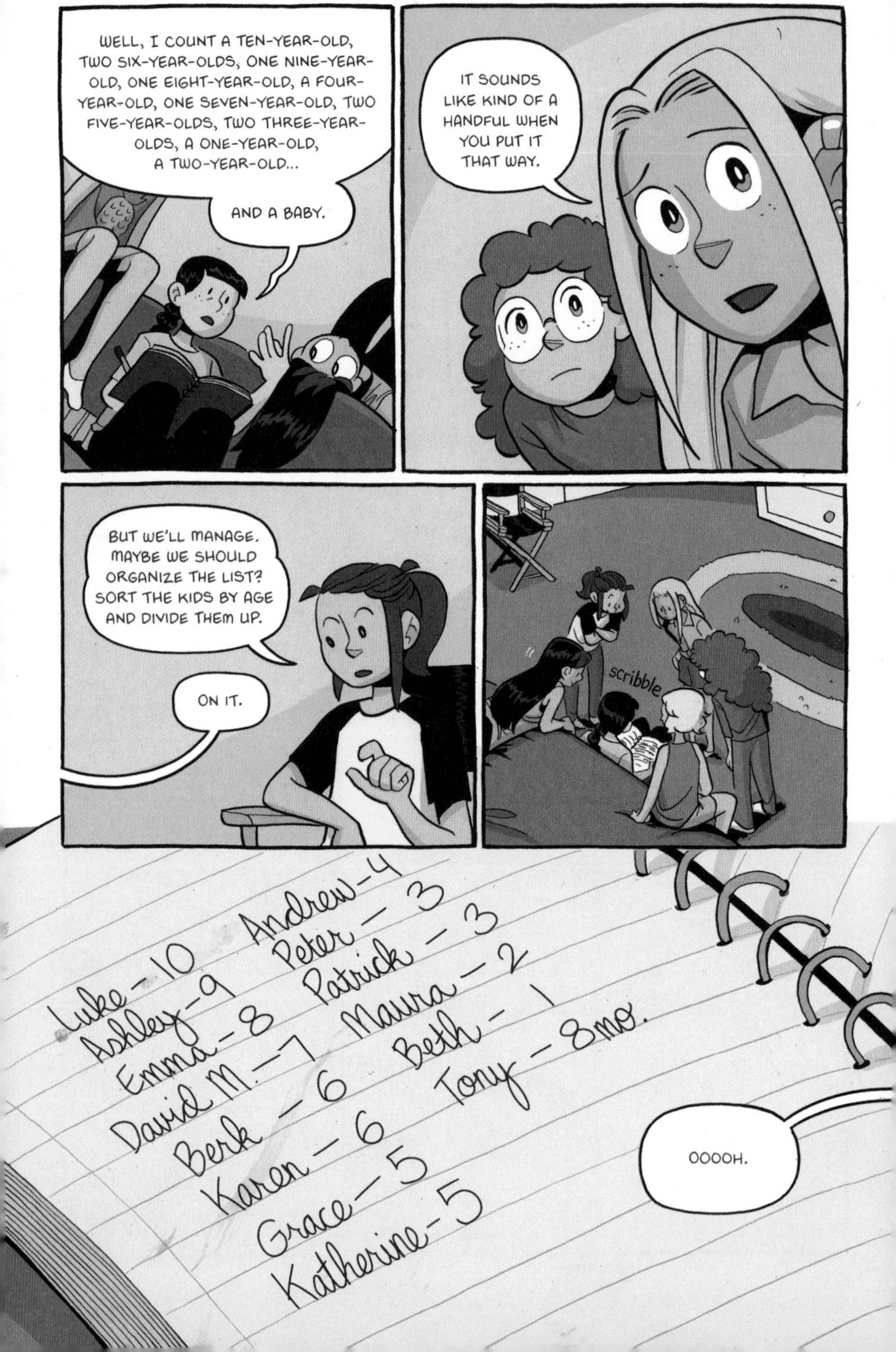
WELL, I COUNT A TEN-YEAR-OLD, TWO SIX-YEAR-OLDS, ONE NINE-YEAR-OLD, ONE EIGHT-YEAR-OLD, A FOUR-YEAR-OLD, ONE SEVEN-YEAR-OLD, TWO FIVE-YEAR-OLDS, TWO THREE-YEAR-OLDS, A ONE-YEAR-OLD, A TWO-YEAR-OLD...
AND A BABY.
IT SOUNDS LIKE KIND OF A HANDFUL WHEN YOU PUT IT THAT WAY.
BUT WE'LL MANAGE. MAYBE WE SHOULD ORGANIZE THE LIST? SORT THE KIDS BY AGE AND DIVIDE THEM UP.
ON IT.
scribble
Luke-10
Ashley-9
Emma-8
David M.-7
Berk-6
Karen-6
Grace-5
Katherine-5
Andrew-4
Peter-3
Patrick-3
Maura-2
Beth-1
Tony-8mo.
OOOOH.

55

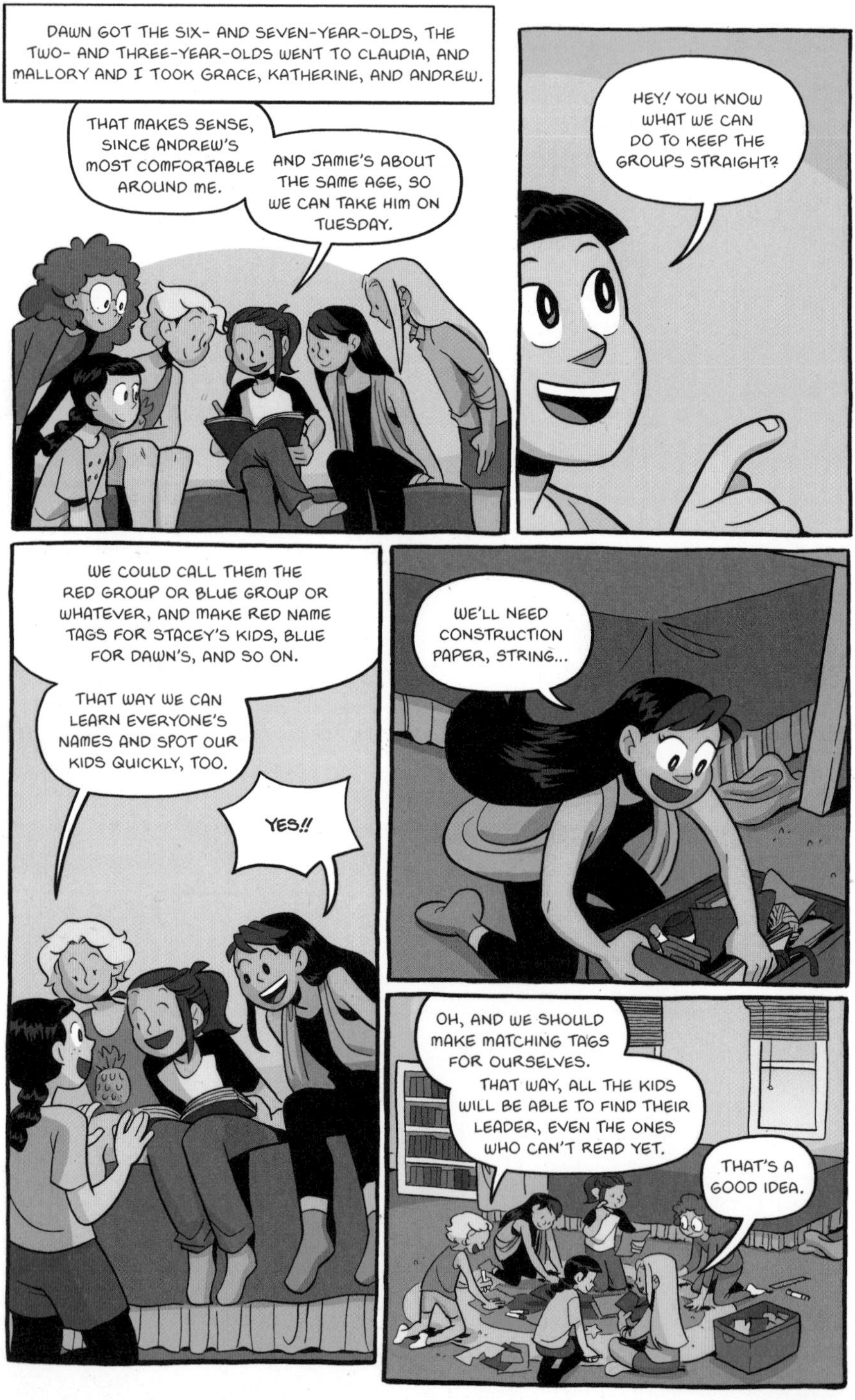

DAWN GOT THE SIX- AND SEVEN-YEAR-OLDS, THE TWO- AND THREE-YEAR-OLDS WENT TO CLAUDIA, AND MALLORY AND I TOOK GRACE, KATHERINE, AND ANDREW.
THAT MAKES SENSE, SINCE ANDREW'S MOST COMFORTABLE AROUND ME.
AND JAMIE'S ABOUT THE SAME AGE, SO WE CAN TAKE HIM ON TUESDAY.
HEY! YOU KNOW WHAT WE CAN DO TO KEEP THE GROUPS STRAIGHT?
WE COULD CALL THEM THE RED GROUP OR BLUE GROUP OR WHATEVER, AND MAKE RED NAME TAGS FOR STACEY'S KIDS, BLUE FOR DAWN'S, AND SO ON.
THAT WAY WE CAN LEARN EVERYONE'S NAMES AND SPOT OUR KIDS QUICKLY, TOO.
YES!!
WE'LL NEED CONSTRUCTION PAPER, STRING...
OH, AND WE SHOULD MAKE MATCHING TAGS FOR OURSELVES.
THAT WAY, ALL THE KIDS WILL BE ABLE TO FIND THEIR LEADER, EVEN THE ONES WHO CAN'T READ YET.
THAT'S A GOOD IDEA.

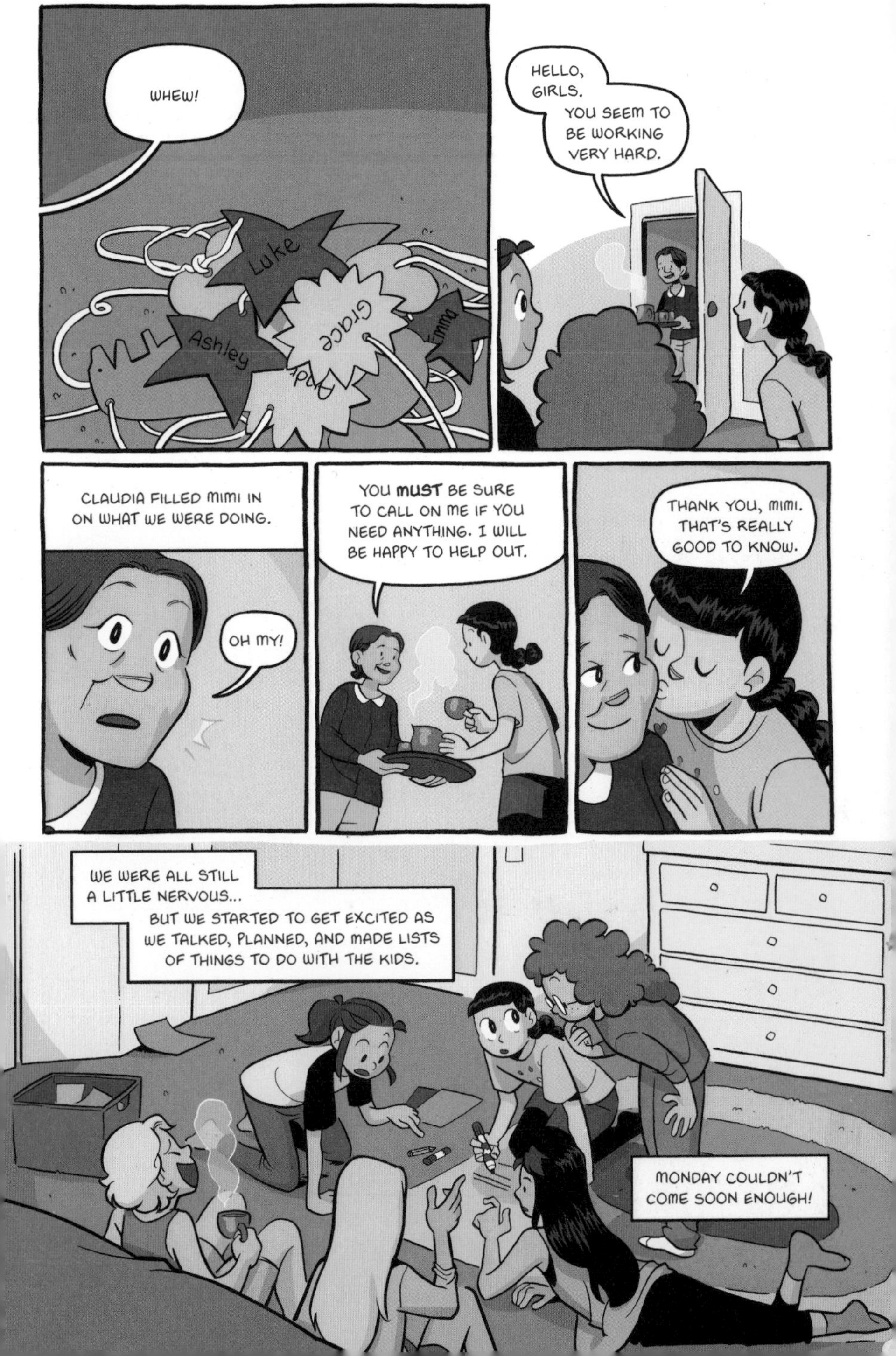
WHEW!
Luke
Grace
Ashley
Emma
HELLO, GIRLS.
YOU SEEM TO BE WORKING VERY HARD.
CLAUDIA FILLED MIMI IN ON WHAT WE WERE DOING.
OH MY!
YOU **MUST** BE SURE TO CALL ON ME IF YOU NEED ANYTHING. I WILL BE HAPPY TO HELP OUT.
THANK YOU, MIMI. THAT'S REALLY GOOD TO KNOW.
WE WERE ALL STILL A LITTLE NERVOUS...
BUT WE STARTED TO GET EXCITED AS WE TALKED, PLANNED, AND MADE LISTS OF THINGS TO DO WITH THE KIDS.
MONDAY COULDN'T COME SOON ENOUGH!

Beth
Stacey
Red Star Group
•Luke (10)
•Ashley (9)
•Emma (8)
Dawn
Bluebird Group
•David Michael (7)
•Berk (6)
•Karen (6)
Kristy & Mallory
Yellow Sun Group
•Grace (5)
•Katherine (5)
•Andrew (4)
Claudia
Green Dinosaur Group
•Peter (3)
•Patrick (3)
•Maura (2)
Mary Anne
Pink Heart Group
•Beth (1)
•Tony (8 mo.)

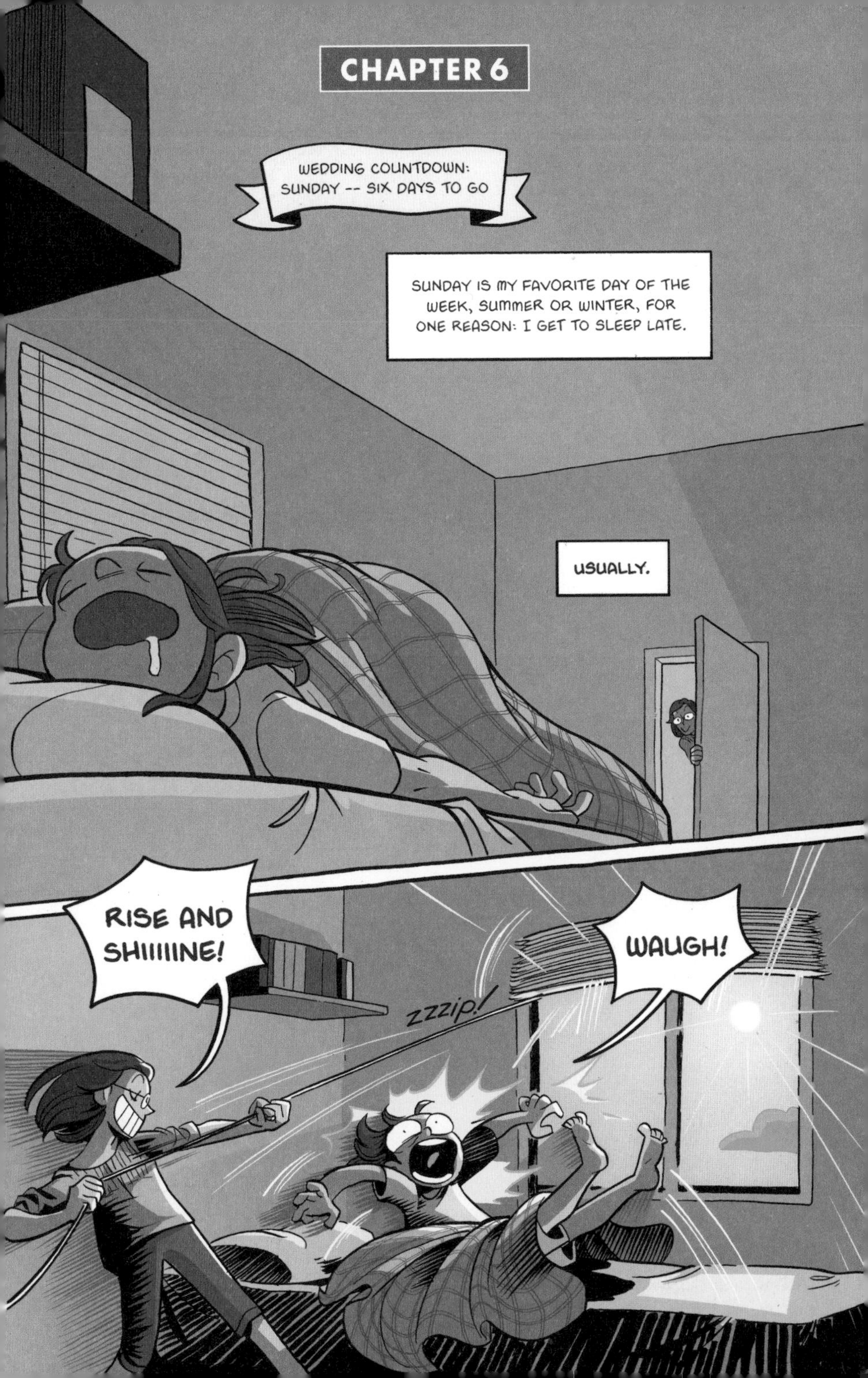
CHAPTER 6
WEDDING COUNTDOWN: SUNDAY -- SIX DAYS TO GO
SUNDAY IS MY FAVORITE DAY OF THE WEEK, SUMMER OR WINTER, FOR ONE REASON: I GET TO SLEEP LATE.
USUALLY.
RISE AND SHIIIIINE!
zzzip!
WAUGH!

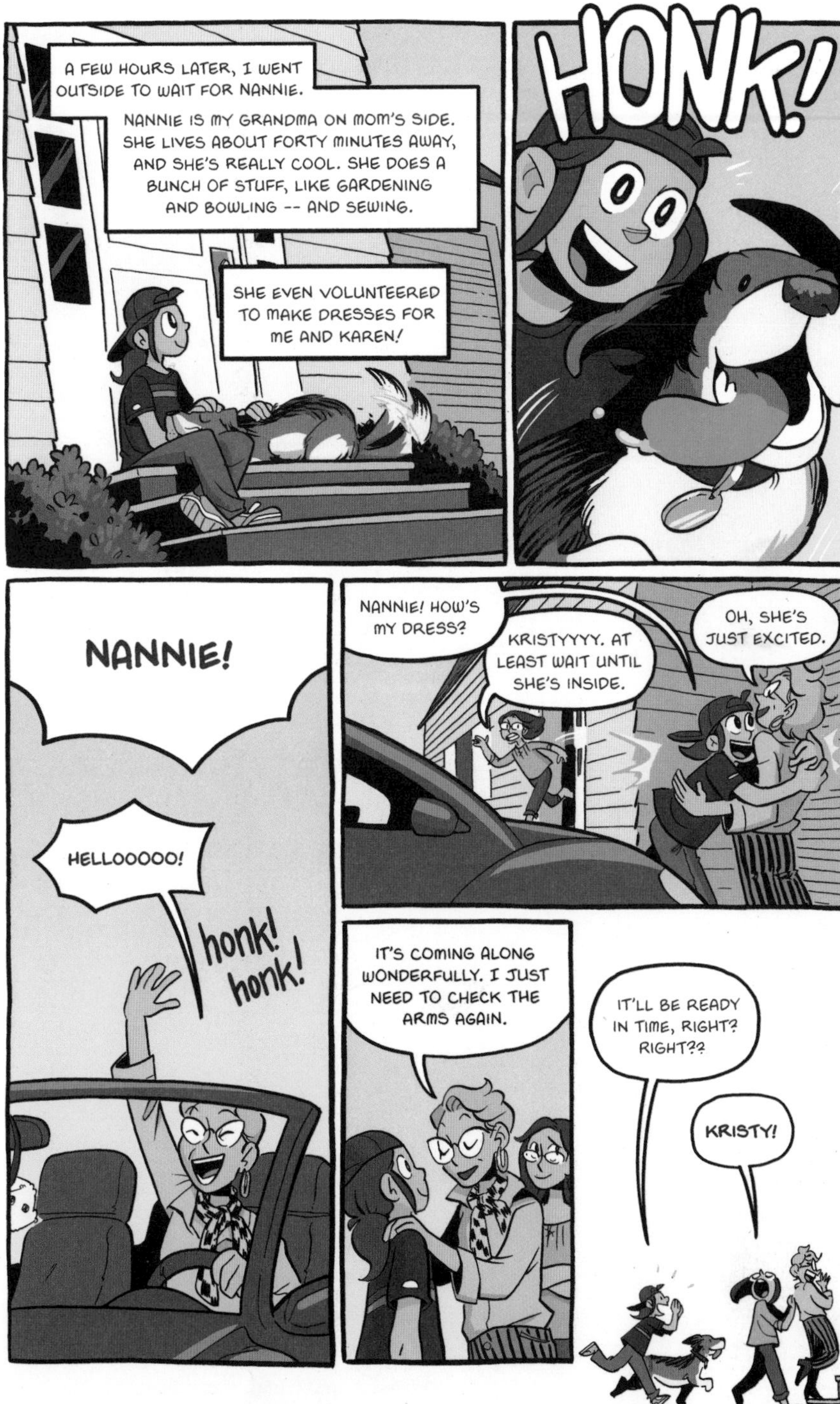
A FEW HOURS LATER, I WENT OUTSIDE TO WAIT FOR NANNIE.
NANNIE IS MY GRANDMA ON MOM'S SIDE. SHE LIVES ABOUT FORTY MINUTES AWAY, AND SHE'S REALLY COOL. SHE DOES A BUNCH OF STUFF, LIKE GARDENING AND BOWLING -- AND SEWING.
SHE EVEN VOLUNTEERED TO MAKE DRESSES FOR ME AND KAREN!
HONK!
NANNIE!
HELLOOOOO!
honk! honk!
NANNIE! HOW'S MY DRESS?
KRISTYYYY. AT LEAST WAIT UNTIL SHE'S INSIDE.
OH, SHE'S JUST EXCITED.
IT'S COMING ALONG WONDERFULLY. I JUST NEED TO CHECK THE ARMS AGAIN.
IT'LL BE READY IN TIME, RIGHT? RIGHT??
KRISTY!

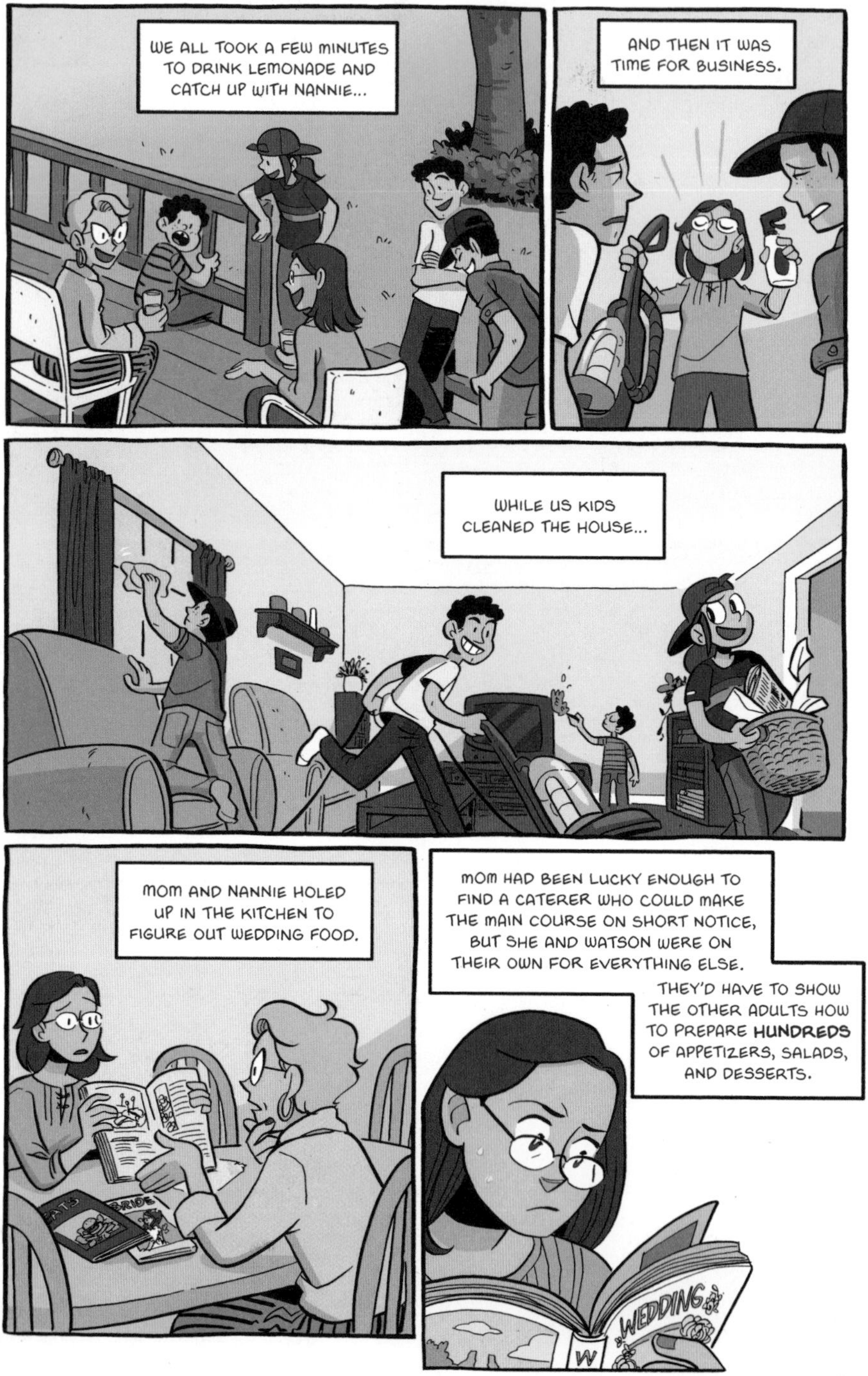
WE ALL TOOK A FEW MINUTES TO DRINK LEMONADE AND CATCH UP WITH NANNIE...
AND THEN IT WAS TIME FOR BUSINESS.
WHILE US KIDS CLEANED THE HOUSE...
MOM AND NANNIE HOLED UP IN THE KITCHEN TO FIGURE OUT WEDDING FOOD.
MOM HAD BEEN LUCKY ENOUGH TO FIND A CATERER WHO COULD MAKE THE MAIN COURSE ON SHORT NOTICE, BUT SHE AND WATSON WERE ON THEIR OWN FOR EVERYTHING ELSE.
THEY'D HAVE TO SHOW THE OTHER ADULTS HOW TO PREPARE **HUNDREDS** OF APPETIZERS, SALADS, AND DESSERTS.
EATS
BRIDE
WEDDING
W

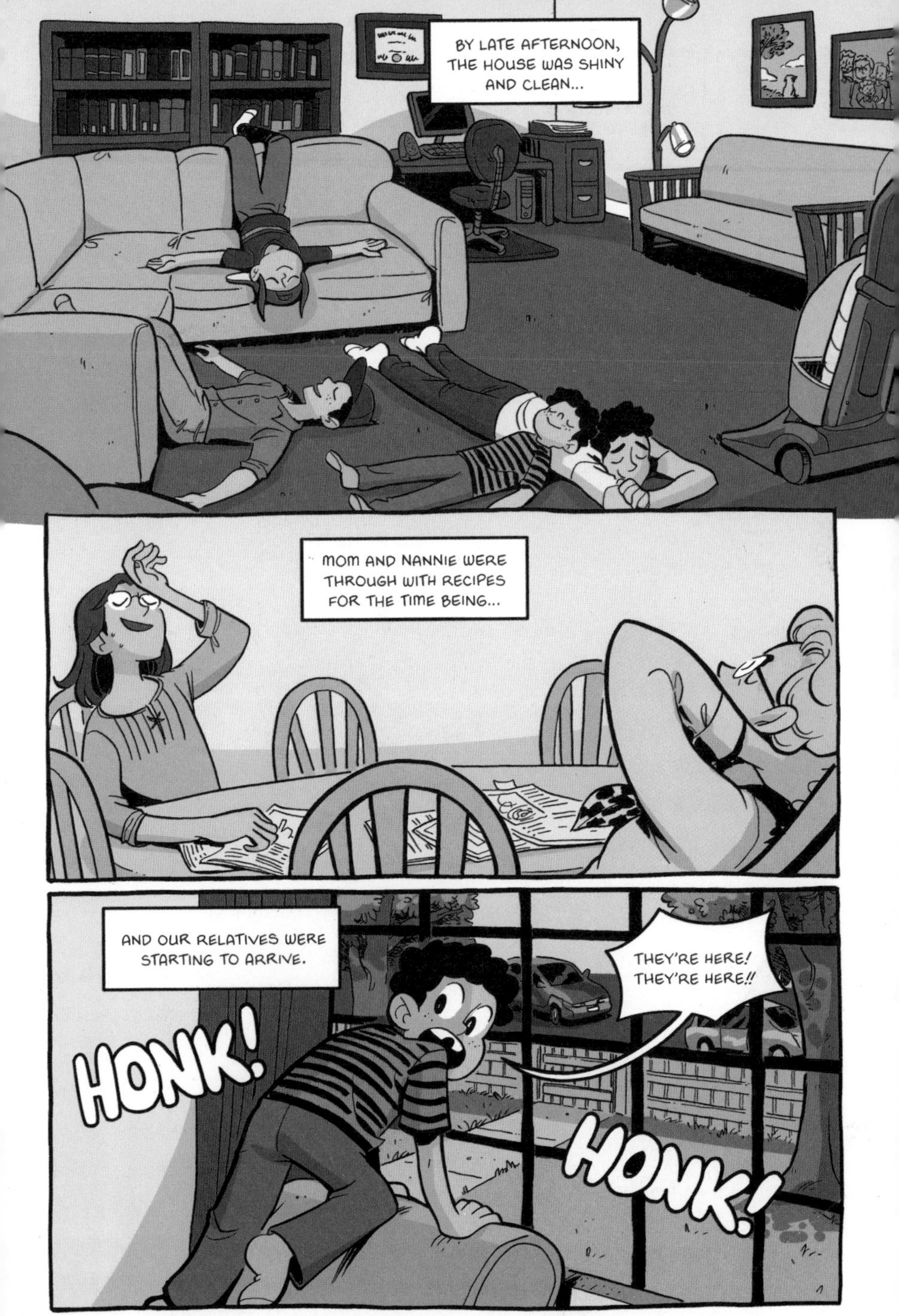
BY LATE AFTERNOON, THE HOUSE WAS SHINY AND CLEAN...
MOM AND NANNIE WERE THROUGH WITH RECIPES FOR THE TIME BEING...
AND OUR RELATIVES WERE STARTING TO ARRIVE.
HONK!
THEY'RE HERE! THEY'RE HERE!!
HONK!

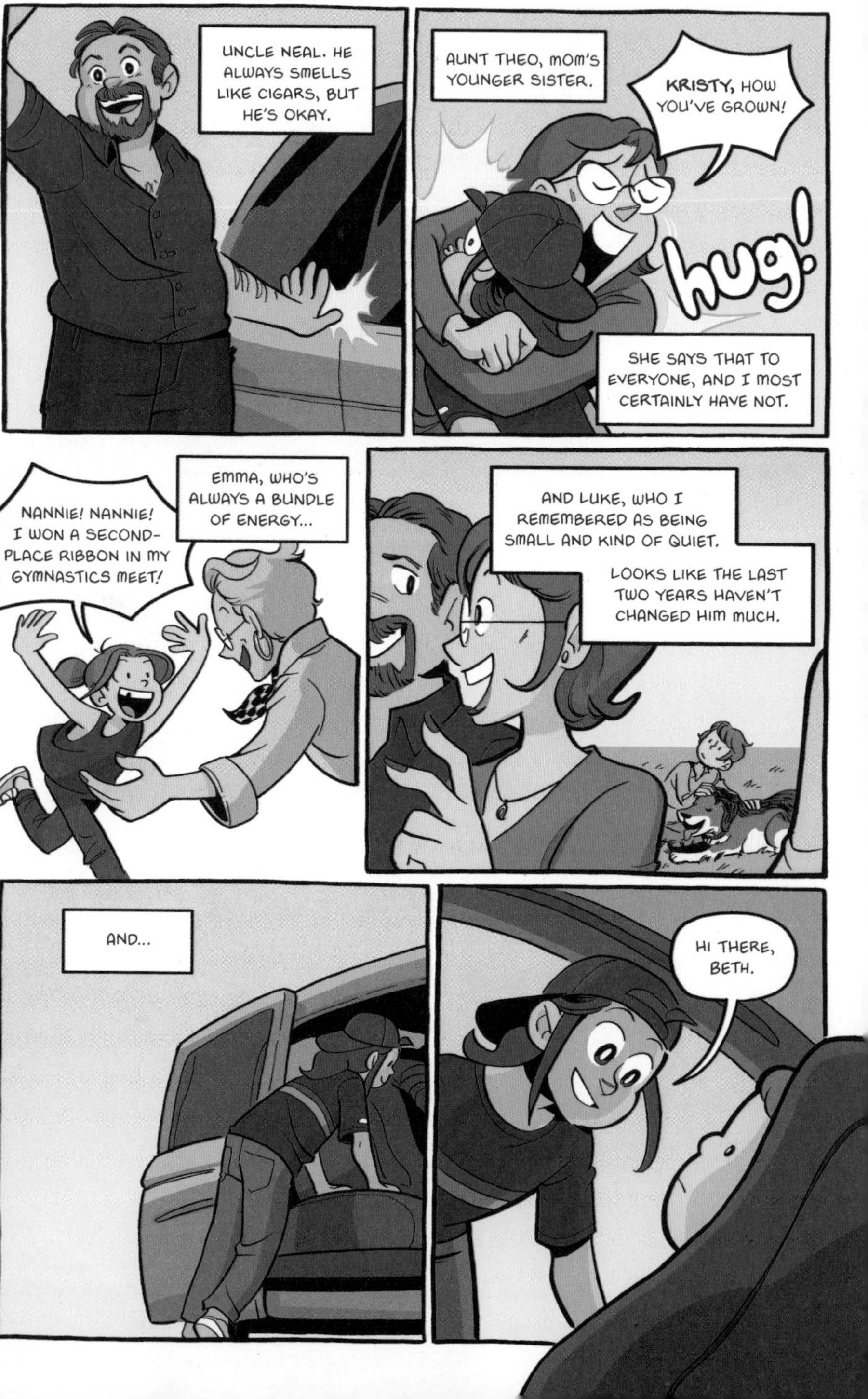
UNCLE NEAL. HE ALWAYS SMELLS LIKE CIGARS, BUT HE'S OKAY.
AUNT THEO, MOM'S YOUNGER SISTER.
KRISTY, HOW YOU'VE GROWN!
hug!
SHE SAYS THAT TO EVERYONE, AND I MOST CERTAINLY HAVE NOT.
EMMA, WHO'S ALWAYS A BUNDLE OF ENERGY...
NANNIE! NANNIE! I WON A SECOND-PLACE RIBBON IN MY GYMNASTICS MEET!
AND LUKE, WHO I REMEMBERED AS BEING SMALL AND KIND OF QUIET.
LOOKS LIKE THE LAST TWO YEARS HAVEN'T CHANGED HIM MUCH.
AND...
HI THERE, BETH.

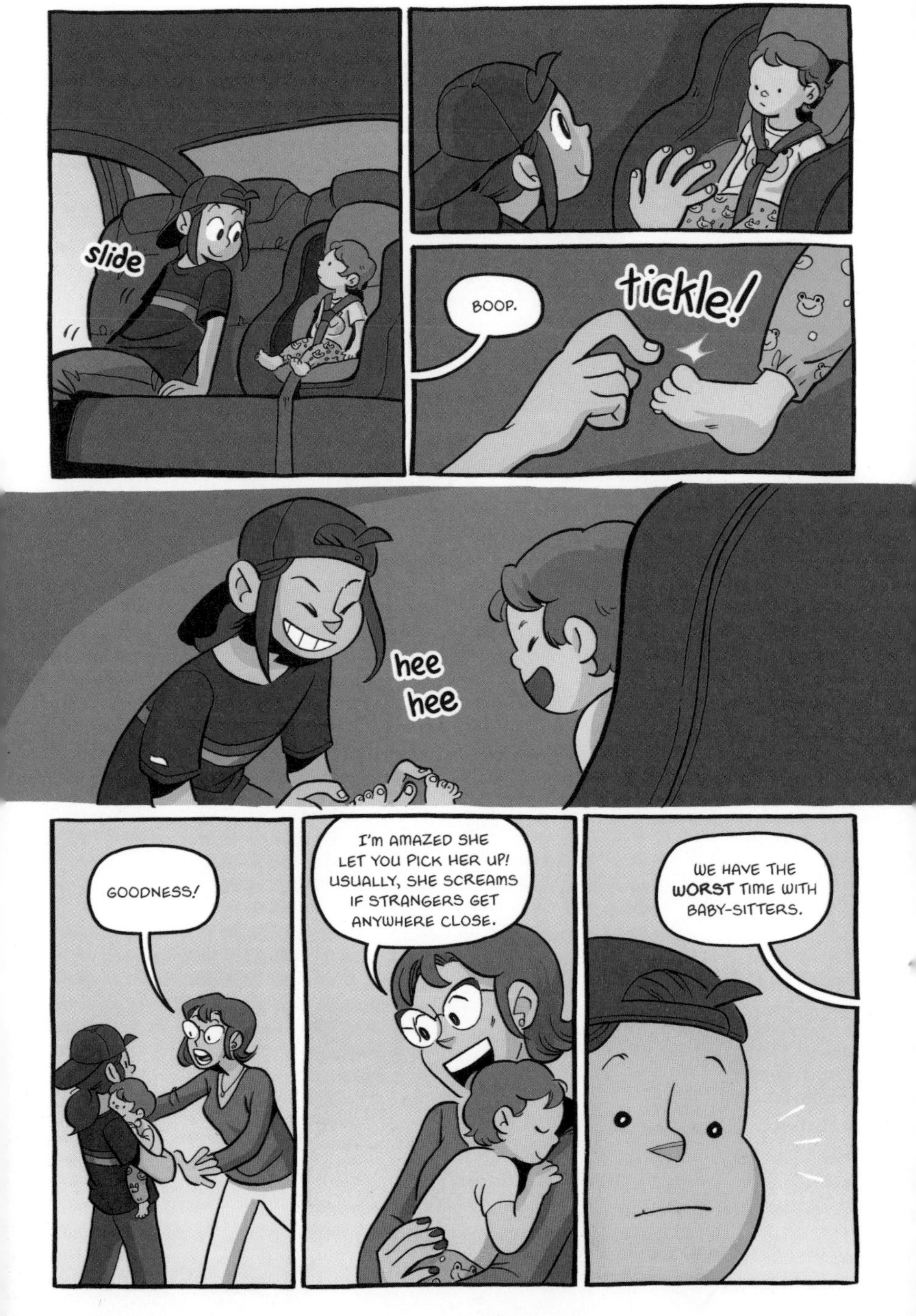
slide
BOOP.
tickle!
hee
hee
GOODNESS!
I'M AMAZED SHE LET YOU PICK HER UP! USUALLY, SHE SCREAMS IF STRANGERS GET ANYWHERE CLOSE.
WE HAVE THE **WORST** TIME WITH BABY-SITTERS.

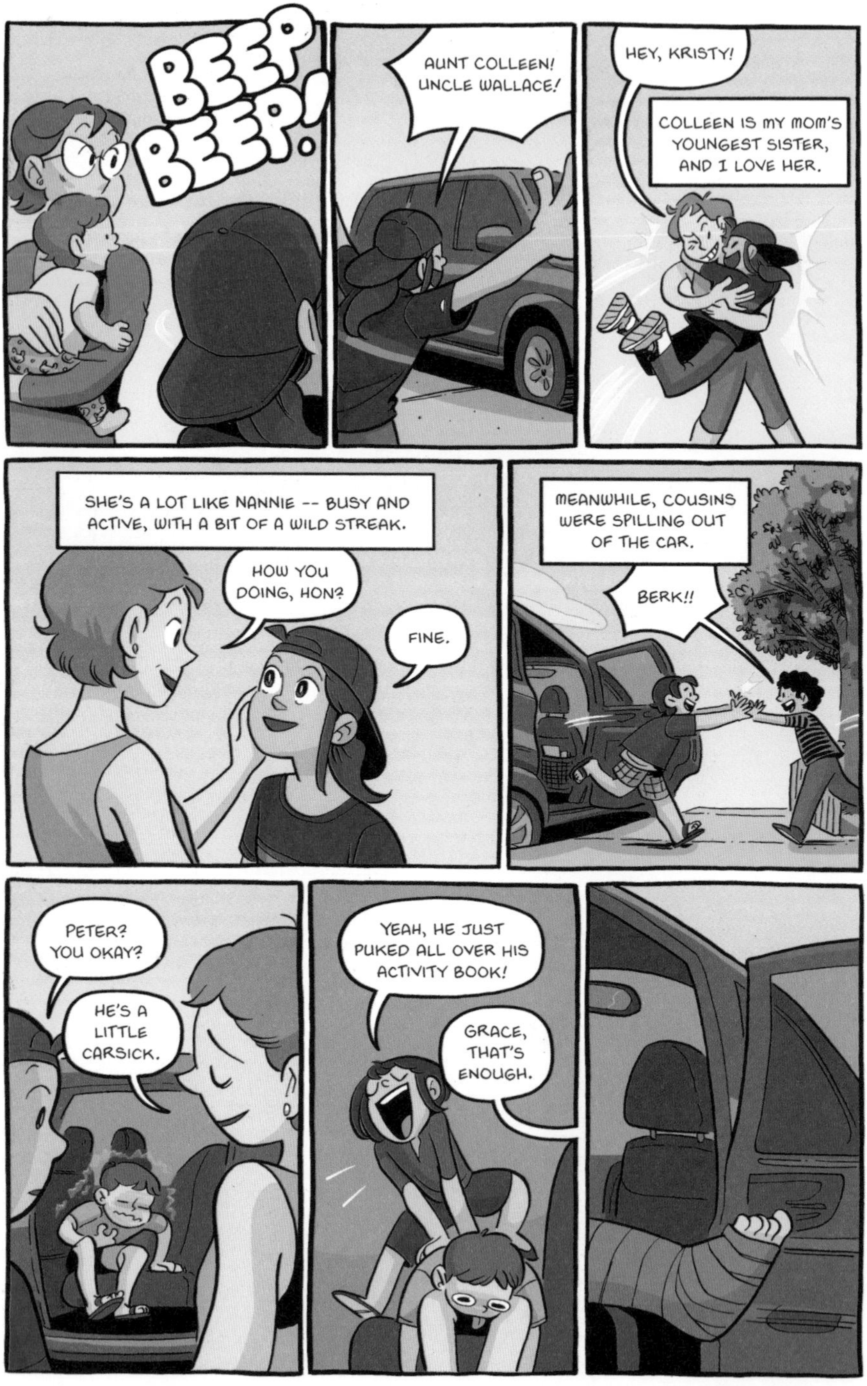
BEEP BEEP!
AUNT COLLEEN! UNCLE WALLACE!
HEY, KRISTY!
COLLEEN IS MY MOM'S YOUNGEST SISTER, AND I LOVE HER.
SHE'S A LOT LIKE NANNIE -- BUSY AND ACTIVE, WITH A BIT OF A WILD STREAK.
HOW YOU DOING, HON?
FINE.
MEANWHILE, COUSINS WERE SPILLING OUT OF THE CAR.
BERK!!
PETER? YOU OKAY?
HE'S A LITTLE CARSICK.
YEAH, HE JUST PUKED ALL OVER HIS ACTIVITY BOOK!
GRACE, THAT'S ENOUGH.

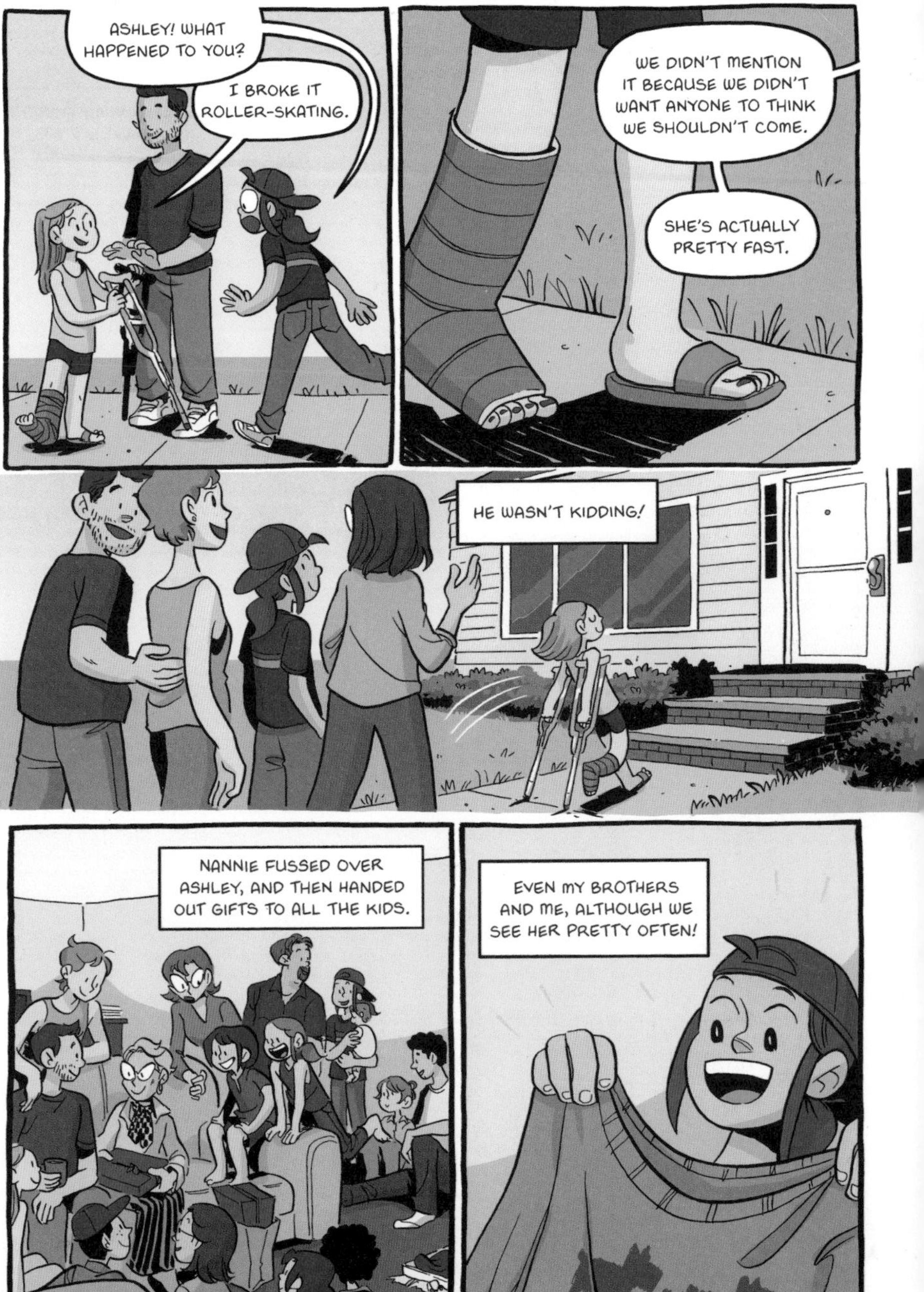
ASHLEY! WHAT HAPPENED TO YOU?
I BROKE IT ROLLER-SKATING.
WE DIDN'T MENTION IT BECAUSE WE DIDN'T WANT ANYONE TO THINK WE SHOULDN'T COME.
SHE'S ACTUALLY PRETTY FAST.
HE WASN'T KIDDING!
NANNIE FUSSED OVER ASHLEY, AND THEN HANDED OUT GIFTS TO ALL THE KIDS.
EVEN MY BROTHERS AND ME, ALTHOUGH WE SEE HER PRETTY OFTEN!

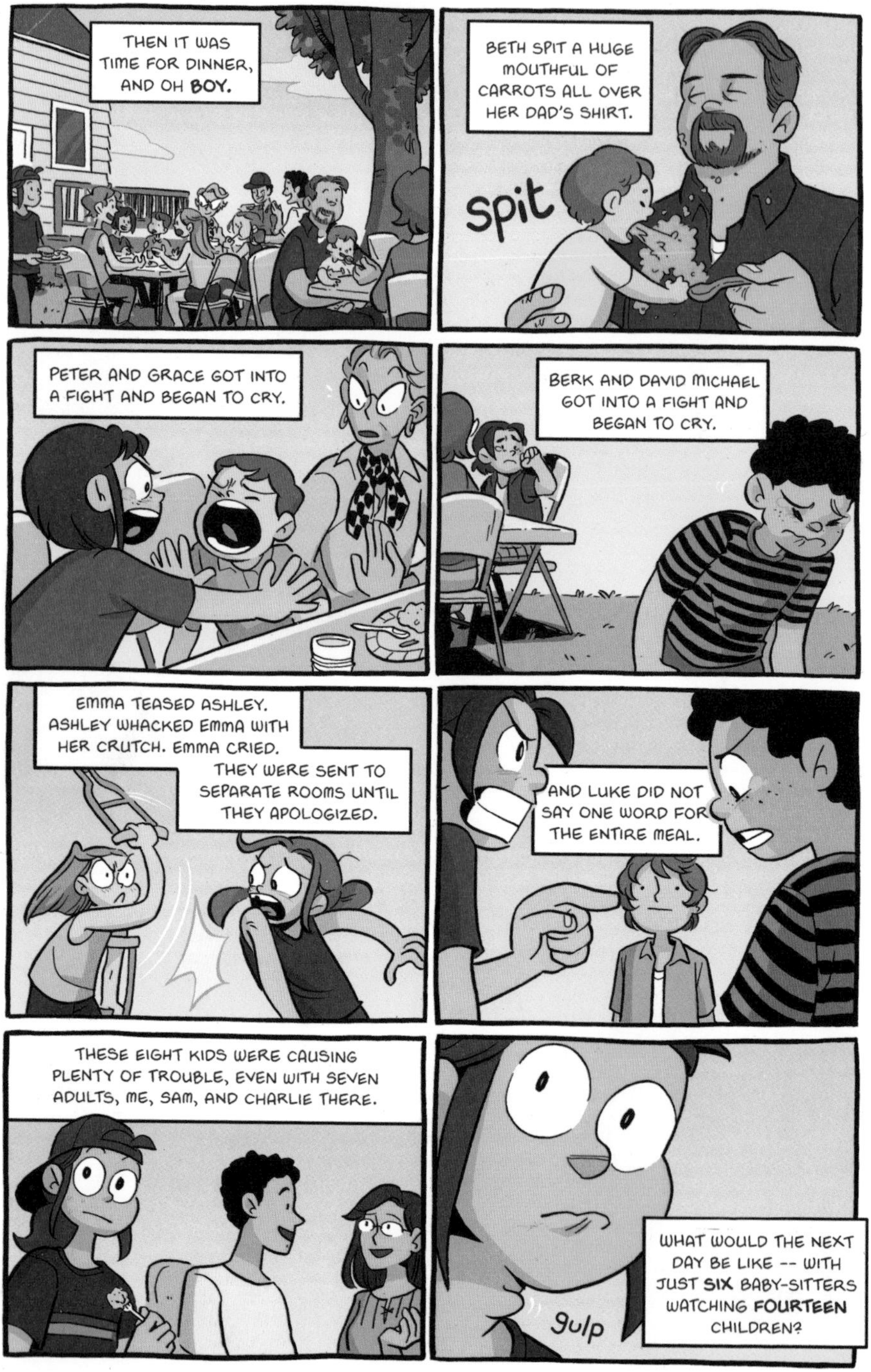
THEN IT WAS TIME FOR DINNER, AND OH **BOY.**
BETH SPIT A HUGE MOUTHFUL OF CARROTS ALL OVER HER DAD'S SHIRT.
spit
PETER AND GRACE GOT INTO A FIGHT AND BEGAN TO CRY.
BERK AND DAVID MICHAEL GOT INTO A FIGHT AND BEGAN TO CRY.
EMMA TEASED ASHLEY. ASHLEY WHACKED EMMA WITH HER CRUTCH. EMMA CRIED.
THEY WERE SENT TO SEPARATE ROOMS UNTIL THEY APOLOGIZED.
AND LUKE DID NOT SAY ONE WORD FOR THE ENTIRE MEAL.
THESE EIGHT KIDS WERE CAUSING PLENTY OF TROUBLE, EVEN WITH SEVEN ADULTS, ME, SAM, AND CHARLIE THERE.
WHAT WOULD THE NEXT DAY BE LIKE -- WITH JUST **SIX** BABY-SITTERS WATCHING **FOURTEEN** CHILDREN?
gulp

CHAPTER 7

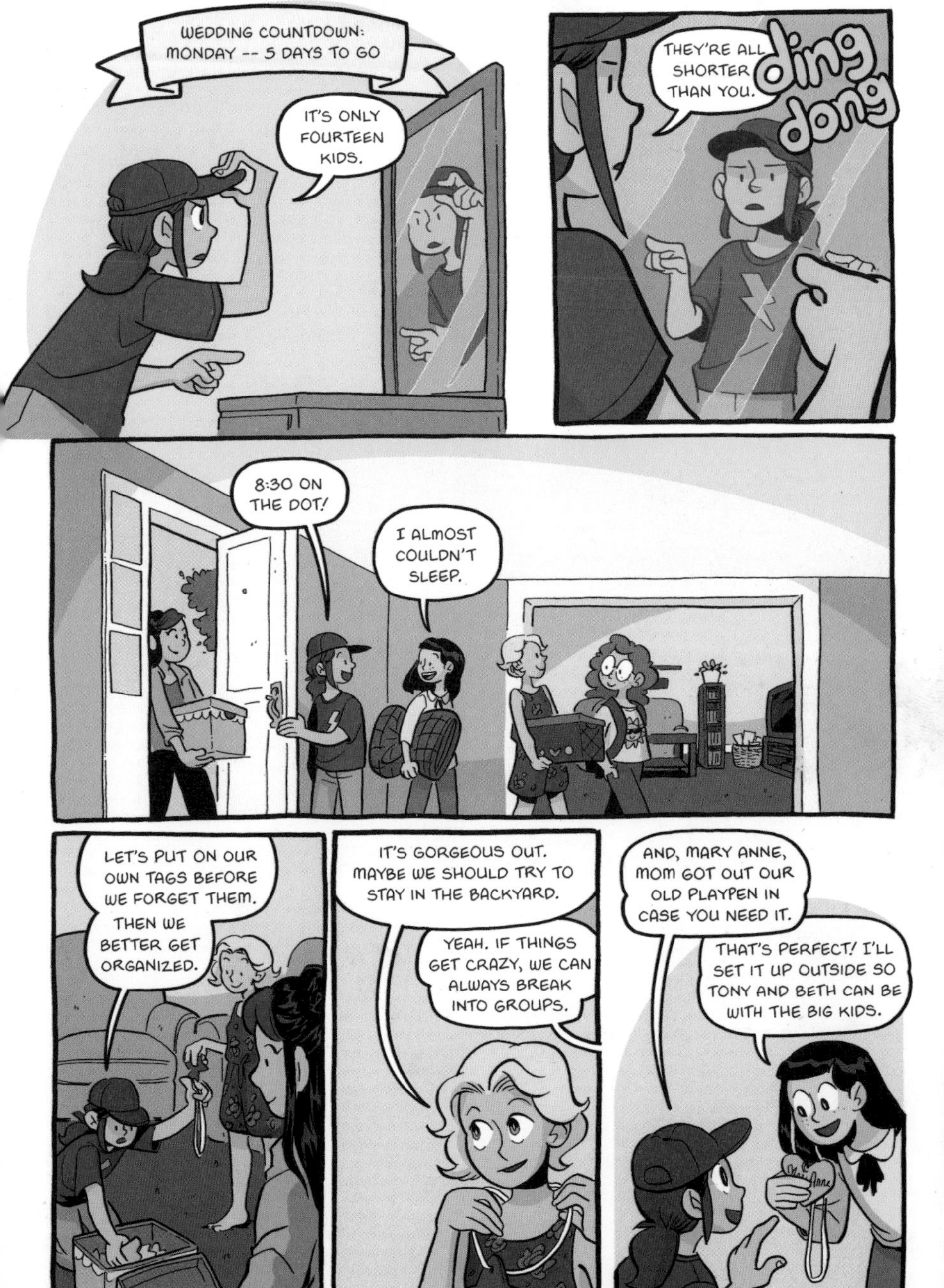
WEDDING COUNTDOWN: MONDAY -- 5 DAYS TO GO
IT'S ONLY FOURTEEN KIDS.
THEY'RE ALL SHORTER THAN YOU.
ding dong
8:30 ON THE DOT!
I ALMOST COULDN'T SLEEP.
LET'S PUT ON OUR OWN TAGS BEFORE WE FORGET THEM.
THEN WE BETTER GET ORGANIZED.
IT'S GORGEOUS OUT. MAYBE WE SHOULD TRY TO STAY IN THE BACKYARD.
YEAH. IF THINGS GET CRAZY, WE CAN ALWAYS BREAK INTO GROUPS.
AND, MARY ANNE, MOM GOT OUT OUR OLD PLAYPEN IN CASE YOU NEED IT.
THAT'S PERFECT! I'LL SET IT UP OUTSIDE SO TONY AND BETH CAN BE WITH THE BIG KIDS.

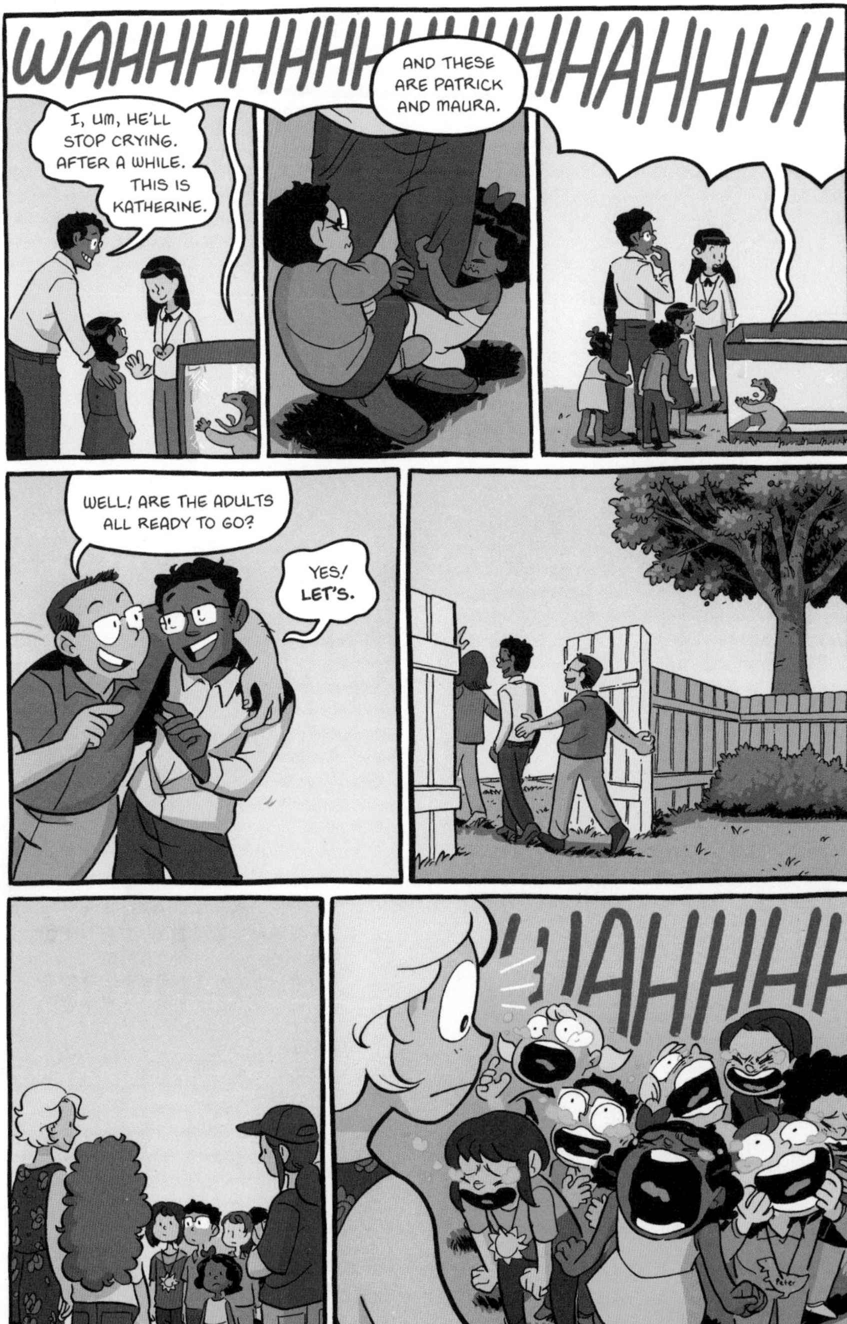
WAHHHHHHHHHHHHHAHHHH
I, UM, HE'LL STOP CRYING. AFTER A WHILE.
THIS IS KATHERINE.
AND THESE ARE PATRICK AND MAURA.
WELL! ARE THE ADULTS ALL READY TO GO?
YES! LET'S.
WAHHHH

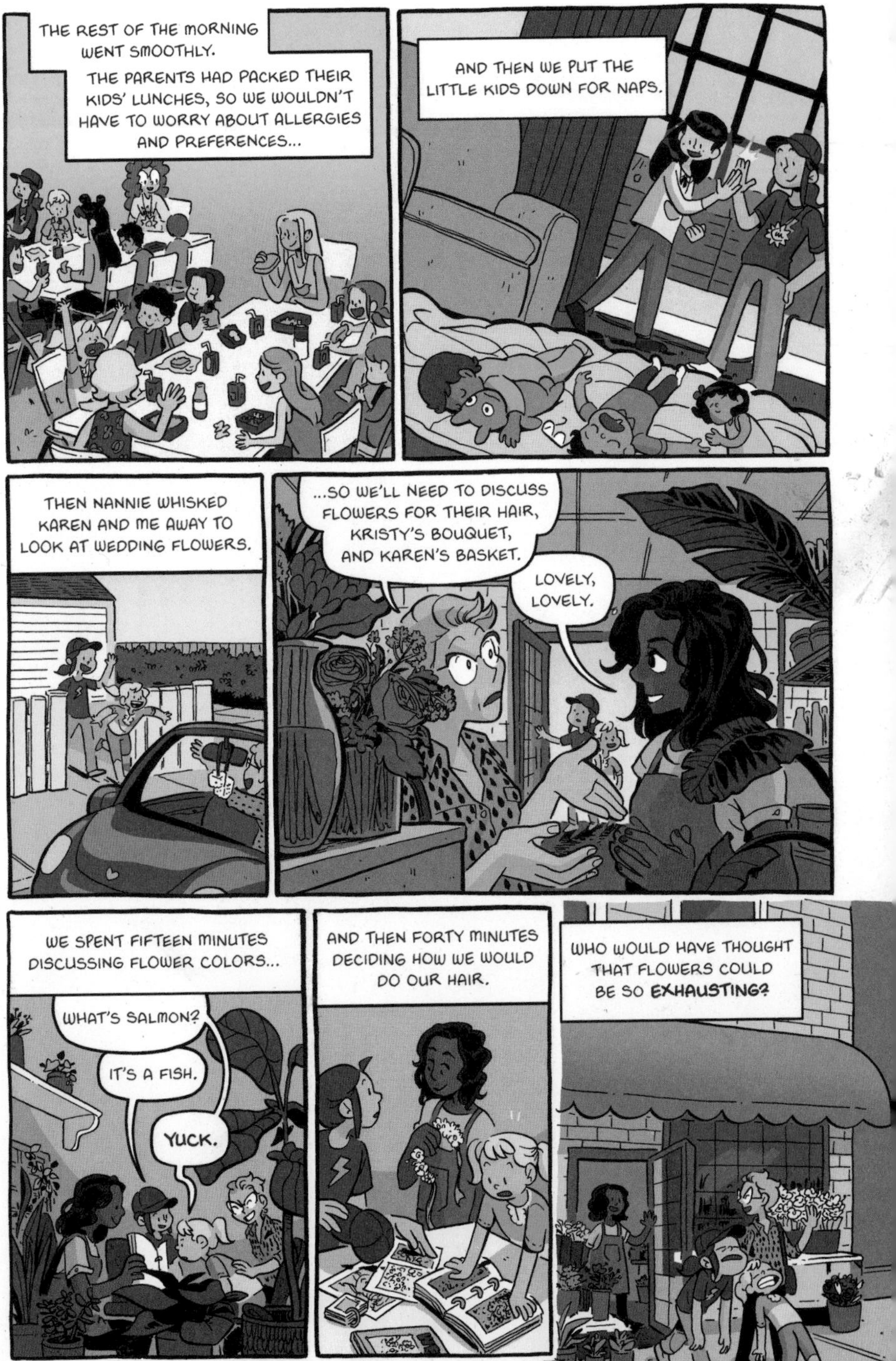
THE REST OF THE MORNING WENT SMOOTHLY.
THE PARENTS HAD PACKED THEIR KIDS' LUNCHES, SO WE WOULDN'T HAVE TO WORRY ABOUT ALLERGIES AND PREFERENCES...
AND THEN WE PUT THE LITTLE KIDS DOWN FOR NAPS.
THEN NANNIE WHISKED KAREN AND ME AWAY TO LOOK AT WEDDING FLOWERS.
...SO WE'LL NEED TO DISCUSS FLOWERS FOR THEIR HAIR, KRISTY'S BOUQUET, AND KAREN'S BASKET.
LOVELY, LOVELY.
WE SPENT FIFTEEN MINUTES DISCUSSING FLOWER COLORS...
WHAT'S SALMON?
IT'S A FISH.
YUCK.
AND THEN FORTY MINUTES DECIDING HOW WE WOULD DO OUR HAIR.
WHO WOULD HAVE THOUGHT THAT FLOWERS COULD BE SO EXHAUSTING?

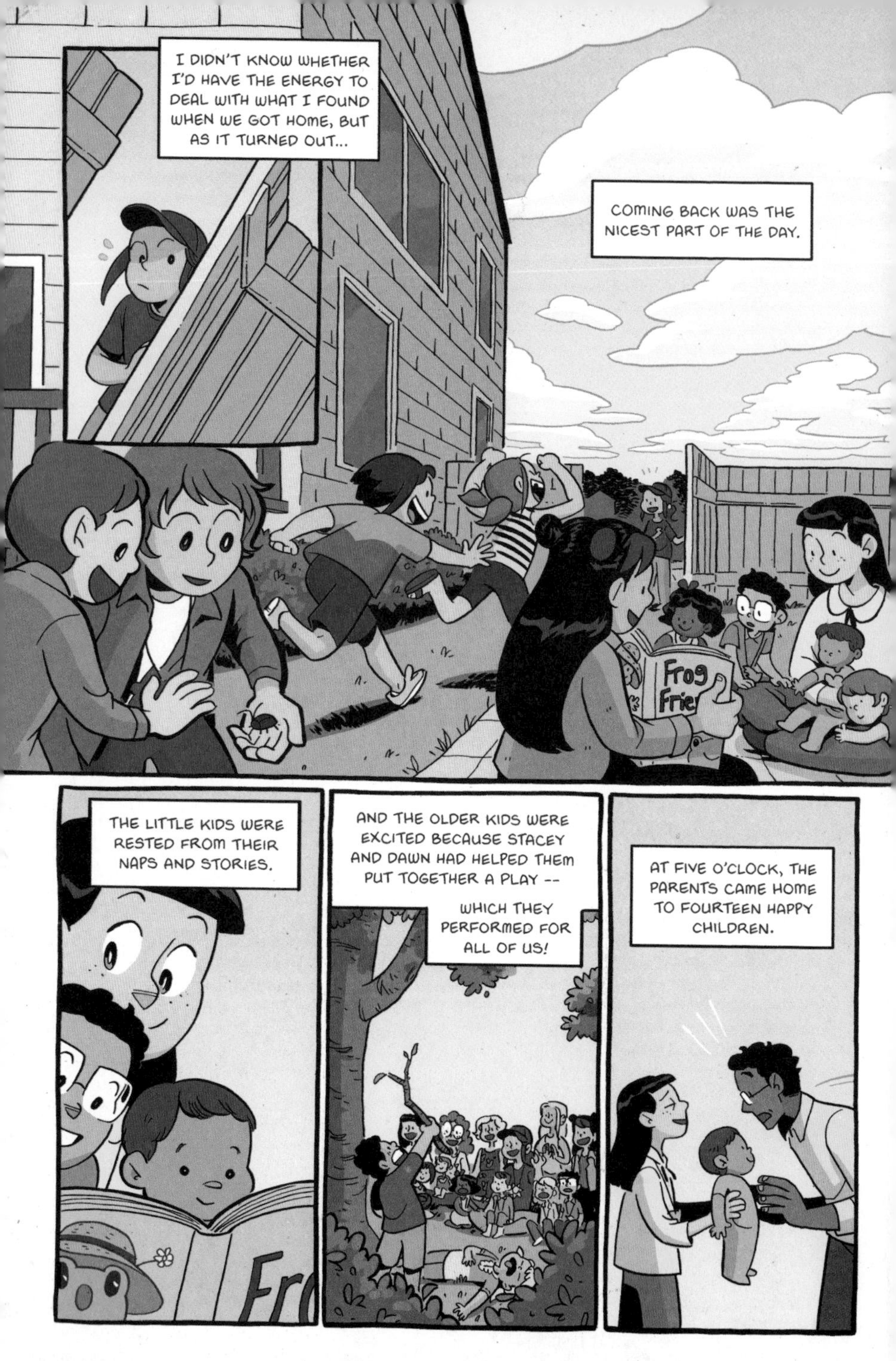
I DIDN'T KNOW WHETHER I'D HAVE THE ENERGY TO DEAL WITH WHAT I FOUND WHEN WE GOT HOME, BUT AS IT TURNED OUT...
COMING BACK WAS THE NICEST PART OF THE DAY.
Frog Frie
THE LITTLE KIDS WERE RESTED FROM THEIR NAPS AND STORIES.
AND THE OLDER KIDS WERE EXCITED BECAUSE STACEY AND DAWN HAD HELPED THEM PUT TOGETHER A PLAY --
WHICH THEY PERFORMED FOR ALL OF US!
AT FIVE O'CLOCK, THE PARENTS CAME HOME TO FOURTEEN HAPPY CHILDREN.

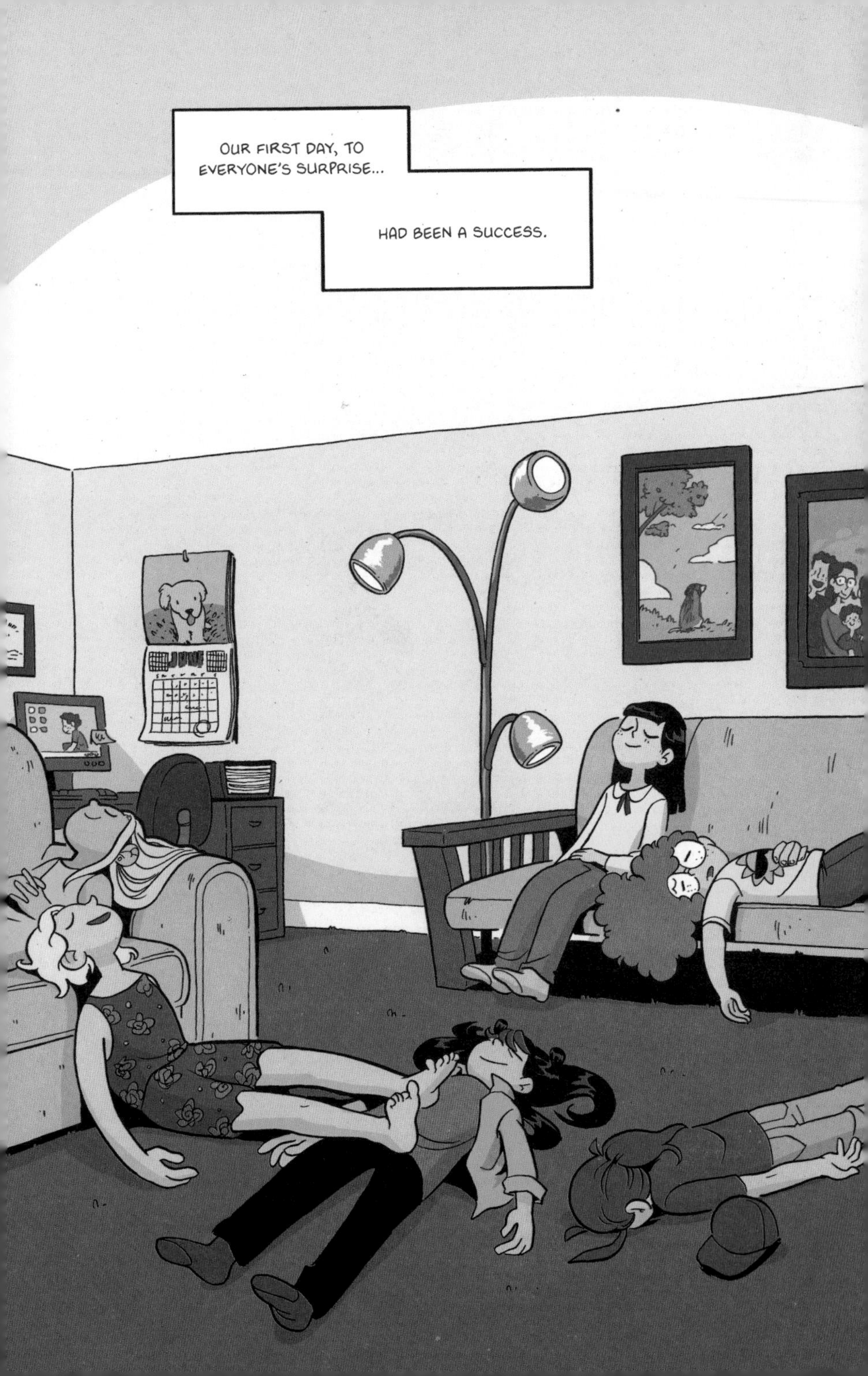
OUR FIRST DAY, TO EVERYONE'S SURPRISE...
HAD BEEN A SUCCESS.
JUNE

TUESDAY, JUNE 23

TODAY WAS ANOTHER BRIGHT, SUNNY DAY, THANK
GOODNESS, AND ALMOST AS WARM AS A NICE SEPTEMBER
DAY IN CALIFORNIA. YESTERDAY WAS FINE WITH ALL THE
KIDS IN KRISTY'S BACKYARD, BUT WE DECIDED TO DO
DIFFERENT THINGS THIS MORNING. THE KIDS WOULD GET
TIRED OF THE THOMASES' YARD PRETTY QUICKLY. SO AFTER
THE PARENTS LEFT, MARY ANNE TOOK THE BABIES FOR A
WALK, STACEY TOOK THE RED GROUP TO THE BROOK TO CATCH
MINNOWS, KRISTY AND CLAUDIA WALKED THEIR GROUPS
TO THE PUBLIC LIBRARY FOR STORY HOUR, AND I TOOK DAVID
MICHAEL, BERK, AND KAREN TO THE SCHOOL PLAYGROUND.

WHAT A MORNING MY GROUP HAD - ALL THANKS TO
KAREN'S IMAGINATION.
                    - DAWN

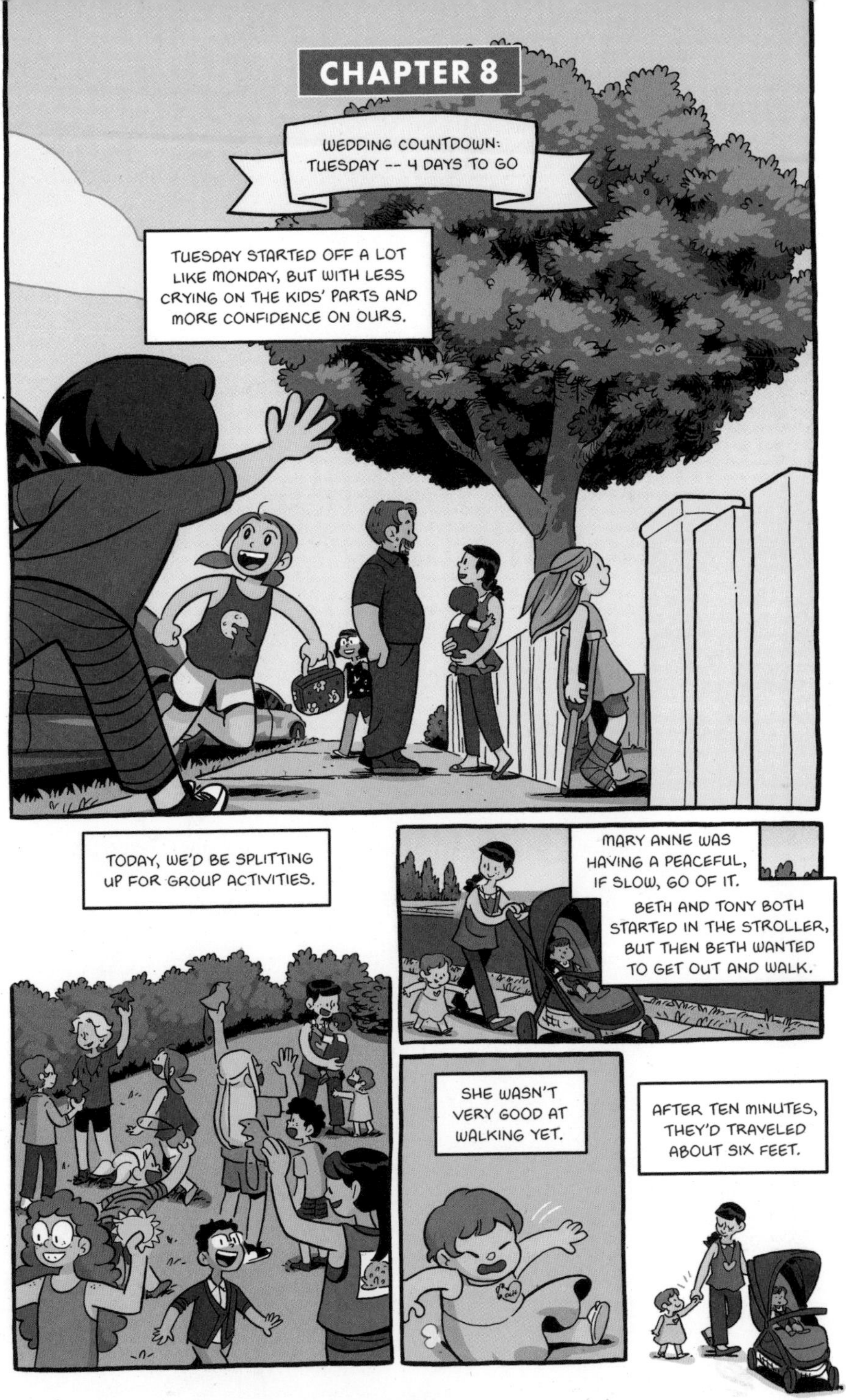
CHAPTER 8
WEDDING COUNTDOWN: TUESDAY -- 4 DAYS TO GO
TUESDAY STARTED OFF A LOT LIKE MONDAY, BUT WITH LESS CRYING ON THE KIDS' PARTS AND MORE CONFIDENCE ON OURS.
TODAY, WE'D BE SPLITTING UP FOR GROUP ACTIVITIES.
MARY ANNE WAS HAVING A PEACEFUL, IF SLOW, GO OF IT.
BETH AND TONY BOTH STARTED IN THE STROLLER, BUT THEN BETH WANTED TO GET OUT AND WALK.
SHE WASN'T VERY GOOD AT WALKING YET.
AFTER TEN MINUTES, THEY'D TRAVELED ABOUT SIX FEET.

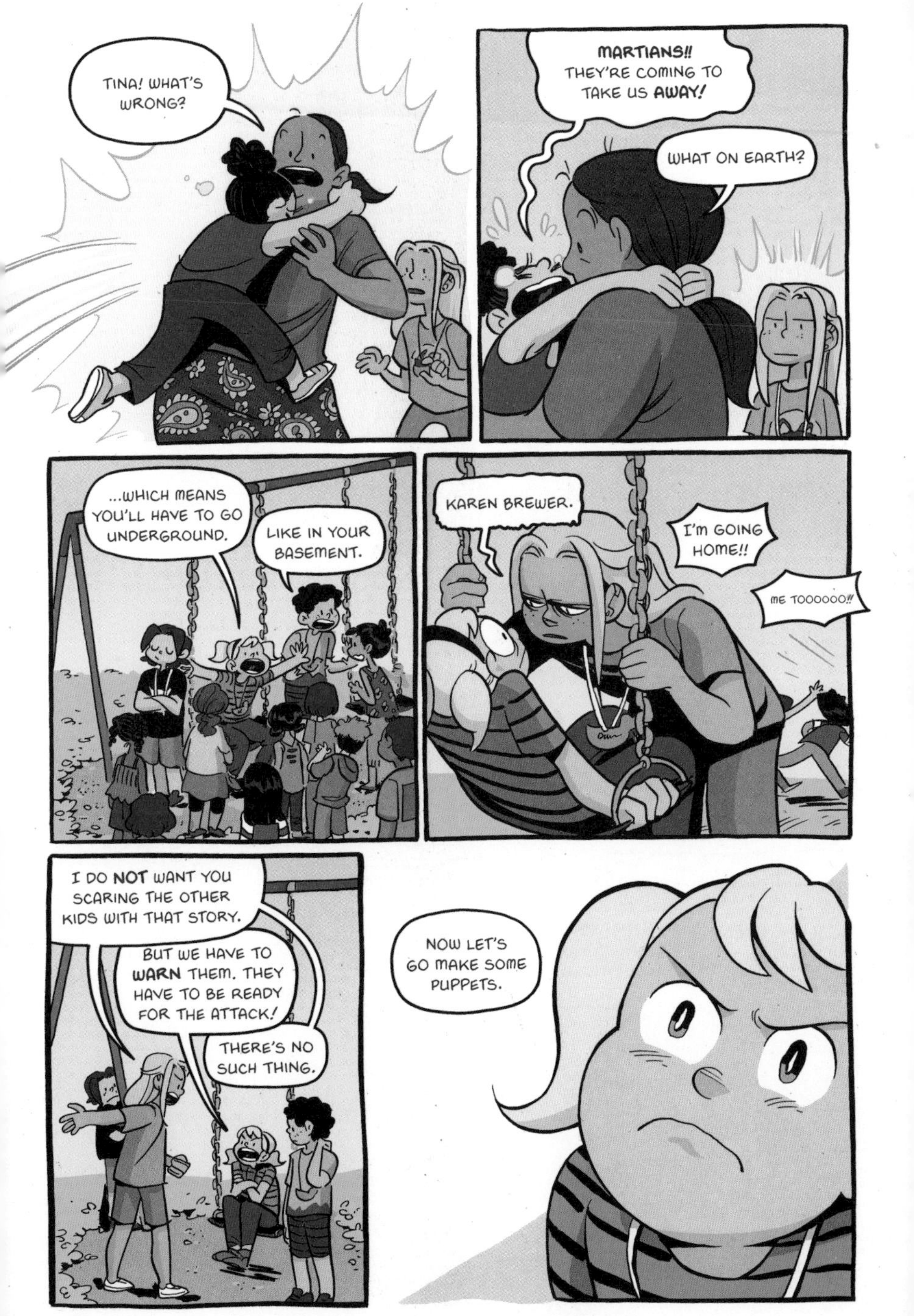
TINA! WHAT'S WRONG?
MARTIANS!! THEY'RE COMING TO TAKE US AWAY!
WHAT ON EARTH?
...WHICH MEANS YOU'LL HAVE TO GO UNDERGROUND.
LIKE IN YOUR BASEMENT.
KAREN BREWER.
I'M GOING HOME!!
ME TOOOOOO!!
I DO NOT WANT YOU SCARING THE OTHER KIDS WITH THAT STORY.
BUT WE HAVE TO WARN THEM. THEY HAVE TO BE READY FOR THE ATTACK!
THERE'S NO SUCH THING.
NOW LET'S GO MAKE SOME PUPPETS.

Wednesday, June 24

    This is a confession, you guys. I know you think I'm so sophisticated, since I'm from New York and everything, but no kidding, my favorite movie is "Mary Poppins." I've seen it 65 times. I know it by heart. Anyway, when I saw that it was going to be at the Embassy Theater for a special screening, I decided I had to have another chance to see it on a big screen. That's one reason I was so determined to take the red group to it. Besides, since it's my favorite movie, I was sure Luke, Emma, and Ashley would love it too. Believe me, if I'd had a crystal ball to see into the future, I would never have taken them.

Stacey

CHAPTER 9

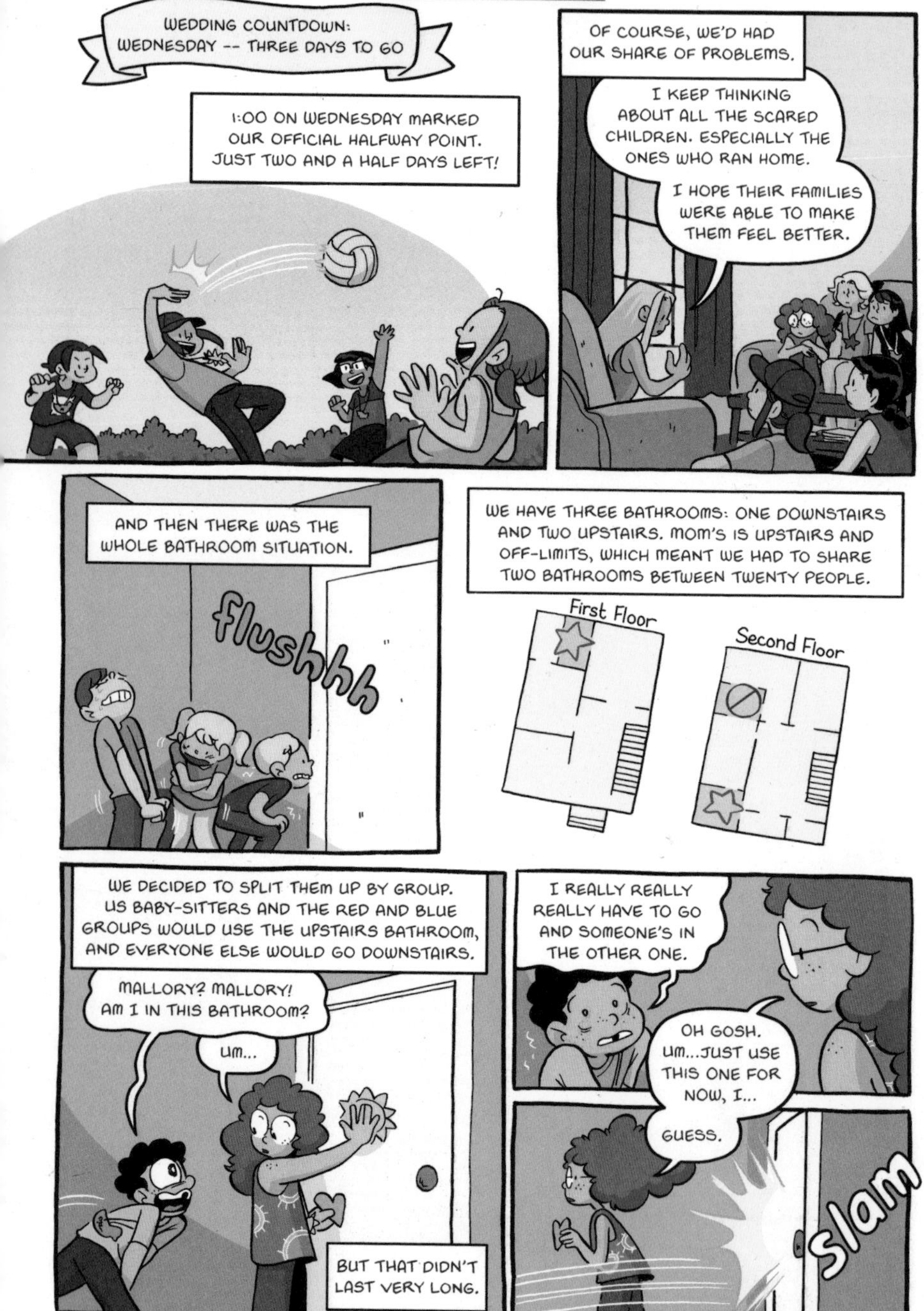
WEDDING COUNTDOWN:
WEDNESDAY -- THREE DAYS TO GO
1:00 ON WEDNESDAY MARKED OUR OFFICIAL HALFWAY POINT. JUST TWO AND A HALF DAYS LEFT!
OF COURSE, WE'D HAD OUR SHARE OF PROBLEMS.
I KEEP THINKING ABOUT ALL THE SCARED CHILDREN. ESPECIALLY THE ONES WHO RAN HOME.
I HOPE THEIR FAMILIES WERE ABLE TO MAKE THEM FEEL BETTER.
AND THEN THERE WAS THE WHOLE BATHROOM SITUATION.
flushhh
WE HAVE THREE BATHROOMS: ONE DOWNSTAIRS AND TWO UPSTAIRS. MOM'S IS UPSTAIRS AND OFF-LIMITS, WHICH MEANT WE HAD TO SHARE TWO BATHROOMS BETWEEN TWENTY PEOPLE.
First Floor
Second Floor
WE DECIDED TO SPLIT THEM UP BY GROUP. US BABY-SITTERS AND THE RED AND BLUE GROUPS WOULD USE THE UPSTAIRS BATHROOM, AND EVERYONE ELSE WOULD GO DOWNSTAIRS.
MALLORY? MALLORY! AM I IN THIS BATHROOM?
UM...
BUT THAT DIDN'T LAST VERY LONG.
I REALLY REALLY REALLY HAVE TO GO AND SOMEONE'S IN THE OTHER ONE.
OH GOSH. UM...JUST USE THIS ONE FOR NOW, I...
GUESS.
slam

THE MOST IMPORTANT THING WAS THAT THE KIDS WERE HAVING FUN. AND STACEY HAD A VERY SPECIAL PLAN FOR HER GROUP THAT AFTERNOON.

THANKS AGAIN FOR TAKING US.

OH, IT'S MY PLEASURE.

I'LL DRIVE VERY SLOWLY. I DON'T WANT TO JAR YOUR LEG.

WHILE NANNIE AND I WENT SHOE SHOPPING, STACEY WOULD BE TAKING HER KIDS TO SEE MARY POPPINS.

TRUE TO HER POSITION AS TREASURER, SHE'D EVEN THOUGHT AHEAD AND ASKED THEIR PARENTS FOR PERMISSION AND TICKET MONEY IN ADVANCE.

putt putt

HAVE FUN! WE'LL BE BACK IN TWO HOURS.

NOW, DO YOU ALL HAVE YOUR MONEY?

YUP.

YUP.

UHHHH.

NEXT?

EMMA? I TOLD YOU THREE TO MAKE SURE YOU BROUGHT YOUR MONEY.

I **DID**, BUT I CAN'T FIIIIND IT.

93

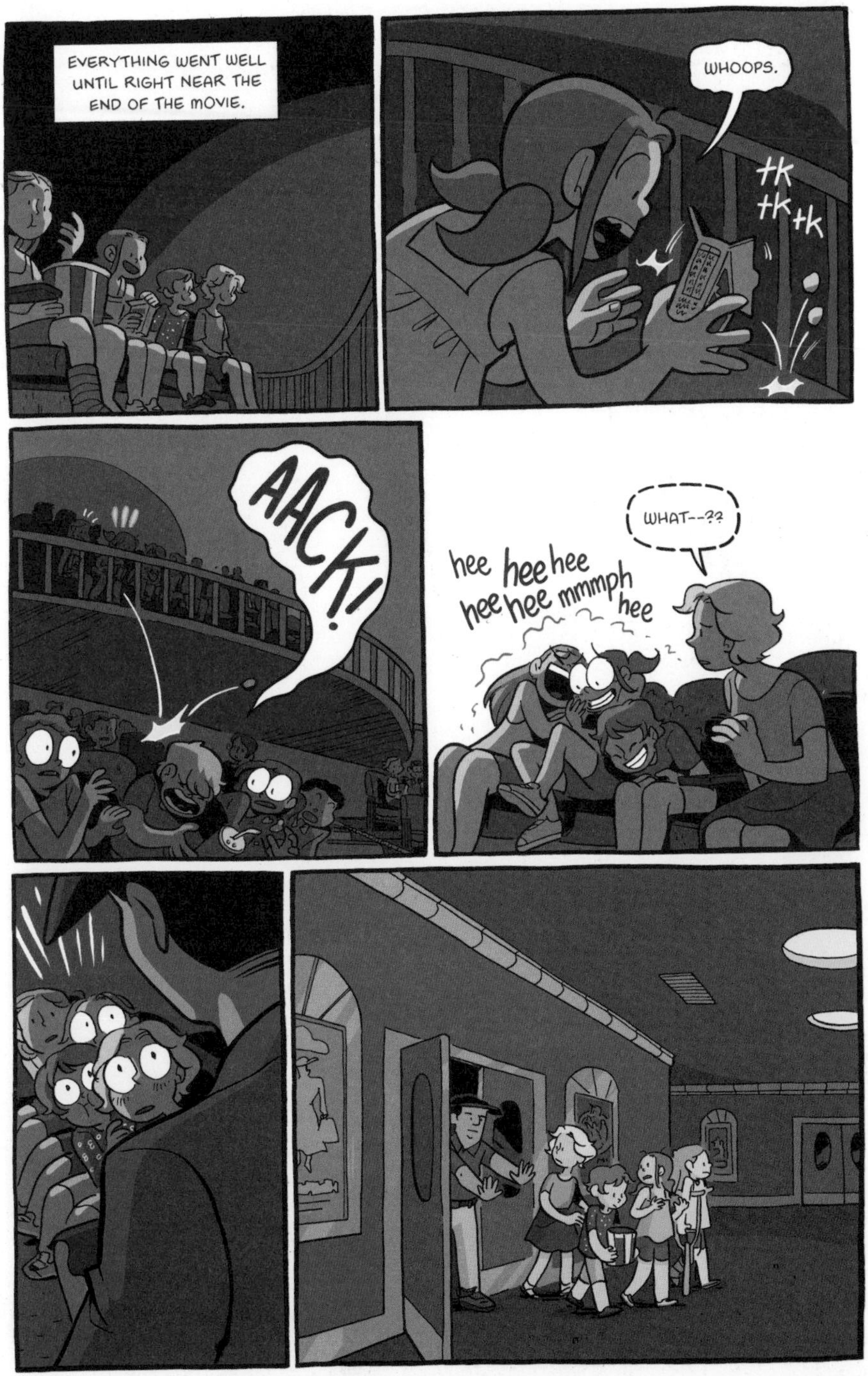
EVERYTHING WENT WELL UNTIL RIGHT NEAR THE END OF THE MOVIE.
WHOOPS.
tk tk tk
AACK!
WHAT--??
hee hee hee hee hee mmmph hee

THANK
GOODNESS.

WHAT HAPPENED?

ASK HER.

WE WERE ON THE
BALCONY AND --

EMMA WAS EATING
JUNIOR MINTS BUT --

snrrk

I GOT SOMEONE
ON THE HEAD!!

mmph

haha
haha

ahahaha

OH WELL.

I CAN ALWAYS
SEE IT ON TV.

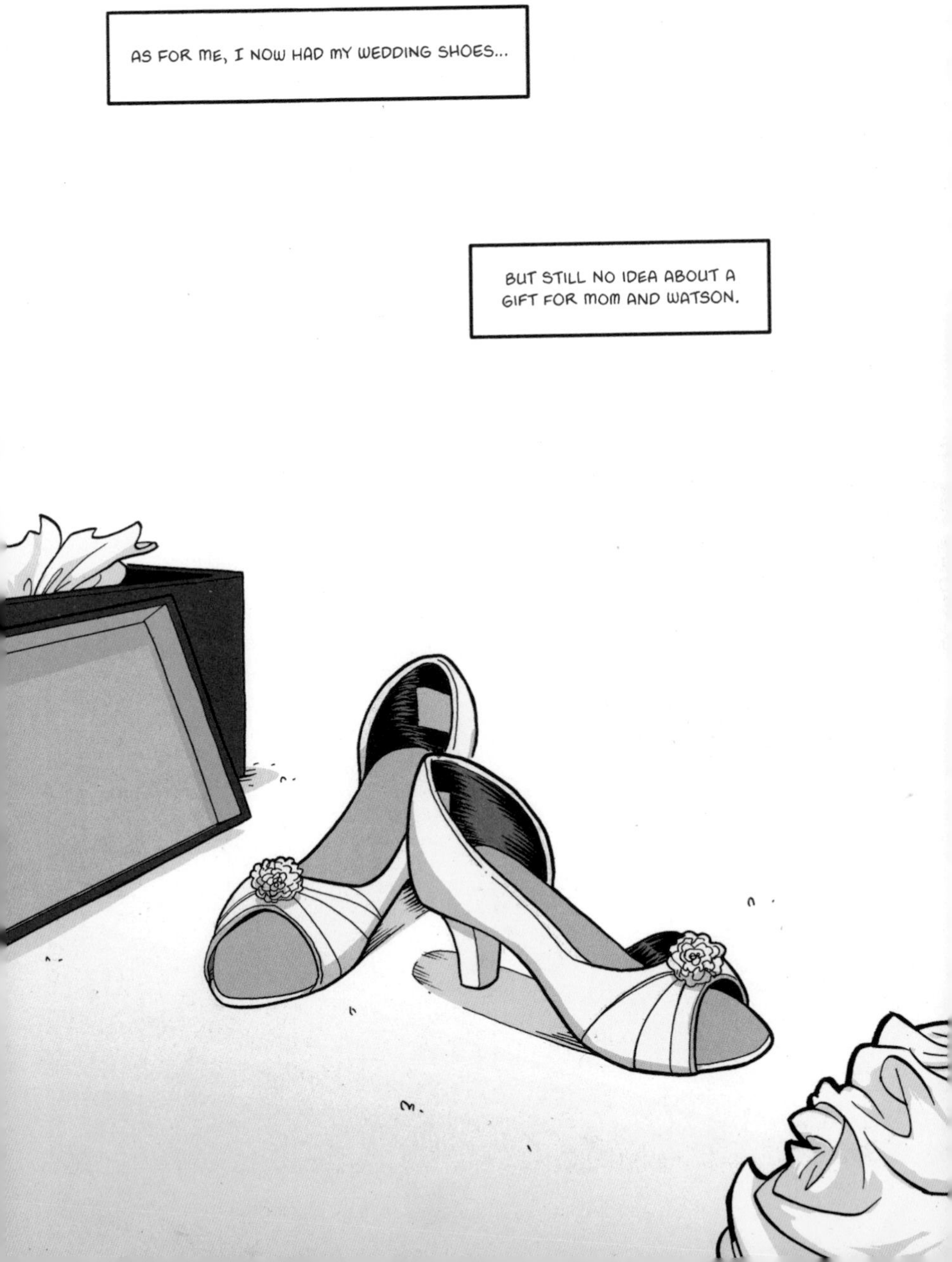
AS FOR ME, I NOW HAD MY WEDDING SHOES...
BUT STILL NO IDEA ABOUT A GIFT FOR MOM AND WATSON.

Thursday, June 25

Until today, I didn't know that 'barber' is a dirty word. But it is - to little boys. Here's how I found out: When the mothers and fathers dropped their children off at Kristy's house this morning, they all looked guilty. It turned out that they'd decided the boys, except for baby Tony, needed their hair cut before the wedding. Since the barber is only open from 9:00 until 5:00, guess what they asked us poor, defenseless, unprepared baby-sitters to do? They asked us to take Luke, David Michael, Berk, Andrew, Peter, and Patrick to poor, defenseless, unprepared Mr. Gates, whose barbershop is just around the corner from the elementary school. When we told the boys about their field trip, all six of them turned pale, then red, and began throwing tantrums...

Mary Anne

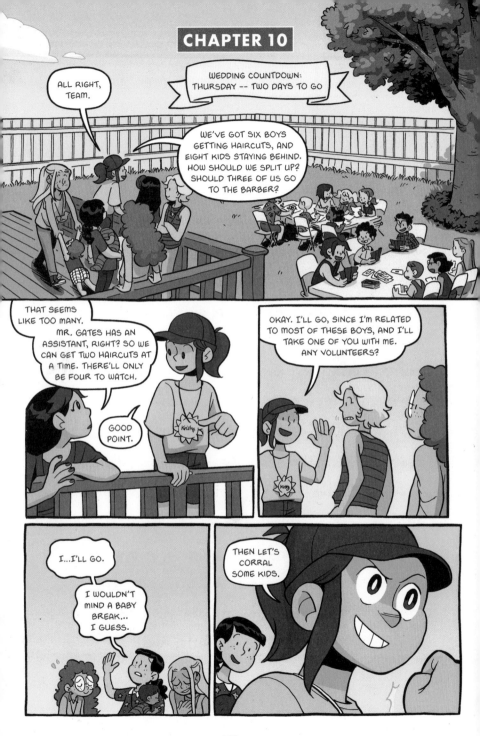

CHAPTER 10

ALL RIGHT, TEAM.

WEDDING COUNTDOWN: THURSDAY -- TWO DAYS TO GO

WE'VE GOT SIX BOYS GETTING HAIRCUTS, AND EIGHT KIDS STAYING BEHIND. HOW SHOULD WE SPLIT UP? SHOULD THREE OF US GO TO THE BARBER?

THAT SEEMS LIKE TOO MANY. MR. GATES HAS AN ASSISTANT, RIGHT? SO WE CAN GET TWO HAIRCUTS AT A TIME. THERE'LL ONLY BE FOUR TO WATCH.

GOOD POINT.

OKAY. I'LL GO, SINCE I'M RELATED TO MOST OF THESE BOYS, AND I'LL TAKE ONE OF YOU WITH ME. ANY VOLUNTEERS?

I...I'LL GO.

I WOULDN'T MIND A BABY BREAK... I GUESS.

THEN LET'S CORRAL SOME KIDS.

Friday, June 26

Unfiar! Today it rained! All day!
  I guess we baby sitters shouldnt complain
to much since this was the first rainy day
all weak. But still it was a yucky day
wether wise. The kids were not to
bad though.
  Hey Kristy how come we have to write
in the diary this weak? We're all sitting
so we all know whats going on right? I
guess its just the rules right? Anyway it
cant hurt.
  Anyway the morning went okay but by the
time lunch was over we were running out
of things to do then I got this really
fun idea ...
                    * Claudia *

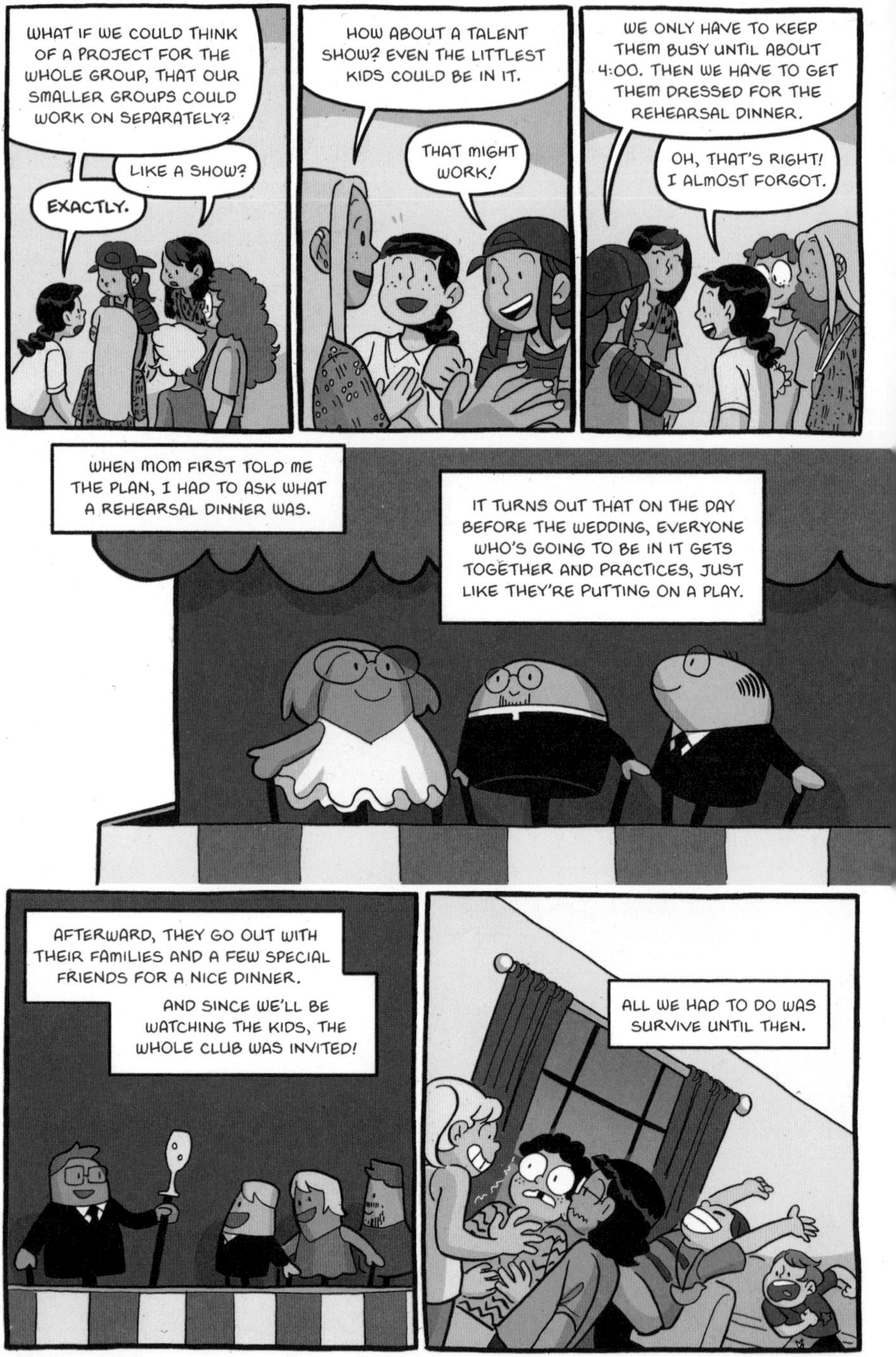
WHAT IF WE COULD THINK OF A PROJECT FOR THE WHOLE GROUP, THAT OUR SMALLER GROUPS COULD WORK ON SEPARATELY?
LIKE A SHOW?
EXACTLY.
HOW ABOUT A TALENT SHOW? EVEN THE LITTLEST KIDS COULD BE IN IT.
THAT MIGHT WORK!
WE ONLY HAVE TO KEEP THEM BUSY UNTIL ABOUT 4:00. THEN WE HAVE TO GET THEM DRESSED FOR THE REHEARSAL DINNER.
OH, THAT'S RIGHT! I ALMOST FORGOT.
WHEN MOM FIRST TOLD ME THE PLAN, I HAD TO ASK WHAT A REHEARSAL DINNER WAS.
IT TURNS OUT THAT ON THE DAY BEFORE THE WEDDING, EVERYONE WHO'S GOING TO BE IN IT GETS TOGETHER AND PRACTICES, JUST LIKE THEY'RE PUTTING ON A PLAY.
AFTERWARD, THEY GO OUT WITH THEIR FAMILIES AND A FEW SPECIAL FRIENDS FOR A NICE DINNER.
AND SINCE WE'LL BE WATCHING THE KIDS, THE WHOLE CLUB WAS INVITED!
ALL WE HAD TO DO WAS SURVIVE UNTIL THEN.

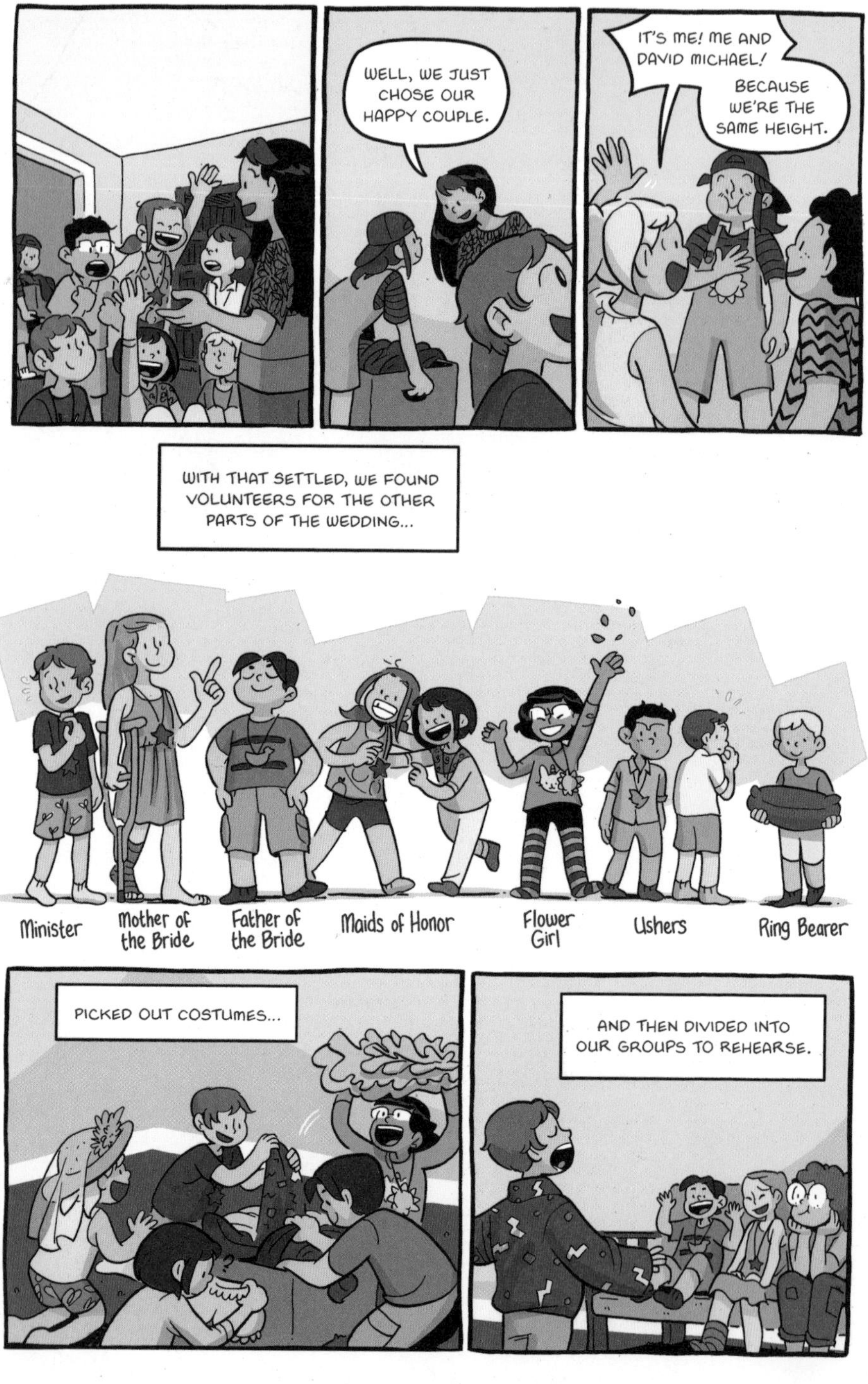
WELL, WE JUST CHOSE OUR HAPPY COUPLE.
IT'S ME! ME AND DAVID MICHAEL!
BECAUSE WE'RE THE SAME HEIGHT.
WITH THAT SETTLED, WE FOUND VOLUNTEERS FOR THE OTHER PARTS OF THE WEDDING...
Minister
Mother of the Bride
Father of the Bride
Maids of Honor
Flower Girl
Ushers
Ring Bearer
PICKED OUT COSTUMES...
AND THEN DIVIDED INTO OUR GROUPS TO REHEARSE.

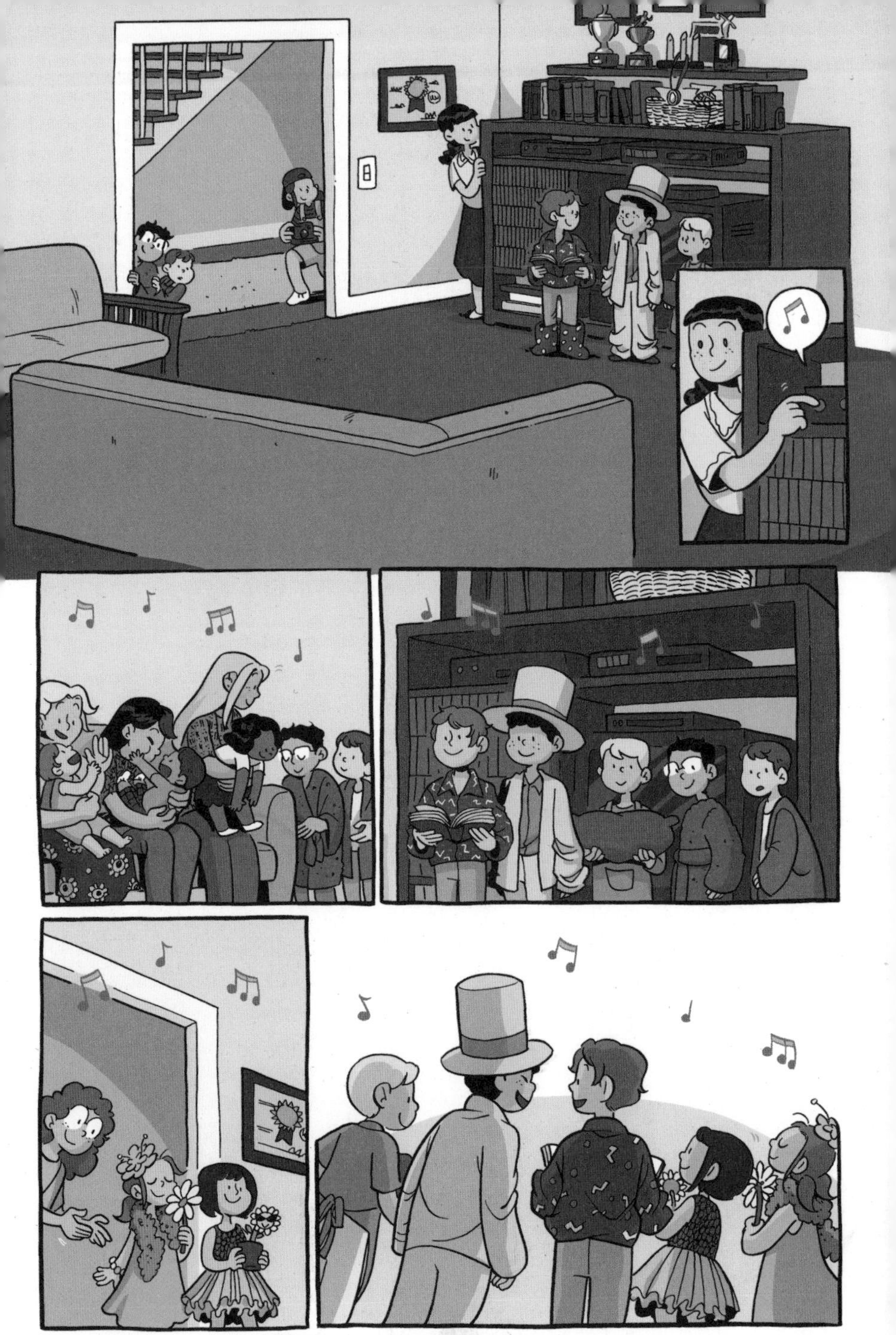

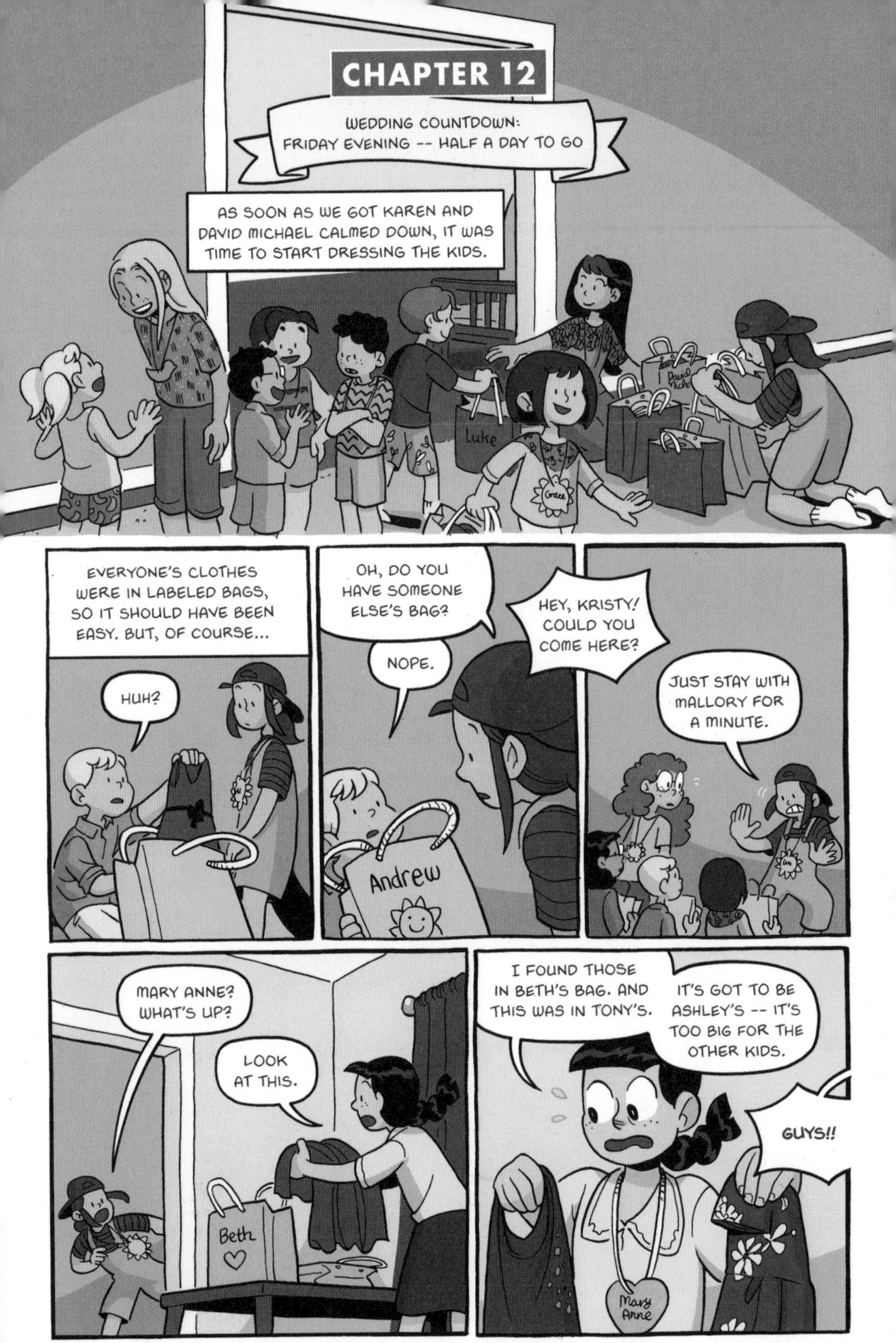
CHAPTER 12
WEDDING COUNTDOWN: FRIDAY EVENING -- HALF A DAY TO GO
AS SOON AS WE GOT KAREN AND DAVID MICHAEL CALMED DOWN, IT WAS TIME TO START DRESSING THE KIDS.
Luke
Grace
EVERYONE'S CLOTHES WERE IN LABELED BAGS, SO IT SHOULD HAVE BEEN EASY. BUT, OF COURSE...
HUH?
OH, DO YOU HAVE SOMEONE ELSE'S BAG?
NOPE.
Andrew
HEY, KRISTY! COULD YOU COME HERE?
JUST STAY WITH MALLORY FOR A MINUTE.
MARY ANNE? WHAT'S UP?
LOOK AT THIS.
Beth
I FOUND THOSE IN BETH'S BAG. AND THIS WAS IN TONY'S.
IT'S GOT TO BE ASHLEY'S -- IT'S TOO BIG FOR THE OTHER KIDS.
GUYS!!
Mary Anne

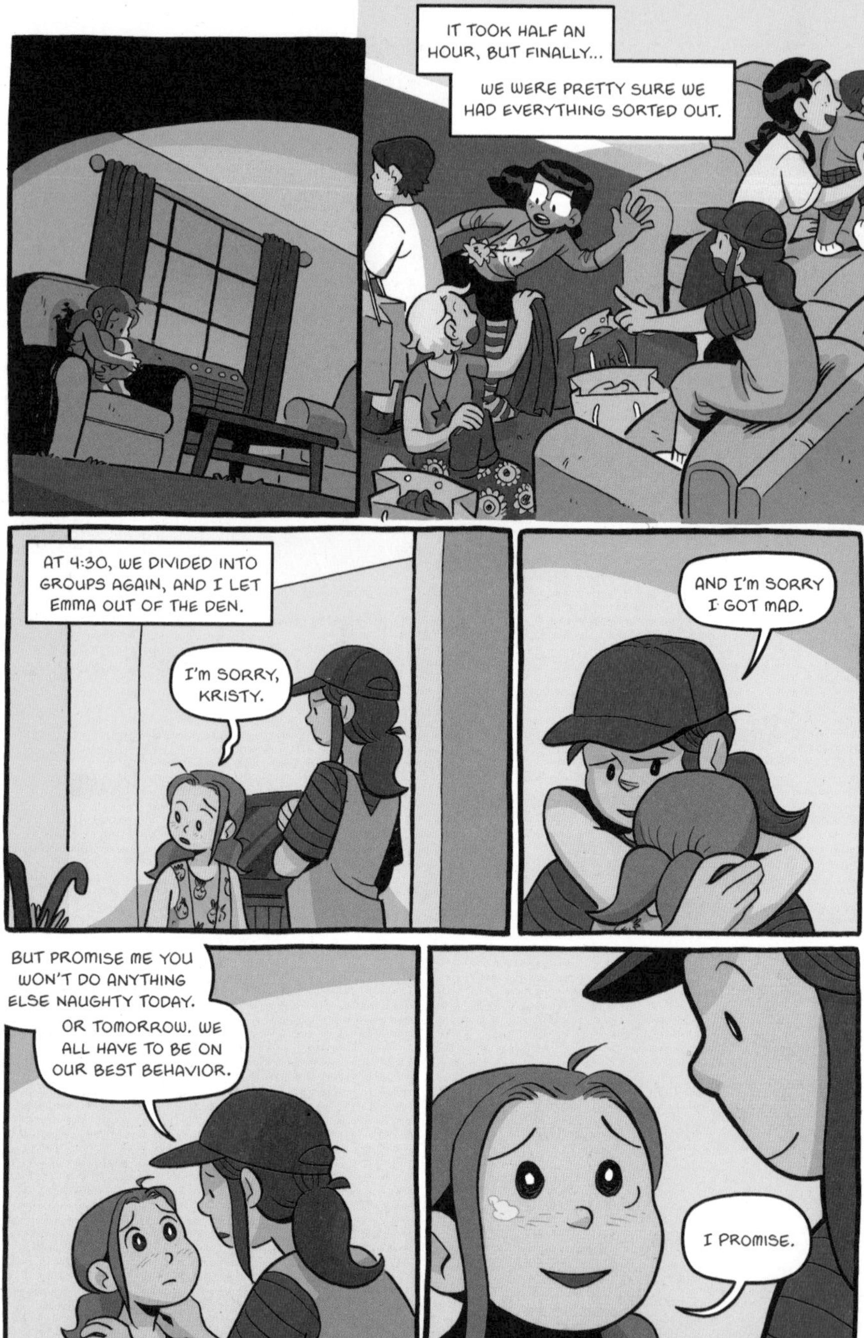
IT TOOK HALF AN HOUR, BUT FINALLY...
WE WERE PRETTY SURE WE HAD EVERYTHING SORTED OUT.
AT 4:30, WE DIVIDED INTO GROUPS AGAIN, AND I LET EMMA OUT OF THE DEN.
I'M SORRY, KRISTY.
AND I'M SORRY I GOT MAD.
BUT PROMISE ME YOU WON'T DO ANYTHING ELSE NAUGHTY TODAY.
OR TOMORROW. WE ALL HAVE TO BE ON OUR BEST BEHAVIOR.
I PROMISE.

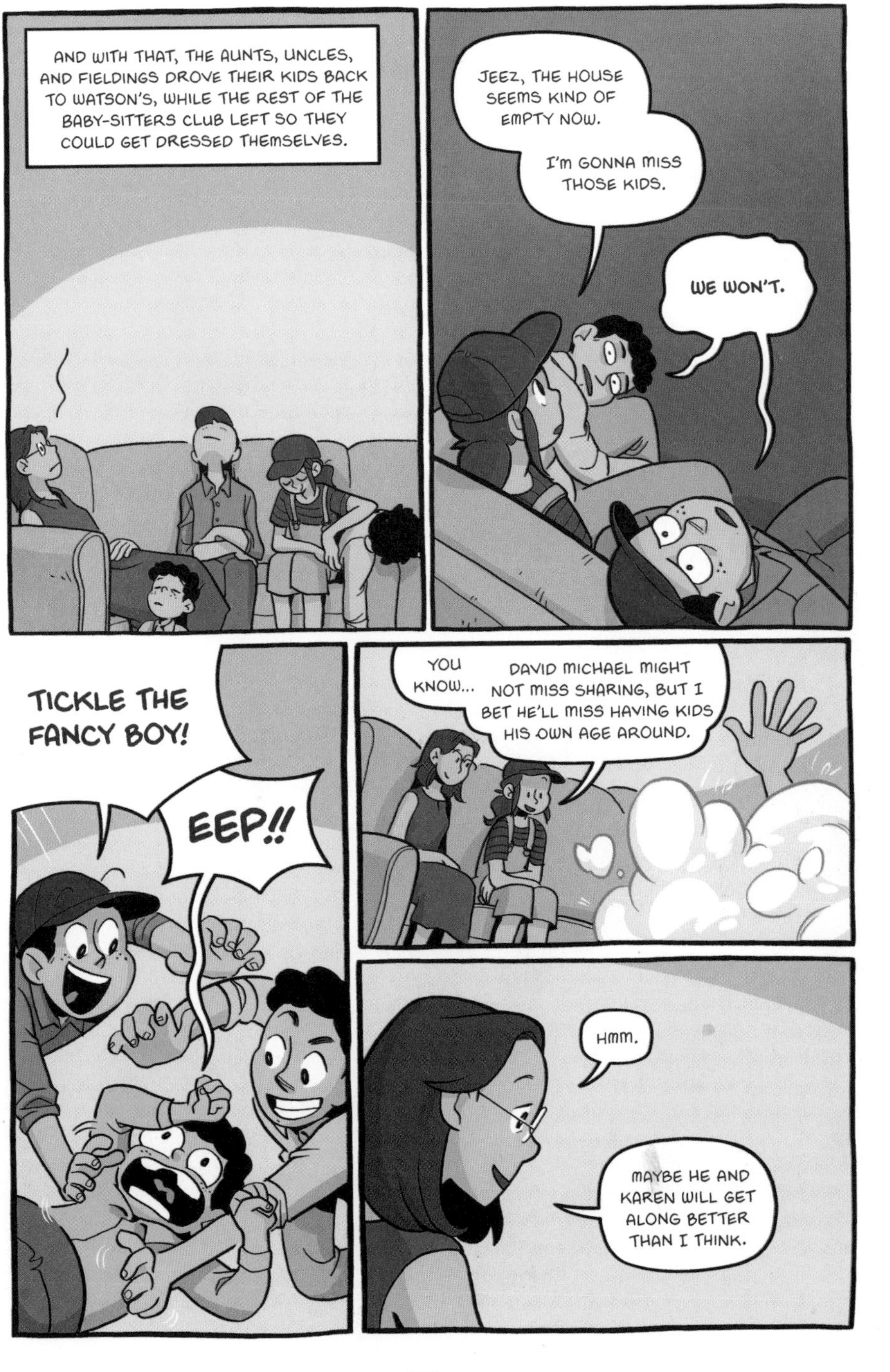
AND WITH THAT, THE AUNTS, UNCLES, AND FIELDINGS DROVE THEIR KIDS BACK TO WATSON'S, WHILE THE REST OF THE BABY-SITTERS CLUB LEFT SO THEY COULD GET DRESSED THEMSELVES.
JEEZ, THE HOUSE SEEMS KIND OF EMPTY NOW.
I'M GONNA MISS THOSE KIDS.
WE WON'T.
TICKLE THE FANCY BOY!
EEP!!
YOU KNOW...
DAVID MICHAEL MIGHT NOT MISS SHARING, BUT I BET HE'LL MISS HAVING KIDS HIS OWN AGE AROUND.
HMM.
MAYBE HE AND KAREN WILL GET ALONG BETTER THAN I THINK.

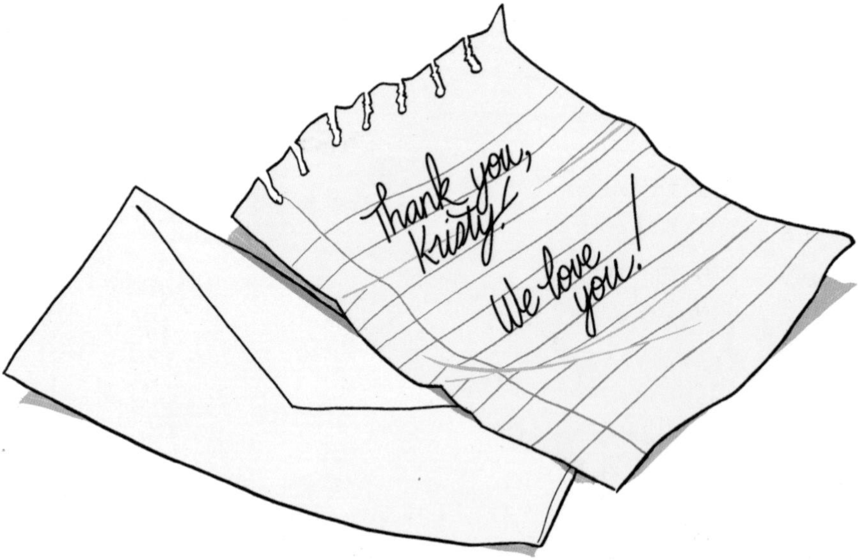
Thank you,
Kristy!
We love
you!

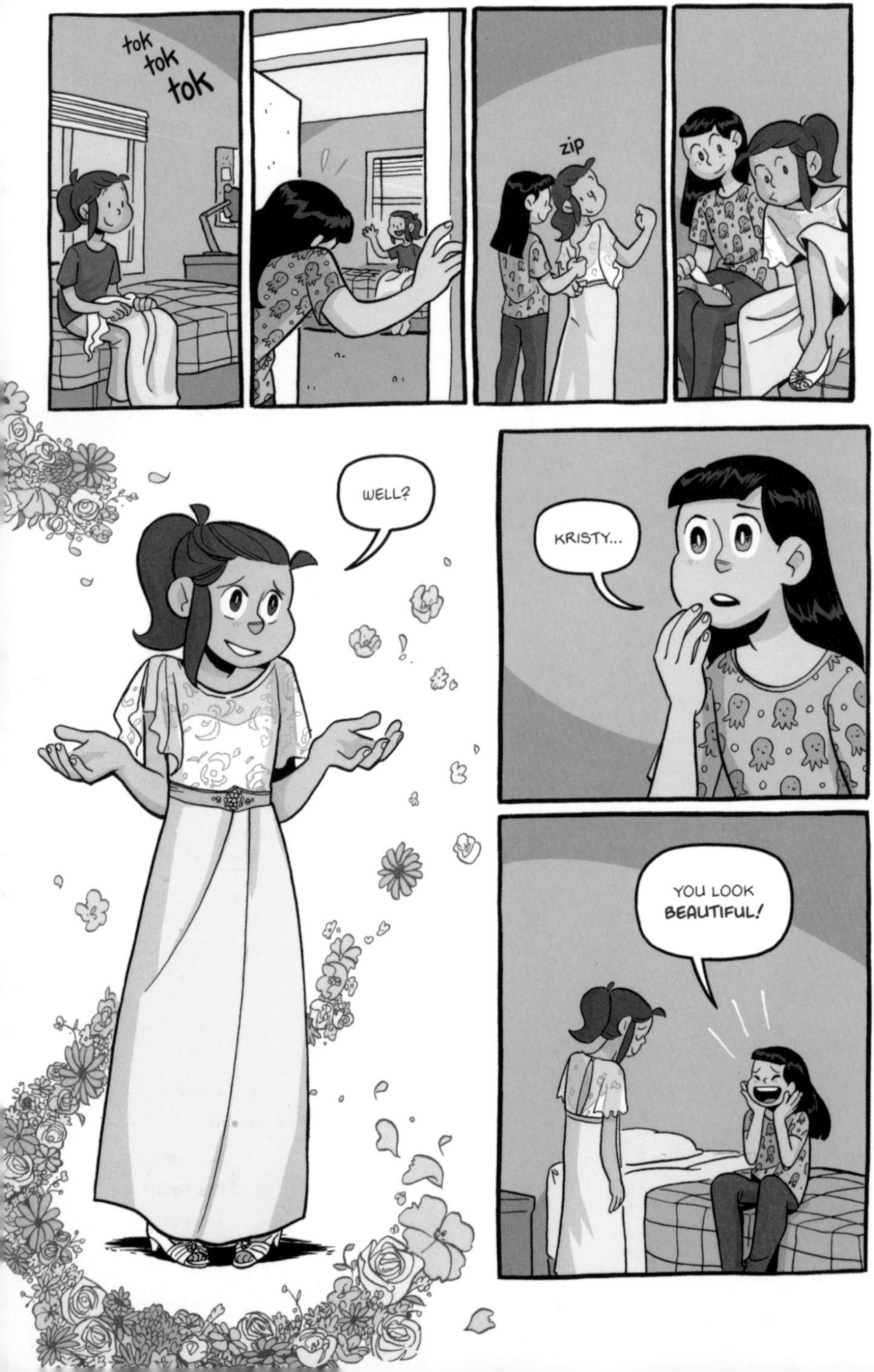
tok
tok
tok
zip
WELL?
KRISTY...
YOU LOOK BEAUTIFUL!

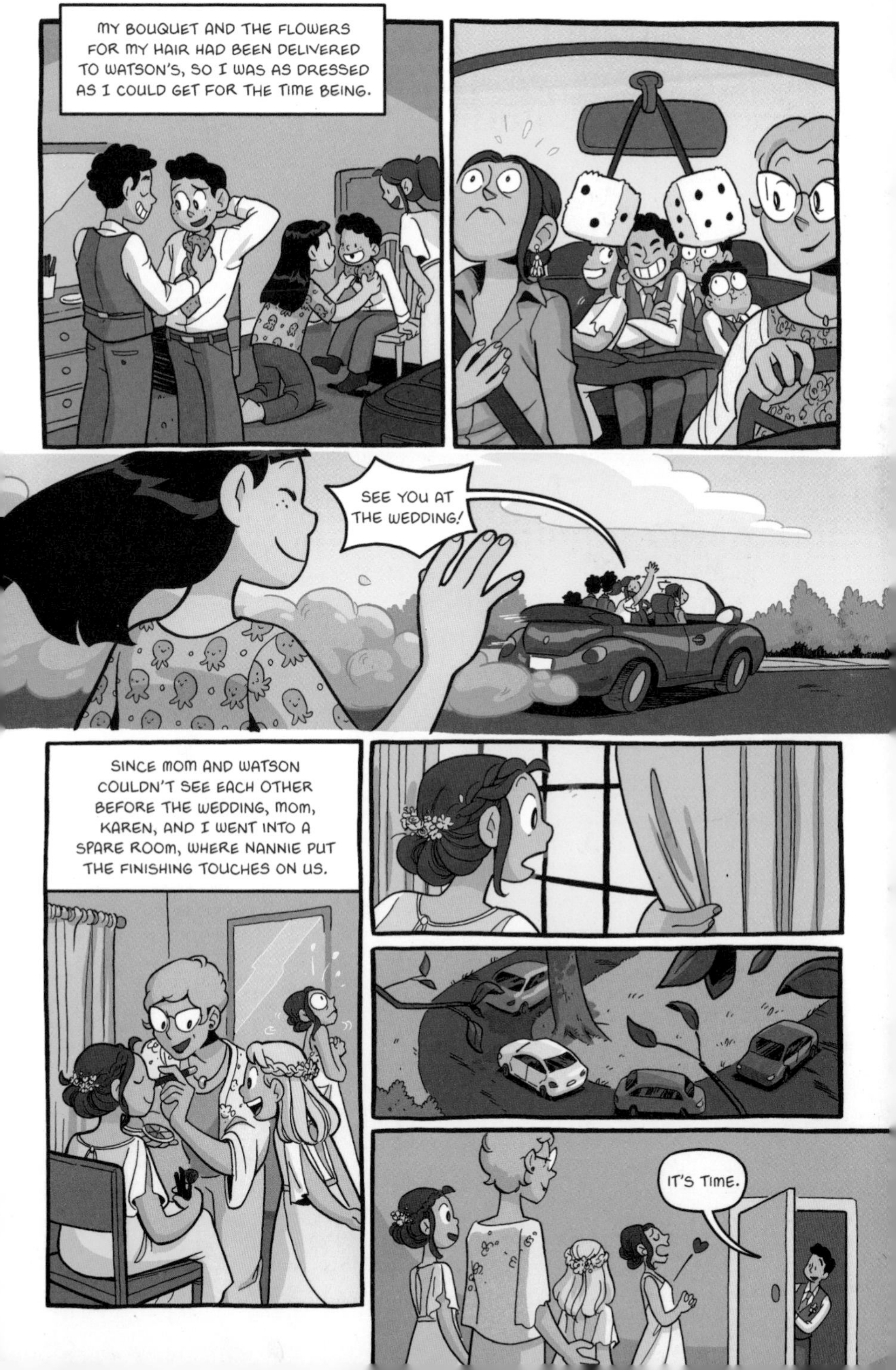
MY BOUQUET AND THE FLOWERS FOR MY HAIR HAD BEEN DELIVERED TO WATSON'S, SO I WAS AS DRESSED AS I COULD GET FOR THE TIME BEING.
SEE YOU AT THE WEDDING!
SINCE MOM AND WATSON COULDN'T SEE EACH OTHER BEFORE THE WEDDING, MOM, KAREN, AND I WENT INTO A SPARE ROOM, WHERE NANNIE PUT THE FINISHING TOUCHES ON US.
IT'S TIME.

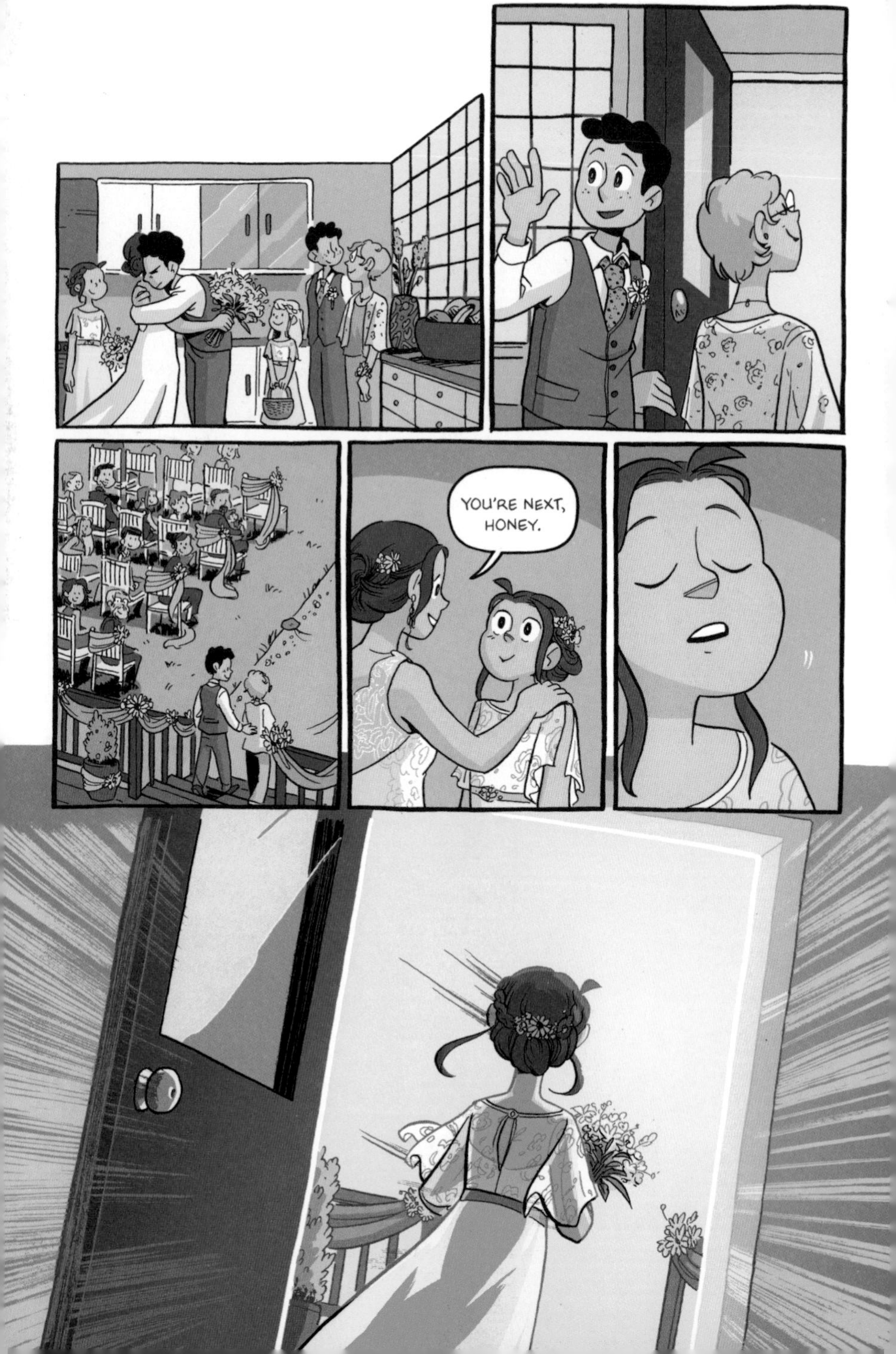
YOU'RE NEXT, HONEY.

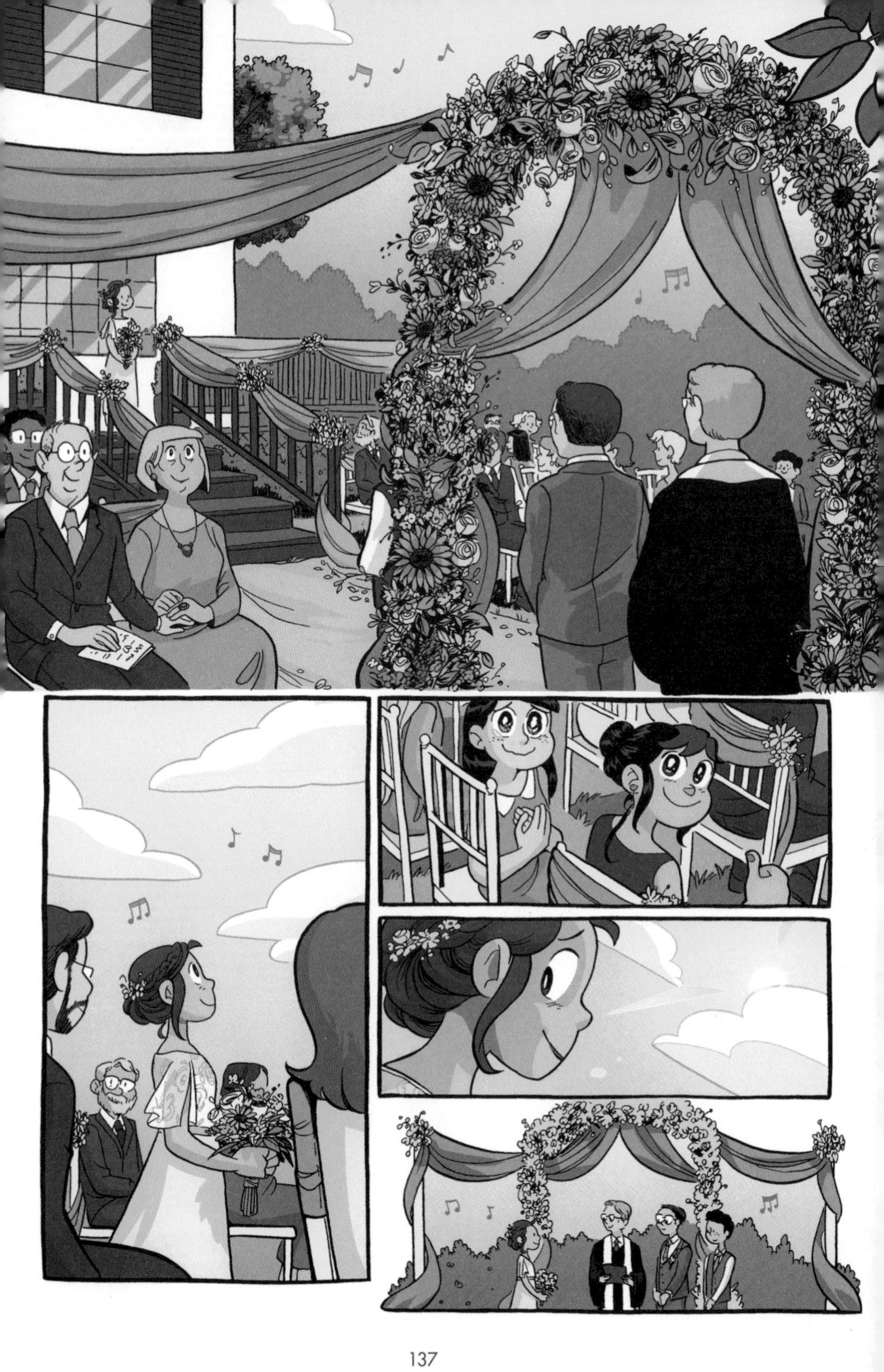

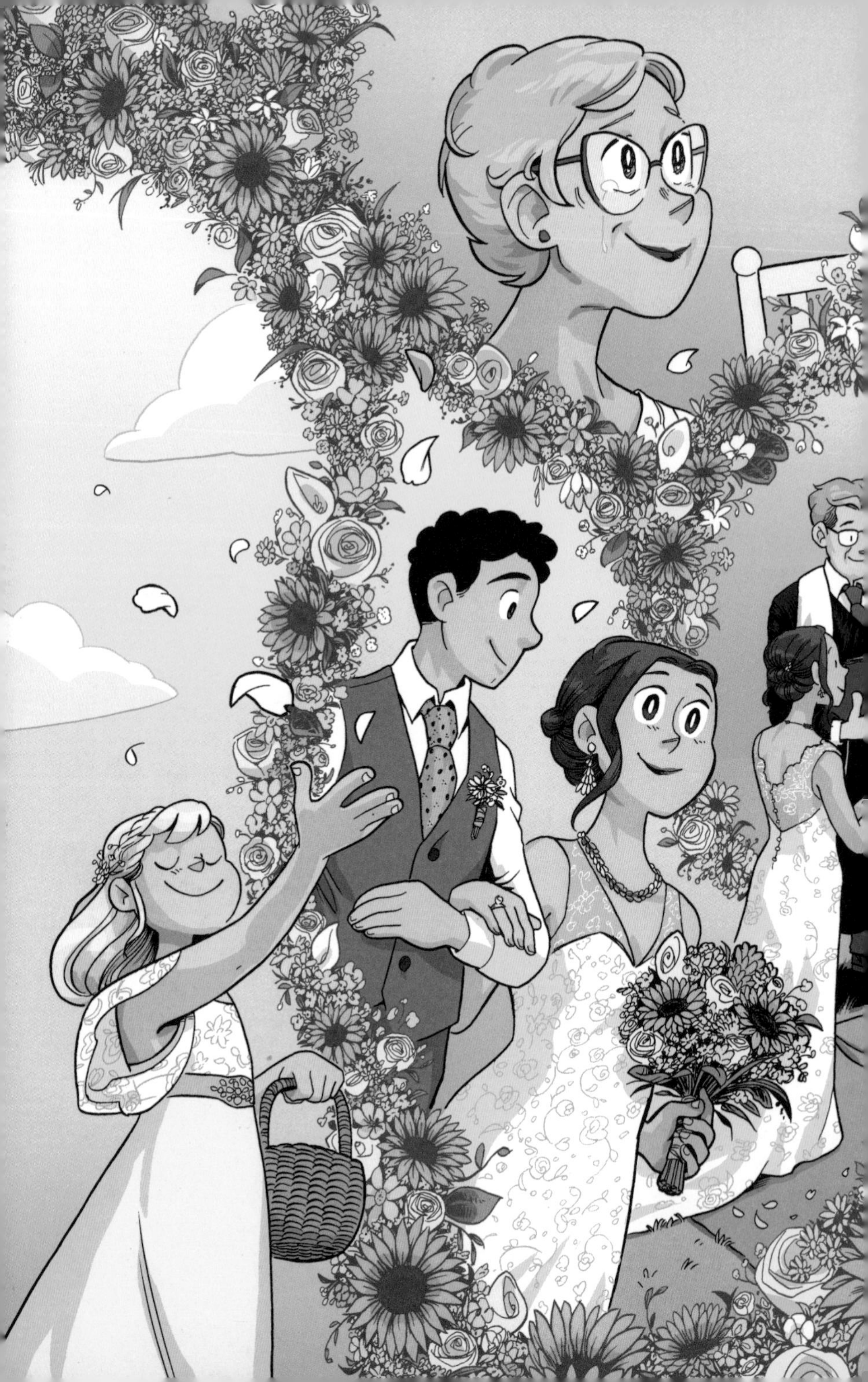

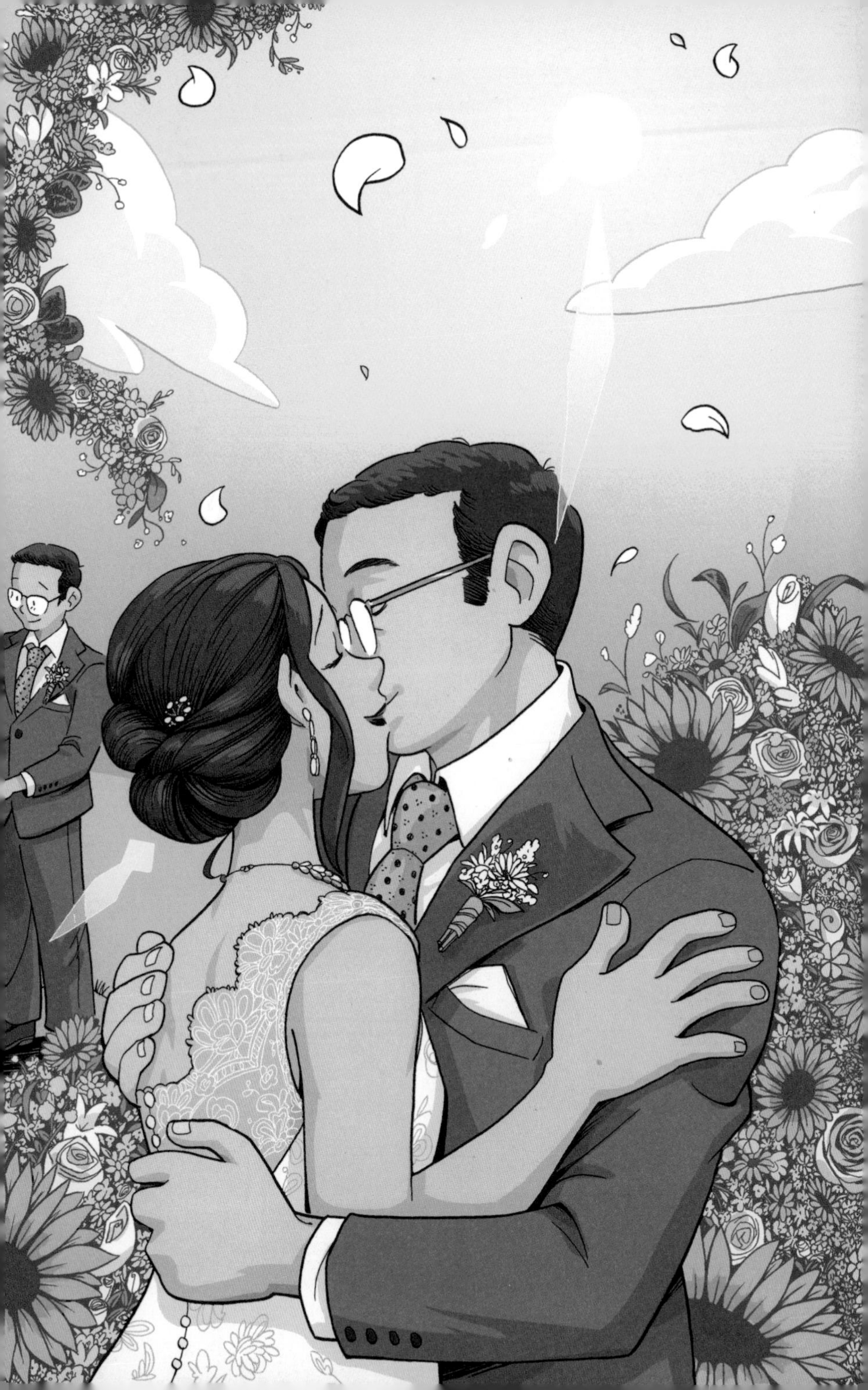

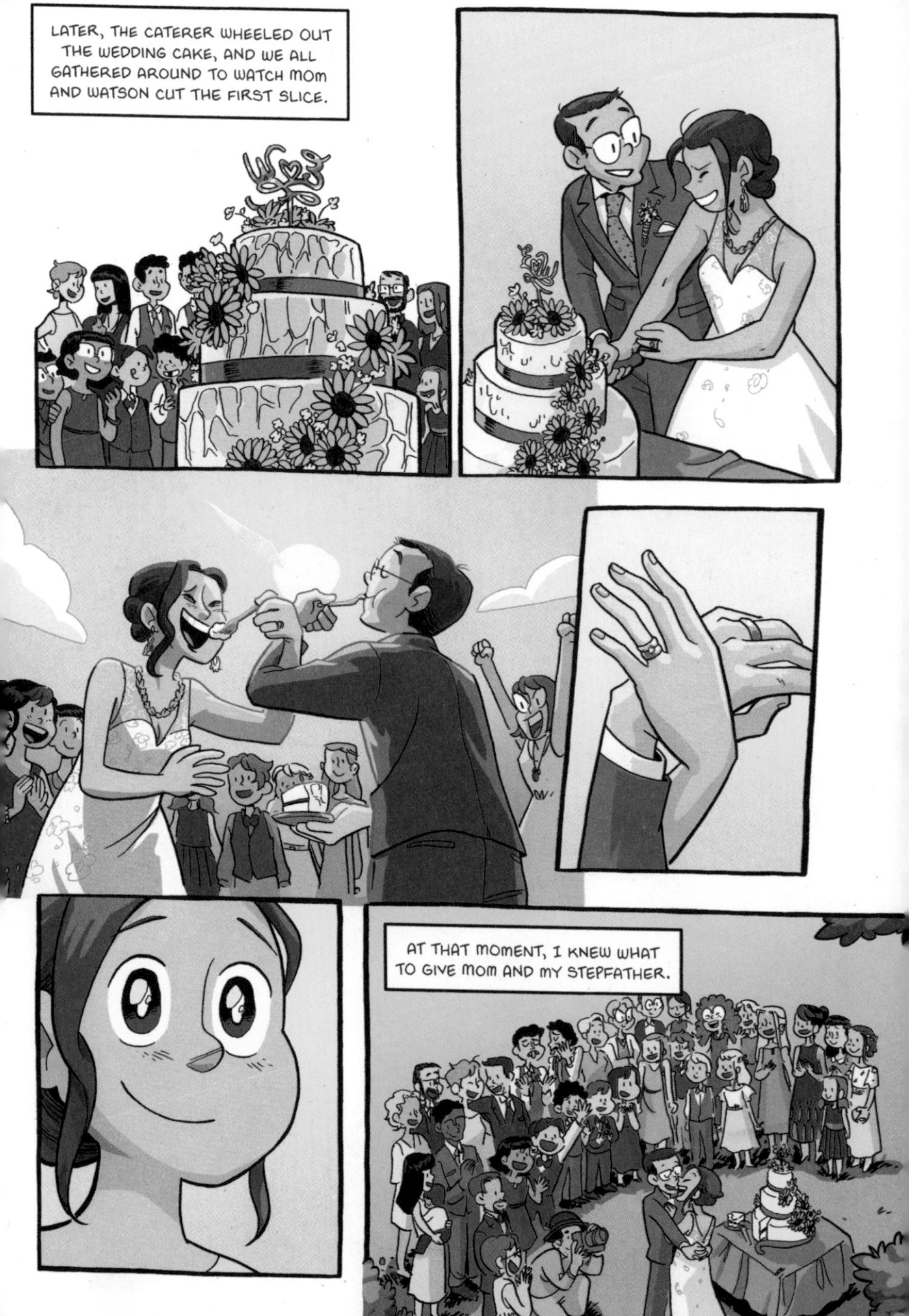
LATER, THE CATERER WHEELED OUT THE WEDDING CAKE, AND WE ALL GATHERED AROUND TO WATCH MOM AND WATSON CUT THE FIRST SLICE.
AT THAT MOMENT, I KNEW WHAT TO GIVE MOM AND MY STEPFATHER.

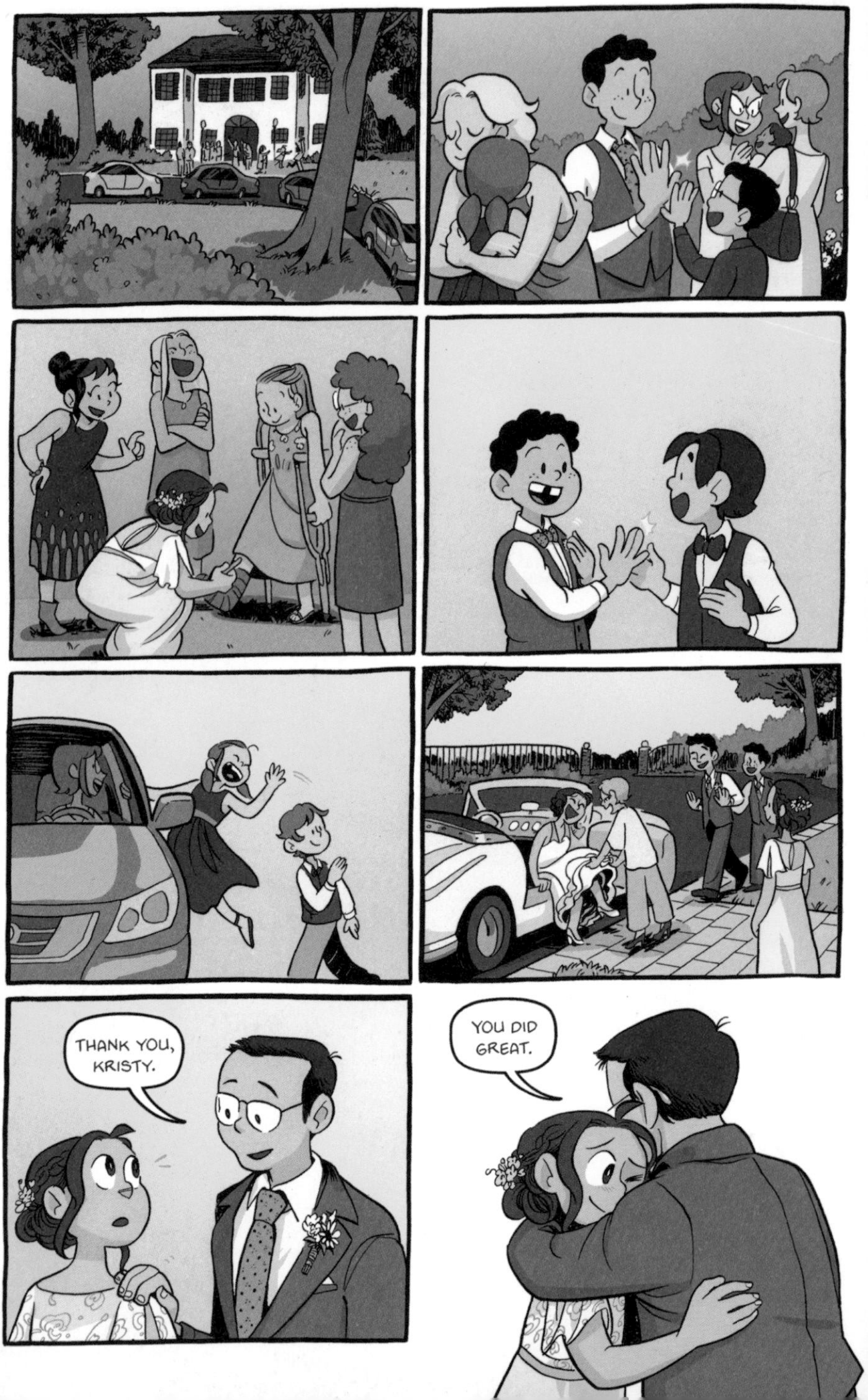
THANK YOU, KRISTY.
YOU DID GREAT.

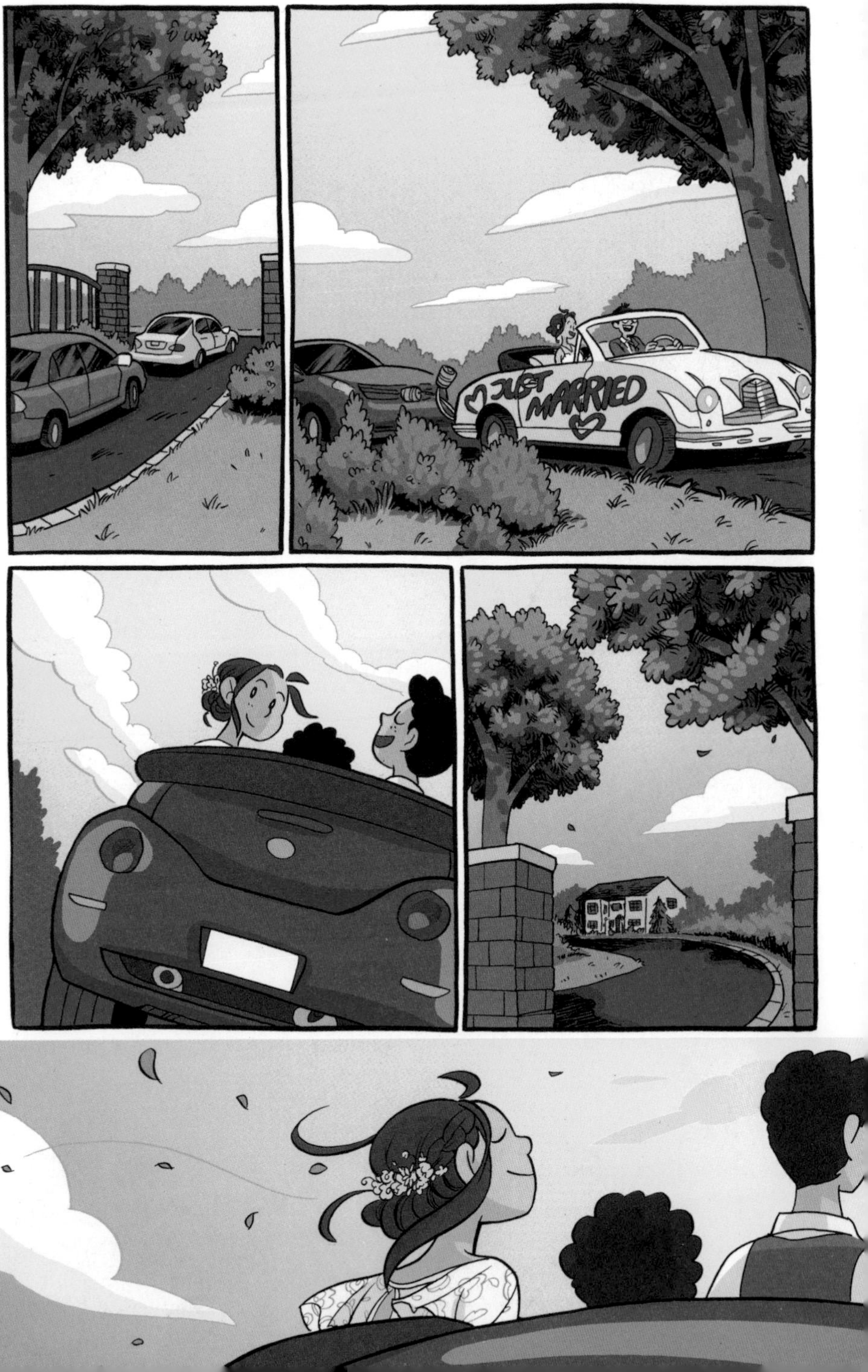
JUST MARRIED

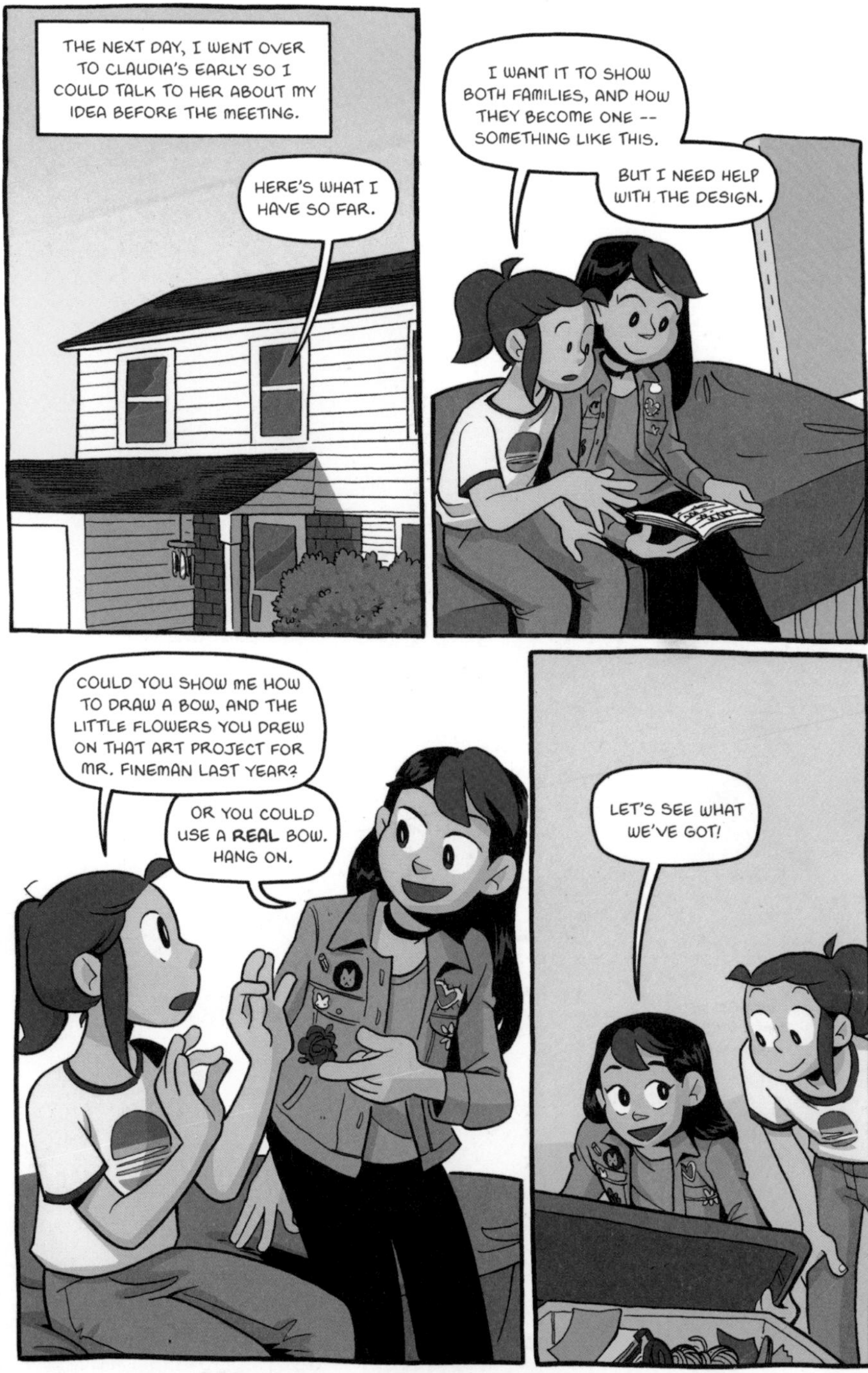
THE NEXT DAY, I WENT OVER TO CLAUDIA'S EARLY SO I COULD TALK TO HER ABOUT MY IDEA BEFORE THE MEETING.
HERE'S WHAT I HAVE SO FAR.
I WANT IT TO SHOW BOTH FAMILIES, AND HOW THEY BECOME ONE -- SOMETHING LIKE THIS.
BUT I NEED HELP WITH THE DESIGN.
COULD YOU SHOW ME HOW TO DRAW A BOW, AND THE LITTLE FLOWERS YOU DREW ON THAT ART PROJECT FOR MR. FINEMAN LAST YEAR?
OR YOU COULD USE A **REAL** BOW. HANG ON.
LET'S SEE WHAT WE'VE GOT!

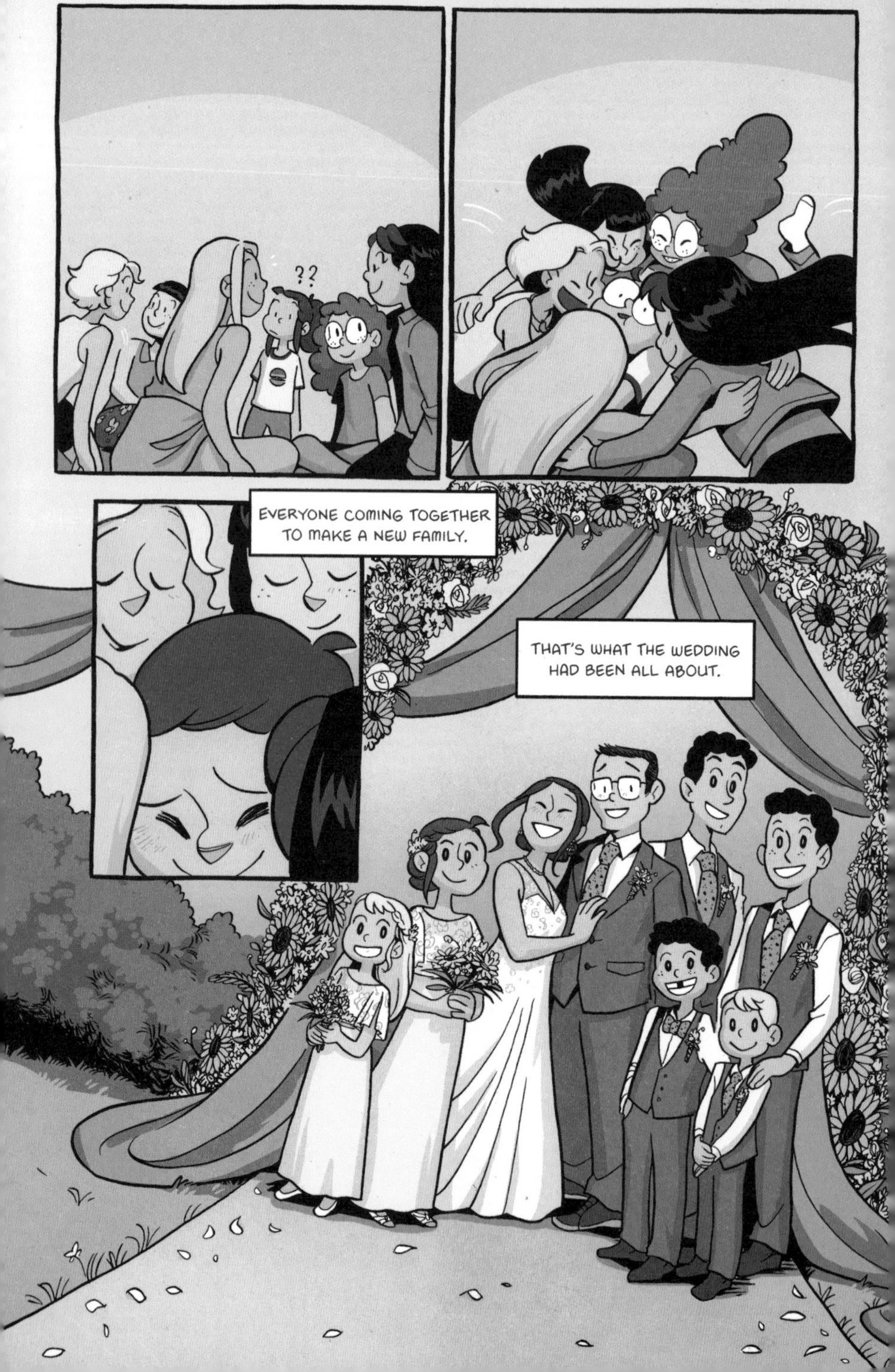
??
EVERYONE COMING TOGETHER TO MAKE A NEW FAMILY.
THAT'S WHAT THE WEDDING HAD BEEN ALL ABOUT.

ANN M. MARTIN'S The Baby-sitters Club is one of the most popular series in the history of publishing — with more than 176 million books in print worldwide — and inspired a generation of young readers. Her novels include *Belle Teal*, *A Corner of the Universe* (a Newbery Honor book), *Here Today*, *A Dog's Life*, and *On Christmas Eve*, as well as the much-loved collaborations, *P.S. Longer Letter Later* and *Snail Mail No More*, with Paula Danziger, and *The Doll People* and *The Meanest Doll in the World*, written with Laura Godwin and illustrated by Brian Selznick. She lives in upstate New York.

GALE GALLIGAN is a graduate of NYU and the Savannah College of Art and Design. She created a *USA Today* bestselling graphic novel adaptation of *Dawn and the Impossible Three*, and her work has appeared in a number of anthologies. When Gale isn't making comics, she enjoys knitting, reading, and spending time with her adorable pet rabbits. She lives in Pleasantville, New York. Visit her online at www.galesaur.com.

DON'T MISS THE OTHER BABY-SITTERS CLUB GRAPHIC NOVELS!

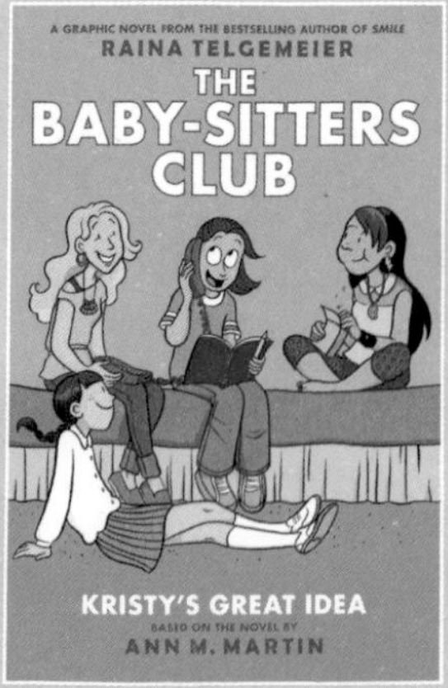
A GRAPHIC NOVEL FROM THE BESTSELLING AUTHOR OF SMILE
RAINA TELGEMEIER
THE BABY-SITTERS CLUB
KRISTY'S GREAT IDEA
BASED ON THE NOVEL BY
ANN M. MARTIN

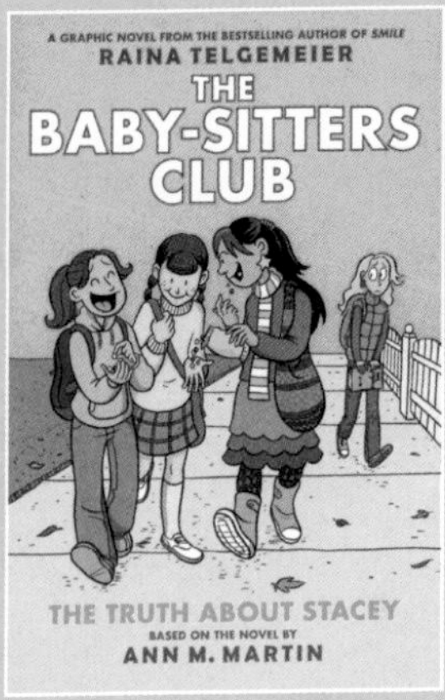
A GRAPHIC NOVEL FROM THE BESTSELLING AUTHOR OF SMILE
RAINA TELGEMEIER
THE BABY-SITTERS CLUB
THE TRUTH ABOUT STACEY
BASED ON THE NOVEL BY
ANN M. MARTIN

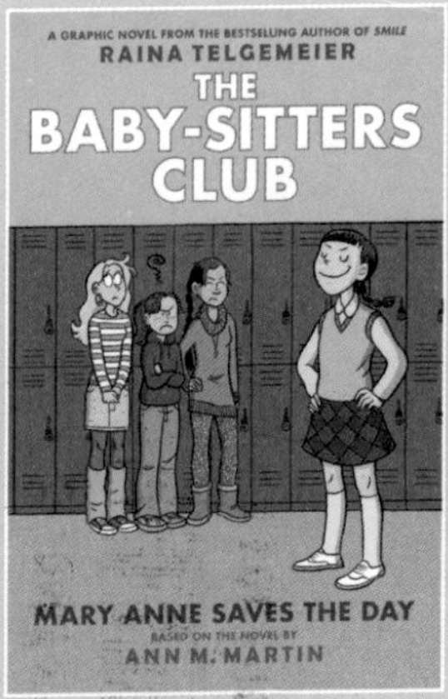
A GRAPHIC NOVEL FROM THE BESTSELLING AUTHOR OF SMILE
RAINA TELGEMEIER
THE BABY-SITTERS CLUB
MARY ANNE SAVES THE DAY
BASED ON THE NOVEL BY
ANN M. MARTIN

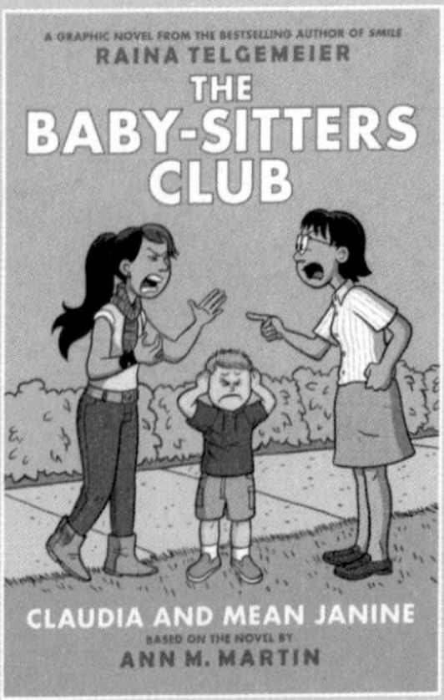
A GRAPHIC NOVEL FROM THE BESTSELLING AUTHOR OF SMILE
RAINA TELGEMEIER
THE BABY-SITTERS CLUB
CLAUDIA AND MEAN JANINE
BASED ON THE NOVEL BY
ANN M. MARTIN

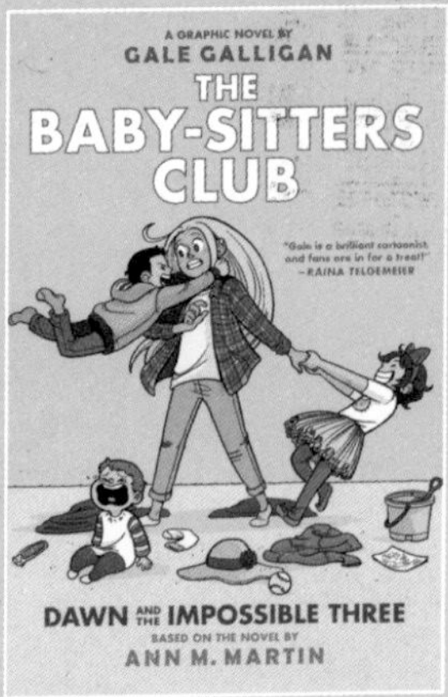
A GRAPHIC NOVEL BY
GALE GALLIGAN
THE BABY-SITTERS CLUB
"Gale is a brilliant cartoonist, and fans are in for a treat!"
—RAINA TELGEMEIER
DAWN AND THE IMPOSSIBLE THREE
BASED ON THE NOVEL BY
ANN M. MARTIN